BOOKS BY JEREMY HODGSON

Historical Romance
Dance on the Terrace

Adventures in Research
Curing Emily
Secret in the Seas

Romantic African Adventures
Leap of a Lifetime
We are One

Egyptian Saga
Take me Instead

Aerial Adventures
Breathe on Me

Science Fiction
TARIK

Historical mystery
The Madonna and the Medallion

The Storyteller

ACT I

An Ecological Adventure

JEREMY HODGSON

ISBN: 978-1-0370-9929-8
e-ISBN: 978-1-0370-9930-4

Jeremy William Hodgson
Villa 99, Tamarina Golf Estate
Black River, Mauritius
90922
jwhodgson42@gmail.com

Illustration of whirlwind used under licence: istockphoto.com/portfolio/ly86

Proofreading by the author
Cover by Nikki Meier
Typesetting and ebook by Liquid Type Publishing Services

For my wife, Michele

...Are thoughts internal? Remaining but an instant before vanishing? Perhaps, but stronger ones endure; they return to remind. Do the most overwhelming thoughts escape the mind to be captured by someone or *something*? – I believe that concentrated thoughts are silent prayers, are heard, and are more effective than whispered words.

Silent prayers – Rev RB Johnson

By polluting the Oceans, not mitigating CO2 emissions, and destroying our biodiversity, we are killing our planet. Let's face it: there is no planet B.

Emmanuel Macron, President of France, addresses the Congress of the United States of America. Washington, DC, April 2018.

Prologue

Except for the history of our universe, a story does not begin from nothing. Events in the past form and fashion the tale; without them, there would be no story. An AI, programmed to identify those that affected this narrative, proposed these events to its programmer.

Why? No one asked for the reasons; they would be a row of probabilities.

54 CE.

Saint Paul wrote: – The Bible: 1 Corinthians 11:4-16. A woman dishonours her head if she prays without covering it... If she refuses to wear a head covering, she should shave off all her hair.

622 CE.

Muhammad preached the Quran verses, Surah An-Nur (24:31):

[Allah] – enjoins believing women to cast down their looks and guard their private parts and not reveal their adornment except that which is revealed of itself, and to draw their veils over their bosoms, and not to reveal their adornment save to their husbands, or those approved: [Defined list].

NB: No restriction on covering heads, although then and now desert dwellers wrap a cloth around their heads, leaving only their eyes visible, to protect them from sand and dust.

627-628 CE. (6 AH).

The Quran defines Ihram as a state in which both sexes must reveal their faces to Allah during Hajj and Umrah (Pilgrimage).

The USA, November 1966.

Committees, sub-committees, and sub-sub-committees lurk hidden in the depths of the US intelligence organisations. One of them is the Committee for Research into Alien Phenomena. Formed at the height of the flying saucer scare decades earlier, when stories of alien invasion filled the newspapers, it had met irregularly for decades whenever someone reported an odd light in the sky, without ever identifying an alien. It provided an amusing diversion from the routine and monotonous work that filled the members' days.

Appointment to one of these committees was unforeseeable; it often occurred when an employee approached retirement, so it was a good survival strategy to ensure the committee had something to do from time to time to avoid closing them down.

A person appointed inevitably thought. *Shit, I'm now a member of the CRAP bunch.*

Africa-June 2026

In an African game reserve, the driver of a specially equipped safari vehicle, designed to carry ten tourists, was slowly driving along a dusty track. Buzi did so twice daily, at dawn and dusk, carefully wending around the reserve. He was a Ranger, the title given to the guide-drivers of the vehicles that game lodges use to provide their visitors with an experience of African wildlife.

Buzi was following spoor. Invisible to the passengers, the tracks were mere smears in the dust; he leant over the door sill every few metres to ensure the hyenas had not left the road. When he saw a jackal loping through the bush, he slowed as he crawled around a corner, then stopped. The excited tourists snapped away at the hyenas eating a kill sixty metres away. Jackals surrounded them, trying to sneak or dash in to bite off a morsel without a vice-like jaw crushing a limb. Only Buzi recognised what the kill was. After two minutes, he put the safari vehicle in reverse and said, 'We must leave; one vehicle is allowed at a kill for two minutes.' He reversed around the corner, then did a U-turn and set off in a different direction while scrolling through radio frequencies. When he found the right one, he spoke in the local dialect so none of his passengers could understand.

The vehicle with four Rangers that came to the kill drove away the scavengers, loaded what remained uneaten and took it to the park headquarters, where a veterinarian determined the cause of the man's death. It was the first occurrence in that reserve, but it had also happened in others. The cause of death was snakebite, and the game guards buried the man that night without identifying him. Human deaths in game parks generated unwanted negative publicity for tourism. The veterinarian added an extra entry to the World Wildlife Fund's statistics database and thought. *Poor bloody poacher never expected it.*

Devon – England- August 2028

On a small, curved beach on the Devon Channel coast, twinkling flashes from a small, shallow pool surrounded by rocks, except for a narrow channel leading to the sea, attracted a sunblock-slathered five-year-old boy. Curious, Louis went to look.

Tiny little fish cavorted in the water when gentle ripples formed from the remains of a surge, when incoming waves crashed on the rocks. The sunlight that entered the pool reflected on the minute fish, and the pool seemed full of twinkling lights.

Louis placed a hand on a rock and leant forward. He thought he had frightened the fish when the light display switched off and then on again at the far end of the pool. But then he noticed something on the pool bottom moving towards him. It took a moment to realise it was a small octopus towing something behind it.

The octopus entered the shallow water before Louis's rock and stopped. He looked into its eyes, and then the octopus held up a tentacle with a plastic shopping bag on it and offered it to him.

A surprised Louis had a thought when he remembered his dad's words. *If you find any rubbish, please bring it to me, and we'll dispose of it in a rubbish bin.* So he said, 'Thank you, Mr Octopus, I'll throw it away for you.'

He took it twenty metres up the beach to the umbrella under which his parents were reading, relaxed on inflatable mattresses with all bared skin suitably oiled. Dad had a book, and Mum a magazine.

Louis carefully placed the bag on the sand and scraped some sand on top.

Disturbed by Louis's movements, his dad asked, 'Where did you find that bag, Louis?'

'Mr Octopus gave it to me, Dad. He wants me to throw it in the rubbish bin.'

'Okay, Louis.' Then, as Louis walked back to the pool, he said quietly to his wife. 'Louis must have remembered the octopus in the *Seaside Holiday* book.'

Without disturbing his parents, Louis placed twenty plastic bags and a rubber thong sandal on his pile before his father called to him. 'Louis, come, it's time to go home.'

He saw his son wave at the pool and then walk towards them, carrying a bag, so he folded the umbrella and deflated the mattresses. As Louis arrived, he saw the pile of bags.

'Louis, did the octopus give you all those bags?'

'Yes, Dad, the crabs brought them into the pool. They dragged the shoe in, but it was too heavy for Mr Octopus, so they helped him push it up to me.'

'Is he still in the pool?'

'No, I said goodbye, so he left.'

His wife answered with a smile, 'Darling, he's only five. Tie a string around the bags, and we'll throw them in a bin on the way home.'

That night, after Louis went to bed, feeling pride in what his son had done, his father posted the story of their day on the beach on Facebook.

Two days later, Louis went to school; his class teacher, who, like thousands of others who needed time to organise themselves on the first day of a new school term, gave her pupils paper and coloured crayons to draw a picture showing something from their holiday. Nearly an hour later, the teacher went around collecting the drawings; on each one, she wrote the child's name. She would pin them on a display board the next day. Most had stick figures of Mummy and Daddy, perhaps a sun in the sky, a ball, a dog, or a beach umbrella. Of all of them, Louis's effort was unique. She asked him what it was about, and he told her.

'That's my friend, Mr Octopus; he gave me lots of plastic bags. That's his friend Mr Crab; he brought the plastic bags, and there are the two crabs who brought me a shoe; they had to help Mr Octopus push it up to me.'

'Lots of bags, Louis?'

'Yes,' Louis showed her with his hands apart, 'I made a pile, high like this.'

'It's a lovely picture, Louis. Did your Daddy throw the bags away?'

'Yes, Miss, and the shoe, in a dustbin on the way home.'

'It's a lovely story, Louis, thank you.' She added a title to the drawing. 'Octopus,' then a note. 'Lively imagination.'

She posted the picture on the Facebook page for the five-year-old class with a comment.

Years later, she would remember Louis' story and wonder about it.

Middlesbrough – England, October 2029

The typical prefab industrial building, a single-story grey block facing a tarmac-surfaced car park for fifteen cars, had one attractive feature. Neatly trimmed and mowed emerald-green grass surrounded the car park and building, finally bounded by a row of trees. The lush growth in the north of England was unsurprising, but a hundred identical buildings where the grass grew poorly proved the exceptional care around this building.

Rob Butler, a small business owner and an intense young man, would speak passionately about the environment at every opportunity. He had completed a university career with a doctorate in chemistry, during which he became a vocal leader of the student movement to save the planet. Like many student movements, they advocated for change but lacked a clear idea of how to achieve it, had no real power, and were too busy studying to take time off. It fuelled his passion, and when he finally looked for a job, employers viewed his activist history with alarm. Without an offer of exciting employment, he thought. *The world is not interested in pollution; they're too busy to bother.* He joined two fellow graduates and started the company. The enigmatic name on the stone sign beside the road read – *Edible Bags Plc*.

Rob, Morry (his French mother had named him Maurice Emmanuel) and Priscilla had started the business with a grant from an eco-foundation, which viewed their passion and history in a different light; some assistance from a government office, and help from the local council. After installing their laboratory in one corner of the building, and following up on several promising leads, they subsequently installed some machinery.

Rob would be the first to admit that several research students at his university, also enthusiastic about saving the world, had conducted illicit lab experiments to help. After four years and numerous manufacturing trials, they had developed an attractive, creamy brown bag that was waterproof, unlike paper.

Before their unpublicised attempt, efforts to replace plastic bags, sponsored by the manufacturers of the products they wanted to replace, had concentrated on making them biodegradable or compostable. Rob and his mates had seen the flaw in the argument: if bags deteriorated within days, rendering re-use impossible, the manufacturers would make far more bags. Profits and pollution levels would rise. He and his mates had decided that a material that bacteria adored or disintegrated was the wrong route. They would make a bag to use many times, which you could then feed to a cow or sheep. Or a fish. The success was encouraging. Chickens pecked it to pieces and swallowed the bits, pigs adored it mixed in with their mash, cows chewed it contentedly, and dogs found it delicious. Cats were picky carnivores, but one minute in the mincer with a spoonful of tuna and a cat would clean the dish. The fish tank in the reception area, sprinkled with pieces, generated a feeding frenzy that resembled piranhas around a carcass.

They had just finished lunch, served with chopped bags sprinkled with salt and vinegar as a salad, as they had done for the last week's lunches. Like many others, it was an accidental decision; they had run out of lettuce the week before.

Rob couldn't help the thought. *We have edible plastic and can make bags, but how do we learn to market them?*

Like many such startups that might make a better mousetrap

but had no idea how to sell it, further technical enhancements were a known route to follow. If awarded more grants, they might continue for years.

Brighton – England, July 2030

Harry, with tattoos on his forearms, and Diana, who wore false eyelashes except in bed, where her tattoos were visible, were a working-class couple. They met when Harry parked his monster machine and entered the London supermarket to buy a frozen pizza, where Diana worked. Harry proudly guided the complicated machine around the streets of a London borough, a new model that resembled a lorry with the cab positioned on top in the middle. It had brushes, a water tank, sprays, an overhead suction pipe Harry could manipulate from the cab for dog poop, and a waste container at the rear. Harry emptied the waste where the depot manager indicated, but never asked where it went. The manufacturer had named his monster a *Guzzler*. Parking was illegal, but the police ignored the infractions of municipal employees.

Their romance had progressed steadily to the point where Harry asked if Diana would like to spend a weekend with him in Brighton, probably England's most famous beach resort. She had agreed, and he had made the arrangements.

The train ride had passed with mounting excitement as hormone levels grew in anticipation of the coming night.

At 7:30 the following morning, dressed for a run on the beach, they left the small hotel with smiles and tender looks that indicated a successful night and, after crossing Madeira Drive, descended the steps from the promenade to the beach. Five metres later, they stopped and stared.

'Harry, what's all this stuff on the beach?'

'I don't know. I once watched an IMAX documentary that showcased undersea marine life. The guy talking called these things jellyfish. They looked beautiful, but there weren't many.'

'Well, there are millions here. Look, they cover the beach from way up to the water. Are there still more in the water?'

'We can look, but the guy in the film said they can sting, so let's find sticks to clear them out of the way, and then we can look. There are always some sticks on a beach, probably up here near the top.'

'Are they alive?'

'I don't think so, Di; they must be dead or near it, washed up like this. I'll call the police.' Harry thought. *'The council has a massive problem. I couldn't drive my Guzzler along the beach to clear them up, and I bet they don't have a machine that can do it. It will cost a packet.'*

With no alternative, they ran on the pavement, then went for breakfast, and Harry posted a picture on Facebook.

The Municipal Council didn't have a machine. Still, between various departments, Agriculture supplied tractors with rakes and trailers, Public Works brought mechanical shovels to load the piles of dead jellyfish, and Police reinforcements arrived with hundreds of traffic cones. Everything returned to normal a week later.

Buckets of jellyfish were awaiting analysis for species identification and the toxins that had killed them in two laboratories associated with the Ministries of Agriculture and the Environment.

The fisheries lab identified them as Caribbean Box Jellyfish. The agricultural lab found molecules common in pesticides but claimed no British pesticide matched the results.

The Ministry of the Environment announced that the incident was due to global warming, a catchphrase that has become a convenient excuse for everything.

1

As Patrick O'Connor walked to the podium at Stamford University's conference, his T-shirt, jeans, and trainers immediately drew attention. After the moderator introduced him, his first words captured Meghali Azzaro's mind. Meghali didn't own her mind; she borrowed it when necessary.

'You have heard from the previous presentations today about various methods to analyse data to forecast the future. If I summarise, they have stated that if there is one extra apple every day in the bowl on the table, there will also be one more tomorrow. If that were true, we would all be millionaires.'

Meghali woke from a half-sleep. Most people enter the half-sleep state without knowing it's not full sleep. Dogs and many animals may not be aware of it; it's their principal sleep mode, where the brain shuts down everything unnecessary to conserve energy, including the conscious mind, but continues to monitor the senses for danger signals. The subconscious continues with daily maintenance, and when blessed with a high IQ, it uses the time to classify information received.

Patrick had noticed her when he approached the microphone. She was the sole woman in the front row of his audience. Besides being blonde and blue-eyed, with regular features, one metre seventy in height, and weighing sixty-two kilograms, Meghali was physically attractive. Unlike her usual low hemlines, her tight skirt revealed attractive legs. She had struggled for years to keep her weight under control with careful eating and regular running. She accepted the extra two kilograms smoothed over the bony bits. Her mind, though, was not ordinary. Three days had passed before she noticed she was now thirty-eight.

Meghali had learnt she could overcome the challenge of advancement in a male society by dressing strategically, so she dressed plainly for work, in long skirts and loose tops, never used makeup, wore rimless spectacles, and left her hair straight – the antithesis of the average woman.

Her eyesight was perfect – the circular spectacles were made for her, flat glass with a thickened outer ring to disguise them.

She had come from Washington, DC, on the Amtrak train to Stamford, her Alma Mater, so she stayed in lounging pyjamas before leaving, which she did, dressed *very* differently. Meghali had registered for a conference on 'Forecasting the Future,' to be held the following day. She had attended classes by three of the speakers while at Stamford, and the abstracts of their presentations included some new formulae that might be useful. However, she had little interest in forecasting the future as a university subject. The date she had noticed was a Friday, so she decided on the expenses-paid outing to visit several of her student friends who still lived in Stamford, including one ex whose muscles and flowing locks she could remember. A weekend away had attractions.

Meghali's train was late, so she checked into the Stamford Marriott Hotel and slept.

The next day, she was on time at the conference venue. A dozen attendees recognised her, and after exchanging news, she settled down for the first presentation in a front-row seat.

By lunch, she was bored. The three papers presented were a rehash of what she already knew, and the conference moderator struggled to hold the audience's attention. The buffet lunch outside the conference room looked excellent, so Meghali stayed for lunch, intending to leave before the afternoon session. Then, while popping a shrimp into her mouth, she met once again the professor who had taught her Boolean logic.

When Meghali asked why he was at a conference on forecasting, he admitted he had not attended the morning session but was interested in the two speakers scheduled for the afternoon. The first was the researcher whose abstract had caught her attention before she registered, and the second was an industry futurist who, he said, was radically different. Meghali stayed. The first speaker that afternoon gave her some ideas to consider. But the second...

Patrick continued his apple allegory, 'Unfortunately, although it might be true tomorrow and the day after, the day will come when a mother decides to make an apple pie, and there will be none.'

The down-to-earth way he began pleased the bored audience, and they laughed in response.

'The rule applies to the stock market, so it explains why we will not be millionaires in the future.'

Someone called out, '*Shame!*'

Patrick noticed her again. It wasn't the stylish business jacket, tight skirt, and blouse that didn't attempt to hide her fit and healthy curves. It couldn't have been pheromones or hormones; he was too far away. The part of his brain that Patrick had never controlled had analysed the changes as she passed from semi-conscious to wide awake. The straightening spine, the rise of her shoulders, her fingers spreading on her lap. The flare of nostrils as the smell program rebooted. Patrick's brain knew what they meant as it used an identical program to wake him, and it would have approved Meghali's breakfasts, which her now rare overnight visitors thought of as '*Yuk.*'

Her preparation method would have raised eyebrows. The collection of fruits, vegetables, and nuts seemed like a haphazard but healthy choice, until spoonfuls of industrially produced protein, collagen, vitamins, and bran followed. Sometimes, breakfast cereal, a raw egg, or a pot of yoghurt would make up the volume when short of ingredients. She didn't decide. Her unusual brain worked out what her body, her brain's life support system, needed, then influenced her morning selection accordingly.

She would reply, 'I'm nearly a vegetarian,' if someone asked.

Patrick continued his lecture.

'Now I promised to discuss forecasting the future in industry. Why do industries need it? The example I'll use is a producer of clothes washing powder, traditionally Brand X in case studies, who pays a sizable percentage of their income for television advertising to promote their product. They want to know if they are spending enough, what the expenditure does for them, and when to change their advert. The gentlemen who spoke this morning will inform them, using market research tools, and when it comes to changing the advertisement, will suggest something like this.'

> "The income from advertising curve dives about a
> month after a new ad from a competitor, so you
> should change your ad just before, but your curve
> peaks about three months after the ad comes out, so
> don't change it for three months."

'That's telling you how to make the future a copy of today. Just like the apples. What those guys need is a mother.'

The laughter was louder the second time.

'I shouldn't make fun of the stats guys because what they do is necessary, and in my example, they have said *when* to introduce a change. What interests me in forecasting is the change, for only when there is a change will the future be disturbed; otherwise, the world would remain constant, although if a mother didn't decide to make an apple pie, her house would fill with apples.'

This time, the laughter bordered on the raucous. Meghali thought the audience ridiculous.

'Brand X decided on a change, and they decided to engage a new advertising company. That company proposed an innovative ad instead of analysing why every ad for washing powder features a woman doing the washing and a small boy who the producers have rolled in a bath of mud or koki pen ink.'

As the laughter trickled away, he said, 'I know you have all seen those ads and may ask why they never vary.

'I assure you, the ads change; the small boy becomes a girl doused with tomato sauce, the woman cycles between blonde, brunette, and redhead, and the colour of the walls in the laundry changes. The T-shirt may always be white, but the Koki pen comes in many colours.

'Back to Brand X, their ad featured a dirty sheet, at least twenty metres by ten; I can't tell you how they dirtied it, but it looked like a dozen dogs had pooped on it and then rolled around.'

The audience had tears in their eyes when the laughing stopped. Meghali didn't laugh; she took a small mirror from her handbag and a tissue, and while feigning a wiping-the-eyes action, she could see the audience with their eyes fixed on Patrick.

Is he an expert in how to capture an audience? Or plain irreverent?

It wasn't that she had no sense of humour; her mind couldn't help seeking relationships.

Being the Director of Analysis at the CIA at thirty-eight was a notable indication.

Meghali had sailed through junior college and Stamford with straight A's in every course she took. Like Leonardo da Vinci, her polymath's brain was interested in everything. A fraction more left than right brain, but both halves were active. Her mentors could never understand her eclectic choice of subjects; maybe she didn't know herself. Her mind, drawn to something interesting, such as Boolean logic, prompted her to sign up. For a brief five years, between seventeen and twenty-two, her hormones had raged as they do in most young women. The sports jocks were attractive, each cast aside for another as her mind, allowing the activity for health reasons, found no matching entity and made her move on. When the hormones returned to lower levels, she obtained her Master's in English, followed by a Doctorate in analytical techniques. The CIA noted her thesis on the delicate balance of Nuclear Armament and offered her a position.

Despite the occasional interest in a healthy male specimen at the gym, she never formed a relationship that lasted more than one night. Once Jack and Jill had climbed the hill to fetch a pail of water, Jill's mind thought there was no reason to climb it again. It knew what was up there; the pail would be no different. Sometimes it leaked, and the water would be lukewarm.

She was still single at thirty-eight, her mind filled with efforts to find the relationships between diverse facts.

That Patrick was still single was unsurprising. Polymaths of the past weren't buried in the enormous mass of humans today.

Finding one is unlikely.

He continued.

'The ad featured the sheet washed in a swimming pool into which a crew poured a hundred packets of Brand X until the pool bubbled with suds. I'm sure the boxes were oversized, so the packaging was easy to identify, and then a helicopter pulled the gleaming white sheet into the sky.

'Brand X sales bombed!'

Patrick paused for effect... 'The reason is that people react to stimuli in a specific fashion. The future that arrives when a change occurs in the world, the government, or the business is entirely determined by how people react. In the case of Brand X, the buyers were the housewives shown in the standard ads. The advertisers know what the viewer wants to do. Those ads demonstrate it, prompting a blonde viewer to identify with the blonde ad woman, conditioning the viewer to buy the brand promoted. It will be a double success if the little boy resembles her son.

'After the failure of Brand X, market researchers reported that women didn't buy it because *"My sheets are not that big."* The consequences of failure can be catastrophic; the manufacturer withdrew Brand X from the market.'

Meghali's mind found the relationship. *He's an expert on audience participation because he knows what they like.*

'I don't discount past facts when I try to imagine the future, but I try to imagine what people will do; their actions will shape the future. Directors and editors of movie films are superb teachers of human expectation. I've studied thousands of hours of movie films, and I find it helpful to imagine the future that will evolve after a singular event, such as how the characters would behave in a movie if faced with that event. In a film, they must act like people; if they don't, the viewer switches channels. However, I'll admit there is an infinite variety of individuals, so I cannot claim to forecast an individual's future, only an average likely future.

'To finish the presentation, I'll tell you who makes money on stock exchanges: Traders who identify an event occurring in a company, like a CEO resigning, then sell the stock immediately. Although not consistently successful, they do better than most; they anticipate what others will do when they learn of the event.

'Thank you.'

Meghali had to meet Patrick; she didn't ask why, but her brain decided she should - it was fascinated by the prospect of meeting another polymath.

There was a crowd surrounding him at the tea and biscuits after the conference, so she found the moderator and asked for Patrick's number. She then left to prepare for her rendezvous with her ex at a restaurant they both knew.

He was bald, had a double chin, and a belly, and told her about his success as the owner of three fast-food outlets in Stamford. Her brain insisted she should reject him by generating a not-unusual desire to throw the *puttanesca* in her bowl into his face or upturn it on his bald head. Suppressing the violent urge, she said she had to draft an urgent report for her boss and then left feeling regret that the *puttanesca* was still in the bowl.

The next morning, after the disappointing evening, she woke up restless with the sunrise and decided she needed to run around Mill Park to work off her feelings, but her brain wouldn't let her go until she phoned Patrick.

'Hello, Patrick O'Connor.'

'Mr O'Connor, I'm Meghali Azzaro. I was at the conference

and heard you speak. I'm the Director of Analysis at the CIA and would like to meet you. I'm calling today because it might be easier before I return to DC on Monday.'

'When are you free, and where are you?'

'I'm in the Marriott on Broad. I'm about to run in Mill Park for an hour, then have breakfast, so I've nothing booked from ten. I intend to look up a few old friends; Stamford is my Alma Mater.'

Patrick ran the video of the audience he remembered. 'Are you the scrumptious lady in the front row?'

'Was there more than one lady?'

'No.'

'Then the adjective is unnecessary. I am.'

'I'm always polite to scrumptious ladies. I run as well. I'm in the Trump condos, and Mill Park is a good place to run. You must know Whitaker Place. I'll meet you at the corner of the boulevard. Say fifteen minutes.'

2

Patrick had been a normal kid until he was twelve, at least, his Catholic accountant father had thought so, despite his mother's insistence that he kept his brown hair as long as his school allowed. But then he developed a mania for watching old cowboy films; they captivated him. Unlike his friends, who all wanted to be cowboys, Patrick couldn't decide. When the old films featured Indians who had never won a battle, he felt sympathy for the Native Americans. When his father remarked on his passion, his mother had said, 'Don't worry, he's only twelve; let him grow up.'

Patrick was *watching* the films, not watching like ordinary people. He was studying them. At first, he counted the number of times the stagecoach hurtled through the gully, chased by bandits or Indians.

The editor had to work with limited footage and two or three camera angles; the coach would go through the gully five or six times in a chase sequence. When he realised the scene with the coach and two or three men shooting towards the chasing bandits was stationary with a moving background, he worked out how long the painted scenery band was before it repeated.

Then he counted the number of times a cowboy fired his six-shooter before reloading. He had counted a record twenty-seven times. A careful examination of a film revealed that one of the Indians, although disguised by grease paint and feathers, had the face of the cowboy wearing boots and a Stetson, so he was shooting at himself.

It launched a new analysis. How many different actors were employed to play the hundred or more characters in the film? His analysis skills developed over the years; by eighteen, he could deconstruct a movie and recount precisely the process of planning, screenwriting, filming and editing. After eighteen, he rarely visited the cinema; he watched his films as digital downloads. His video analysis was the root cause of the incident that triggered his reluctance. With three friends, he had attended a horror film. At the critical moment when a petrified audience was shrinking into their seats, trying not to look when the monster slobbered over a fallen girl, he had thought of the surrounding cameras, director, sound crew, lighting experts, and the overheated actor in the heavy monster costume. He saw the whole scene, not the monster and the terrified girl.

He had laughed. A raucous, loud, hilarious laugh and the entire audience had risen several centimetres in their seats before turning to glare at him and his mortified friends.

When Patrick discovered statistics, the inevitable followed. He became a Doctor of Mathematics. His thesis, *Analysis of Global Warming Trends*, included many more factors than any previous paper, so a global industrial conglomerate snapped him up for their Department of Future Research.

By the time Patrick started his doctoral research, he had concluded the world's history was one long movie. It explained everything in a way he could understand: A producer for the Universe, an associate producer for each galaxy, a director, an editor for each solar system, not to mention the scriptwriters and other associates.

Like on a movie set, moving creatures were actors, and the scriptwriter didn't specify the furniture's exact position, type, and style. Actors often changed the dialogue to phrases they thought were better, like 'Here's looking at you, kid' in *Casablanca.*

So, the details of most of what happened weren't accidental, but slight modifications due to each actor's reaction to the image the script displayed.

Big-screen movies, Patrick decided, especially the historical ones, were excerpts doctored by humans to fit into a two- or three-hour viewing period between pee breaks, and even then, might need an intermission.

Patrick sat or lay in a room with computer screens for over twelve hours daily. He knew it was bad for his health, so with rigid discipline, he divided his day into periods for exercise, eating, and sleeping. Patrick exercised for more hours each week than most, so he had a metre-eighty-three tall body that compared favourably with that of the dedicated bodybuilders and maintained a balance between mental and physical fatigue, allowing him to sleep dreamlessly and deeply. He dressed in a T-shirt, jeans, and trainers. He had bought black ones for a funeral and hoped never to wear them again. He kept his brown hair long; his colleagues thought he was a hippy and believed Patrick smoked pot on the weekends. He didn't; he had better things to do. His colleagues thought he was taking a nap when Patrick levered his modified chair to a horizontal position. He wasn't. The horizontal chair allowed him to stare at the non-distracting white ceiling, like a blank cinema screen where he could play movies from his imagination that began with what Patrick knew. Then, as his mind took control, he could watch until the most likely ending. He might replay the movie in his head many times while he gathered more data until he felt the ending was correct.

At weekends, he made money, not literally, but a rake-off from human stupidity. If he had invited anyone to his apartment, the million dollars worth of super-computer equipment would have raised a warning flag, although it was all legal. While researching the future, he applied his statistical knowledge to an analysis of international finance. – Every exchange that published data, and even a few that didn't. He learnt one thing of significance. When the total value of a bourse dropped due to price falls, other exchanges rose by a percentage of the drop; he assumed bank accounts took the rest.

Frustrated by the result, he wrote a new AI analysis program that could discover who had bought and sold. Even with a powerful computer, it took months for the results to be statistically valid, but one unusual fact emerged. Several traders made money by buying in small lots when one exchange was low and then selling the stocks on another country's bourse when they rose.

It was not unusual, but Patrick became excited when the AI reported it had traced most traders through a series of cut-out companies worldwide to a lone source. He reprogrammed to follow with smaller trades. Each year, he declared a high six-figure trading profit, allowing him to purchase increasingly powerful equipment in one room of his apartment and open more cut-out companies worldwide.

Patrick occasionally wondered. *Does the other guy have enough computer power to discover what I'm doing?*

Meghali and Patrick ran and, between breaths, learnt a little about each other's history. Although Patrick had more right brain than left, he was a perfect match for Meghali. Neither could control the two minds that decided they wanted to learn about each other. Was a gentle tickle of a hormone enough for

Meghali to invite him for breakfast, and a different tickle made him accept? Or because she resembled his memory of the pom-pom girl he had fallen in love with at fifteen, when the pom-pom girl was eighteen, and he had never missed a game. And did Patrick uncannily resemble the sweating wrestler with the dragon tattoo after they had run hard on a final sprint? Neither remembered those tidbits of history, but their brains did and could use them. He returned to his condo to shower and met her at the Marriott.

They argued for the rest of the day; neither could remember where they had eaten lunch. For Meghali, Patrick was an enigma; his approach to analysis was wholly different, yet exciting enough to tickle deep-seated yearnings. They were both, theoretically at least, left-brain people, methodical and analytical. But the theory cannot account for everything. Throughout history, polymaths have emerged. Engineers and left-brainers can examine a chain suspending a massive weight and determine if the chain is strong enough. They might be doubtful, having no experience of Kevlar's strength, but they would notice nothing when walking into a furnished room. The right-brainer would react to the weight instinctively, avoiding it, as they have no idea if the chain or Kevlar tie will break. However, when walking into the same room, they immediately remark that the orange cushion on the couch is the wrong colour.

Meghali's mind associated facts without conscious thought; she believed it was instinct, but the right brain half recognised when the association fitted, like a cushion's colour. Patrick had more of a right brain that analysed images, but the left side strung movie scenes into an understandable sequence and analysed their content and interconnectivity. They both felt contented during their discussion.

Patrick asked, 'Do you watch movies? TV or big screen? Adverts?'

'Not much; I've books and reports to read.'

'A shame because it's one of the best ways to learn about humanity. I've been doing so for years; it's how I predict the future, which is no more than what humans will do. Our Civilisation is one long movie film from pre-history, a series of shorter episodes that succeed each other with intermissions of different lengths. If you can figure out the plot, you can forecast the future.'

'Can you explain a bit more? That can't be true; the movie for different races and countries can't be a serial.'

'Those run in parallel or overlap and sometimes get mixed up – like wars. We see our movies; our culture dictates what we see, hear and understand. Others may be quite different.

'Movies are all stories told to relate something, an idea, knowledge, or explain a feeling. Each scene must evoke a reaction that prompts a desire to see the next scene. Teaching something takes many subtle steps to ensure it's not forgotten, and missing out on one is the difference between a brilliant editor and an amateur.

'They are all reflections of society. Watch movies, and you learn a lot about humans and cultures.

'If the good guy shoots the bad guy, the cheering viewers are not all murderers; they show what humans want to happen. The mothers who watched that Brand X ad didn't see a soap powder; they saw a big sheet, a size they don't have, so they didn't buy Brand X.

'Ads in distinct cultures can be quite different, even when the product is identical. If you know how a culture thinks and behaves, it's possible to forecast their reactions; they will act like the movies they watch.

'An ad in India must be colourful; their culture is colour-sensitive. It will show joy and happiness through dancing. If you want to influence how they will behave, show them a different movie or ad, but not too different, with a minor change each time.'

Meghali asked, 'An example?'

'Say Brand X doesn't make dog shampoo; it would kill sales if it placed an ad showing a dog washed with Brand X. The viewer would immediately learn Brand X was a dog shampoo. However, if the ad featured a woman washing a dog with Proper Pooch Shampoo and showed her mixing in some washing powder while displaying the Brand X box, stating that she does so to reduce the cost of a dog wash, sales would likely increase. The ad shows the dog-washing viewer what she wants, not the clothes-washing one.'

'You said ads in distinct cultures can be quite different, even when the product is identical. Do you have examples?'

'Of course, but I would have to lure you into my lair, where my computer can show an ad for the product in different countries. I'll bet you can't explain why they are different.'

That's a lure. 'Then I'll wait.'

They had dinner together that night, and, unusually, Patrick took her to a movie.

On Sunday morning, they ran again and discussed it, and they couldn't remember where they had lunch.

They had reached a level of interest in each other that permitted personal questions, and Patrick asked, 'Can I call you Meg?'

'Why? No man has ever called me that.'

'Why not?'

'I don't know, and you didn't answer my question.'

'Then I'll say you never drop your guard; the men felt insecure and didn't dare. I'll add that three-syllable names don't show affection; they're too long, so I want to call you Meg for a reason I can't explain.'

Meghali tried to think about his statement, but didn't have a chance; her delighted mind ordered her to *say yes*.

'You can, but it raises a question, "What makes you tick?"'

'Literally, food.'

'Then change tick to jump for joy.'

'I don't, Meg.'

Somehow, although new, Meg sounds right. Does that make me different?

'Meg, if you're asking what gives me a feeling of satisfaction, it's when a forecast matches what happens.'

'How can it, when you said you can't forecast individual reactions?'

'Then I reckon ninety per cent right. If it's a detailed forecast and I have enough data on a person, I can forecast his reaction, but in marketing, that's not possible.'

'What do you consider a failure?'

'I'll guess fifty per cent, although I haven't had one for years. It wouldn't happen unless I had failed to collect sufficient data before the event.'

'Have you had less?'

'I did when I began, Meg. The most depressing were those where I didn't read the first signs as an opening scene and didn't have the time to collect data before the scenario matured. These days, I collect data worldwide, and I treat each item as if it should be an opening scene and wait for more data.'

So he's driven to get it right; there must have been a failure in his past that caused it.

'What about you, Meg? What makes you tick?'

'I analyse events, looking for who is behind them; the more events and data points I have, the more links I can infer, and when they build, I feel the thrill researchers must have when finding the right formula.'

'And have you had failures?'

'Regretfully, yes, and they leave me stressed for weeks, wondering if I missed something. I'm glad I was a junior in 2017. It broke me up for months, although I wasn't involved.'

I wonder if she had a family member in the Las Vegas catastrophe?

'Meg, if you note two events and believe they are linked, what are you seeking?'

'Who's behind those events.'

'Not what?'

'No. *What* is not sentient. It doesn't make decisions and can't cause another event. Only a human can threaten to damage or destroy my world.'

'Do you fear that happening?'

'I didn't before 2017, but I did for a brief period. Once I recovered my balance, my fear disappeared, but I live with the knowledge that there are people out there who wish to harm our country and, therefore, me.'

'So you don't consider Global Warming a threat?'

'There's no *who* unless you include the entire world's population. It's not a targeted harm.'

Late that afternoon, she offered him a job at the CIA.

On Monday, she called the CIA, arranged a job offer for Patrick and told him, then left for Langley. His security clearance took six weeks for the CIA and FBI to complete. Meghali received the full report. The FBI is thorough. She read it, approved it, and noted that his parents had died in an avalanche. *Was that the event he failed to forecast?*

Meghali's brain connected the dots when she read his Stamford address in the FBI report. The Trump condos were big and expensive; she had assumed he was staying with a friend in Stamford, not living there. Jeans, T-shirts and trainers can be deceiving. Her brain tickled a memory, and Meghali gave him her address. She said it was a good area, and he rented a condo. It took him two more weeks to install his computers and report for work.

Meghali was doing what she did best, trying to discover relationships between events and seeking the cause. She had found nothing of note since meeting Patrick, but a feeling that had begun long ago had grown steadily; she felt sure that signs indicated a delicate balance existed between several countries, and something might break.

Patrick had equivalent thoughts for months, but understood the signs differently. The events his search AI recorded didn't fit the current scenario; the cowboys didn't have Colt revolvers, some had bows, and others had machine guns. He waited for the cosmic editor to change the scenario to fit the events.

The massive intelligence gathering organisation that collected billions of data bytes for the CIA to analyse soon found something interesting for Patrick and Meghali.

3

Light oozed slowly into the black void over the eastern horizon. The vague skyline wavered between the pink-tinged sky above and the hold of the night on an invisible black wasteland of sand humped in places like a turbulent sea. Shadows developed as the light strengthened. Hardy tufts of vegetation grew on the humps, a vast field of spiky alien heads outlined against the ripening sky.

A cautious scratching came from inside a jumble of stone and sun-baked mud blocks, haphazardly piled as happens when a building meets a sudden and explosive end – the sound of a lizard creeping from its lair after hiding to avoid the night predators.

An extra alien head joined those visible, but though the un-moving others grew sharper as the light spread over the land, this one slowly rose to join them. Eyes, visible as two patches of a darker shade, scanned carefully and slowly from side to side, and then the little head turned slowly to check, peering in every direction.

The head and eyes continued to scan for several minutes while the light strengthened. The first signs of the day dis-turbed the night's total silence, the quiet susurration of sand grains rubbing one over another as the promised heat brought a light breeze from the chilly night sucked slowly towards the eastern horizon. The occasional faint pop as a flake of mud, heated by a direct ray of light, gave up its tenuous hold and then dropped to the ground.

Satisfied that no danger lurked in the gloom, the shadow of a small body followed the head slowly and with extreme caution around a large mud block into a deeper patch of shadow to one side of the pile. A mini-amphitheatre with a sand floor lay between the broken mud bricks and stones.

Soraya, a small, thin ten-year-old girl, raised her dusty cotton and wool shift to squat down in the still-intense shadow of the eastern block to relieve her bladder, the dry sand below greedily absorbing the moisture as it fell. Finished, she eased forward onto her knees, then crawled forward until she could turn to lean against the block opposite her makeshift toilet. The position gave her a view, between a block and the shattered remains of a concrete pillar, of the incoming roadway passing her hiding place.

She slowly extracted a rolled-up cloth package from the large pocket on the front of her shift. Sudden movements were dangerous. She had learnt from more experience than any ten-year-old should have had to endure. She laid the rolled-up object beside her, unrolling it to reveal a plastic water bottle and a misshapen lump of bread. Carefully, she tore it into two, replaced half on the unrolled cloth for later, then slowly, tearing off a small piece at a time, she put it in her mouth to chew slowly and methodically, wetting her mouth from time to time with small sips of water to soften the hard, dry bread.

While eating, her eyes never ceased scanning around her and the dusty sand road in front to the horizon over which the sun's orb would shortly creep. The road was rough, potholed, and corrugated, with two distinct wheel tracks separated by a narrow strip and sandbanks on either side. However, she knew every shadow and shape from many days of observation.

On the far side, beside a small sandy lump, was her friend, the lizard. He had crawled slowly out of a hole to gather the morning sun. Opposite the lizard were the two dried sticks, the remains of an ancient bush. The spider living there was already beginning to spin its daily web, glistening in the sun's first rays. Each day, her friends assured her. If they survived, so would she.

Soraya liked this time; she couldn't have said why without giving it some thought. With time to reflect and words to describe, she would reply that it was a time of peace and tranquillity before the overriding fear of the day, the horrors that might explode unexpectedly, and the terrifying wait in claustrophobic spaces with no knowledge of what horrors and terrors the day might bring. When Soraya finished the bread, she wrapped the rest in her cloth with the water, tied it with a string, and carefully looped it around her neck. She removed a piece of a broken comb from the pocket, then slowly, starting on one side and working her way around her head, she combed her shoulder-length blonde hair, removing the tangles formed by movement during the night caused by troubled dreams no child should have. Her hair was blonde and unusual; all the other children she knew had dark hair, but the only memory remaining of her mother was of a blonde angel.

Suddenly, a tiny movement caught her eye; they flicked to the side, a puff of dust in the roadway where it shouldn't be.

She watched with increasing wonder as the tiny puff started to spin instead of falling back to the sand of the track. As it did so, it became a small, pointed cone of dust, slowly growing higher until it was a few centimetres tall.

Light from the sun galloped across the serried dunes from the horizon, bringing dark shadows and brilliant yellows and browns as the first arc of the sun broke above the horizon, lighting the rotating cone of sandy dust. The cone whirled and grew even faster with the coming sunlight, picking up sand and dust from a widening circle until it was too dense to see the desert on the other side.

Soraya had seen many sand whirlwinds, but never such a perfect cone, nor so early in the morning when all was cool after the cold, dry night had drained the heat from the land. She watched, fascinated, as the cone grew until it was much taller than a man; she suddenly realised it had not moved; every whirlwind she had seen moved slowly or rapidly on an erratic path.

Her attention focused on it to the exclusion of all else; fortunately, she was well hidden.

Suddenly, the whirlwind collapsed, and Soraya gasped as standing where it had grown was a man with a deeply lined face and a long white beard wearing a white *thawb*, a *keffiyeh* on his head, held down with a golden cord *agal*. The beard and clothing were the same colour, making it difficult to see the beard's length.

Although she didn't analyse it, the apparition was startling because of the sheer whiteness of his clothing. Every white thing she had seen had an ochre tint due to the sand, dust, and dirt; this white was so clean and clear it appeared to glow. He held a long, polished staff in his right hand. As he stepped forward, she saw hide sandals on his feet and a wool satchel, woven from wool of many colours, hanging from his left shoulder. Soraya thought he looked like the Sage described in a story told to the children to keep them quiet.

He had taken a few steps when he stopped, turned, and looked directly at her hiding place. It seemed impossible that he had seen her motionless shadow, but he reached out his left hand and beckoned her to him.

Hesitantly, Soraya slowly rose and went out to him. As she approached, she saw he had brown eyes and a kindly smile. As she reached him, she took his outstretched hand in a child's natural gesture with a parent.

'Hello, Soraya,' he said quietly, 'Walk with me.'

She didn't wonder how he knew her name, but the fears that had developed and honed over two years made her speak, 'Can't.'

'Why?'

'Bad men – dangerous.'

Gently and quietly, with a sad, compassionate expression, he replied, 'You walk under the protection of Allah. No harm will come to you.'

The words, the assurance, and perhaps something else quietened her fears, so as he stepped forward again, she trotted beside him, holding tightly to his hand, her two steps matching one of his.

The town had once been a collection of small, rectangular buildings, some of which touched one another, sharing a common wall. In contrast, others were separated by a narrow, irregularly wide alley, permanently shaded by the buildings to protect against the sun's oppressive heat. The buildings were of different heights, but this was an illusion. The flat roofs all had perimeter walls built to surround an open living and sleeping area, providing relief during the night from the exhausting heat radiated inside the rooms by the overheated mud brick and stone walls. The perimeter walls, not the buildings, varied in height. All desert countries are similar.

On the sides of the road, a building might appear intact, but two in every three buildings had suffered from a bomb or grenade blast. The result was a chaotic landscape, huge roof slabs lying at drunken angles supported on one side by a remaining piece of wall or forming a lintel between two piles of rubble, making passage through the narrow alleys a tortuous route under or over debris piles. A crumpled steel roller shutter leant on a rubble pile nearby; it had once been green but was now scratched and faded; the indeterminate colour made it difficult to read the word, but despite a missing letter, where a hole blasted through the shutter had cut the letter from the black painted word, it read *alhilaq*. Whether the remains of the building behind and below it had once been a barbershop, no signs remained; the crumpled shutter may have hurtled hundreds of metres in the blast that wrecked it. Farther up the street, in a hidden nook between blocks of rubble, the remains of a barber chair, propped on blocks, provided a comfortable seat for a young soldier, dozing although on guard, his Kalashnikov lying on his lap.

A woman, wrapped in an abaya – a shapeless, all-encompassing black robe with a hood bearing signs of wear, dust, and grime – was well-hidden between and behind slabs of a broken wall as she looked out from a ruined house. Her age was impossible to tell, as only her eyes were visible. She scrutinised the roadway; her eyes moved, stillness in her body. As the man and Soraya stepped into her view, she gasped as her chest constricted in fear. Fear not for her but for Soraya, one of several orphaned children she and two other women looked after. She started to move forward but stopped at once; the fear of exposure and the terror of what might follow if she entered the open street with an unknown man, despite his apparent age, was too great; her legs would not move.

Horror engulfed her as she sensed movement up the road into the remains of the town. Her eyes jerked to it. Stepping into the street from the other side was the soldier; his swagger and youthful step implied youth, but over his left shoulder hung the strap of his Kalashnikov cradled in his hands.

She watched, shrinking back as far as possible to remain invisible, her stomach cramping in fear and anticipation of horrors.

The man and Soraya stopped to watch the ragged soldier approach. He had not washed or shaved for weeks; a dark stubble beard disguised his jaw, and a dirty grey T-shirt and oversized jeans tied with a cord around his waist, above a pair of open sandals, completed his attire.

He stopped five paces before them, took a cigarette stub from behind his ear, placed it between his lips, took a lighter from his pocket, and lit the stub nonchalantly. Despite the exaggerated *look at me, Grandad, I'm a hero* swagger; his left hand didn't move from the Kalashnikov while he lit the stub.

He blew a cloud of smoke and looked the man in the face. His first reaction was stupefaction. In every earlier encounter, the person he confronted had an abject look of fear and terror on their face, but this man was smiling at him!

He angrily asked, 'Who are you, and where are you from?'

The man didn't react to the tone and quietly replied, 'I am Allah's Storyteller.'

The soldier replied abruptly without taking his eyes off the ancient's face, 'Well, you can tell the lieutenant about it. Come with me.'

Soraya had moved right next to her protector, as close as she could, still clutching his hand. She watched the soldier from the corner of her eye as if she could pick the right moment to run. Her eyes widened as she saw the Kalashnikov barrel slowly bend downwards as if made of wax melting in the growing heat.

'Why?'

'Because I order it.'

The Sage bent down to Soraya as the bemused soldier watched. He whispered to her, 'Point at him and say, "No Clothes." '

She reacted instantly. The usual binding constraints had fallen away under unusual circumstances. Without hesitation, her free arm shot out with the typical childish gesture children use in the playground. She pointed her index finger at the man and, in a high piping voice, cried, '*NO CLOTHES!*'

Instantly, their interrogator felt the strap of the Kalashnikov vanish from his shoulder. He tried instinctively to grab the falling Kalashnikov but failed and screamed as the Kalashnikov landed on the ground, coiled like a snake, and the barrel wound itself around the magazine. In the next second, he realised he was completely naked, barefoot, standing in the middle of the road in front of the man and the girl. His still-burning cigarette fell from his lips onto his bare foot between two toes. Seconds later, as his mind tried to encompass what had happened, the burning cigarette brought him back to reality. He kicked his burned foot forward to shake off the cigarette, turned, and ran.

4

The Jihadi's pale buttocks, emphasised against the darker skin of his legs and back, wobbled in the sunlight as he ran, with irregular hops into the air as the sharp pain from his burned foot or a jagged stone chip jabbed into his sole. The accompanying squeals of 'Ow, oh, ow' were a sight to bring a simple reaction. Delighted laughter pealed from Soraya's lips.

With a child's natural curiosity, Soraya asked, 'Can I do that to anyone?'

'No, Soraya, only if I tell you to.'

A galvanised Fatima dashed out to them. 'Come,' she pleaded, 'you must escape before they return.'

The man smiled gently at her. 'Fatima, there is no danger. Please uncover your head and show your face so Allah may see you. Never cover your face from Him except in a sandstorm.'

Fatima looked at him, felt his charisma engulf her, then slowly reached up and dropped the hood of her *abaya*. She whispered, 'Who are you?'

Soraya replied, 'He is the Storyteller of Allah.'

For a reason Fatima didn't understand, this seemed natural and satisfied her.

'Now, we shall walk on.'

The three of them then continued to walk up the road towards the centre of the town.

Fatima's mind filled with confused thoughts. She didn't know why she was walking with them. She was just twenty years old and had been about to marry when the Jihadis invaded the town. The fierce fighting between the garrison of soldiers and the Jihadis had been horrifying. The bombing was even worse, and the consequences when the soldiers left the town to the Jihadis were terrible. The young man she was to marry had disappeared, and she had been lucky not to be at her parents' house when the soldiers took her father away. Her mother died a few months later of typhoid from infected food or water. Fatima had lived in the twilight for three years, out of sight from anyone she didn't know, hidden from the world by her black *abaya* and careful discretion. She lived with three other women and had taken on the care of several children, orphaned when bomb explosions killed their parents, or the Jihadis shot their parents or arrested them and took them away, never to return.

Two hundred metres ahead, the lieutenant of the east end post had risen from his sleeping carpet; it also served as his prayer carpet; he was buckling his belt to prepare for his morning prayers. An excited babbling of voices at the entrance, hidden from his sleeping mat by a threadbare hanging carpet, disturbed his routine. The east end post was once a shop or workshop, if the twisted metal shutters spanning three bays on the roadside justified the name. A pile of rubble from the building's collapsed upper floors blocked two of the bays, but a cleared, narrow path provided access to three rooms, which supplied shelter and storage. Due to the limited access through the high rubble to the street, no one had noticed anything until the night guard sitting in the path was shocked into full wakefulness by the noise of running bare feet and shouting, '*Djinns! Djinns!*'

The lieutenant had risen to his position through a series of bloody and cruel executions during the three years he had been fighting. The promotions had ceased because his superiors, although recognising his usefulness, had sensed his psychopathic behaviour could be a danger to them. He could control inner dementia most of the time. Still, when the opportunity arose, he reached a level of near-orgasmic personal pleasure in terrifying his victims and sadistic ecstasy in their torture and final execution.

When the naked soldier, followed by the guard and two other recently woken fighters, appeared in front of him, the repeated *'Djinns-Djinns'* cut off abruptly when the lieutenant smashed his open hand forcefully on the side of the gibbering man's head. Knocked to the floor, semi-conscious, it took a few moments before he came to his senses.

'What is this about?' He screamed at the floored man.

'Djinns, t-t-took my clothes and gun, c-c-coming up the road,' stuttered the fallen man.

'Give him some pants; everyone on alert in here, *now!'*

There was a sudden rush of activity as the eight men in his command scrambled to obey. He issued an order when they were standing to attention in front of him with their weapons ready.

'Mohammed, look down the road and report what you see. Do not show yourself.'

Mohammed quickly followed the passage, knelt on the packed sand and dusty ground, carefully brushed any concrete or stone chips from under his knees to one side, and peered around a stone block. He had to move forward on his knees until he saw the figures far down the road. The sun was now entirely above the horizon, and he was looking directly into it, so although he could see a dark shape outlined against it, he could not decide if the object was human or animal or how many made up the shape. The sandy road was beginning to warm as the wave of heat from the early sun spread across the desert; the dust lifted by the morning wind and the warming air distorted the image further. He checked the rest of the road from his position for activity and saw none. He slid back out of sight, quickly ran up to the lieutenant, and reported on what he had seen, adding, 'No other visible movements except down the road.'

The Sage said to Fatima, 'Hold my arm tight.' When she did, he said, 'Now, both of you close your eyes.' They did so and felt a brief puff of stronger wind. 'Now, open your eyes,' he said. Fatima did and gasped when she found they were not at the place where she had closed her eyes. She knew every pile of ruined concrete along the road and wonderingly guessed they were now about twenty metres before the eastern headquarters.

The bright light from the rising sun reflected from the broken stones and mud blocks, emphasising deep shadows in the spaces and caves between them.

'Here is a cool place in the shade on the left with comfortable blocks to sit on. We shall sit here,' said the Sage. In dazed wonder, Fatima took a few steps with him and Soraya to the place he indicated, and they sat in the deep shadow, looking out at the road, hidden from a direct view of the headquarters path. Unaware of the impossibility of what had happened, Soraya nonchalantly sat swinging her legs. She believed something interesting was about to happen and was thoroughly enjoying the experience.

The lieutenant looked pensive momentarily, then ordered, 'Take my binoculars and return to watch; report as soon as you can identify what is happening or coming.' Mohammed did so rapidly; it was unwise to execute an order slowly.

He was back in less than a minute. 'There is nothing there now, no sign of anything or any movement,' he reported.

The lieutenant turned to look directly at the man, now wearing a cast-off pair of pants, standing trembling to his left. The scorn in his voice left no doubt that punishment would come later.

'So, your *Djinns* have now gone! We shall now see if they have left your clothes and gun behind; Spirits would have no use for them.'

'Corporal Ahmed, lead the men out and spread across the road with your weapons ready. I shall join you, and we will take a morning stroll.'

The men cradled their AKs in their arms, formed a line, and shuffled out to spread across the road at a jog, then moved forward by several metres to allow the lieutenant to take his usual place behind them. He believed his men should withstand the worst of any attack and protect him for better things. Still, he waited for the sounds of an attack before following the men.

Naturally, they glanced fearfully up the road into the blinding sunlight for the supposed enemy, mostly keeping a close watch for stones on the street in their path.

As the first of them reached the far side, prudently staying as close to the available cover as possible, he turned to face down the road. The second-to-last man suddenly yelled and swung his gun as he turned to see the shocking sight he had finally noticed. A man, a woman wearing an *abaya* with her head uncovered, and a small girl sitting unconcernedly on blocks in the shade on his side of the road, looking at them with interested expressions.

The others switched their gaze to the man who had yelled, and although they registered the presence of the three, it was the mad dance of the man who had shouted as he tried to throw away his Kalashnikov, which riveted their attention. He had held it in the approved two-handed grip, with one hand around the forward pad of the barrel, when the barrel had suddenly turned snake-like and was trying to wrap itself around his arm. It terrified him. In a split second, they were all leaping and yelling as the barrels of their guns coiled and writhed, accompanied by peals of laughter from Soraya, uncontrolled chuckles and a broad smile from Fatima.

The last soldier out was the still half-naked soldier. Throwing down his AK, he turned and accelerated up the road with an impressive gain in speed. He had not gone far but had accumulated sufficient momentum when the lieutenant stepped out from the path to see what was happening. The collision hurled him back against the stones. The naked man staggered upright and continued to run.

At the sight of their leader prostrate on the stones and one of their number running west, the remaining Jihadis decided retreat was the most sensible choice. They followed the runner, who, with bare feet, was already fifty metres ahead and still accelerating.

The Sage stood, as did the two who seemed glued to his side. They stepped forward a few paces until he stopped before the dazed lieutenant, who looked up at him first with the terror of the unknown, then with cunning tinged with fear as he saw it was a Sage with a staff, a woman, and a child.

'Who *are* you?'

'I am Allah's Messenger, Ahmed Mahmoudi; I have a message for you.'

'What is this message?' Mahmoudi had no fear of words.

'You are to look on your past and future,' said the old man, lifting his staff a few centimetres and bringing it down with a thump.

Mahmoudi grinned at him and started to rise, then fell back

with terror written on his face as his eyes focused on something in the sky that he alone could see.

The Sage turned, and, followed closely by his companions, walked westward.

'What will happen to him?' asked Fatima.

'*Inshallah*,' said the Sage, 'God will judge him; no one will see him again.'

Although the morning was still young, many pairs of eyes peered out into the road, watching for danger and trying to gauge whether the time was opportune to collect water or search for food. Seeing the eight soldiers running hard up the road, led by one without a shirt and all of them without weapons, was too much for curiosity. As men were the prime target for unwanted violence, the first person to come out of the ruined concrete's shadows was a woman who came slowly to them.

As she approached, the Sage whispered to Fatima, 'You will tell all women to uncover their heads to Allah; it is your first task.' When they stopped, the woman approached them, her face showing growing amazement as she looked in wonder at Fatima's bared head and the Sage. Fatima spoke to her.

'Zorah, it is Allah's will that women must uncover their heads to Him so he may see their faces. They shall not cover them except for protection from wind and dust. Do so, and He will protect you.'

Like Fatima before her, Zorah looked at the Sage. Seeing his smiling face and gentle eyes, she didn't understand why she obeyed, lifting the hood of her *abaya* to let it drop behind her.

They continued to walk ahead, and as they did, more women emerged to greet them. When told, they dropped their head coverings. Children came too and joined Soraya, who happily told them the man was the Storyteller of Allah and, with glee, told them of the naked soldier.

'I just pointed my finger and said, *"No Clothes,"* and his clothes vanished.' The other children listened in awe and significantly didn't approach too closely.

5

When the Storyteller, Fatima and Soraya reached what was once the central square of the town, now a ruined heap of rubble easily identifiable as the remains of a mosque due to a remaining piece of a minaret, they had gathered a crowd of several dozen. A cleared area before the Mosque served for prayers; the Sage crossed it to the rubble. Choosing a comfortable-looking block, he sat on it and looked at the crowd. Fatima and Soraya stood on either side of him. He noticed one or two older men behind the women and children. The entire group was dirty and dusty, exhibiting signs of starvation that had persisted for many months. Several limped, and there were significant signs of vitamin deficiency, particularly among the children.

'Fatima, where do you obtain your water?' he asked.

'There was a well behind the Mosque; it lies behind this ruin. It had a pump to bring water to the Mosque's fountain, where we could wash our feet and hands before prayers. There were pipes around the basin from which we filled our containers. Then the water flowed north, south, east and west, to places where we could collect water without walking far. The water flowed in channels lined with stones, tiles, and flat rocks as a roof. Before the destruction, they had been there for hundreds of years. A small well with a removable cover allowed us to fetch water at several places. The bombs destroyed them; if water flowed into the channels, it would disappear into the sand.

'When the soldiers destroyed the Mosque, the well collapsed, but the men dug down from the side, and we can crawl down the tunnel and draw water from the well as it comes up through the bricks and stones, but in small amounts.'

'For heating food and cooking?'

'We had gas, but now we have a small amount of kerosene oil; we use it sparingly.'

'This you will do. Find who has the most oversized pots in town and tell the women to fetch three and two large baskets. Place them here in front of me. I shall also need a little kerosene, three teaspoonfuls, and a match.

'But first, stay with me; I shall talk to the men.'

He stood and looked out over the growing crowd of people. He didn't shout, but such was the silence when he stood; every person could hear his words when he spoke without raising his voice. Looking over the women's heads, now without the *abaya* hoods or headscarves, he studied the men at the back of the crowd. As expected in a Muslim community, the men remained separated from the women. He beckoned to the nearest of them, an elder with a curly white beard and dusty white *taqiyya* on his head. '*Hajji*, come forward with the men.'

Leading the way, the elder he had called came straight towards him. The crowd of women and children split to either side to let him pass, followed by the other men, until they stood before him.

'I am Allah's Storyteller. I come to tell you all a story, but first, you must all eat and drink.'

The elder looked at him fearlessly. 'You say Allah has sent you, yet the women stand shamelessly without hiding their hair and faces from the sight of men. They say you have promised them protection from the fighters who claim to be fighting for Allah in Jihad. They have killed many in this town. What will you do when they come here and fire on us all?'

'Only Allah alone can protect. The women show their faces, not to men, but to Him, claiming his protection. No one will fire weapons at those whom He protects. – I have spoken.'

The *Hajji* stared at him, first with doubt, then in resignation. 'So be it. What do you want?'

'The men must find a rope long enough to reach the water in the well, as before the destruction of the Mosque. They will attach it to a bucket, the largest they can raise in the well with water inside, and as many containers for the water as they can find. They shall bring them here, and I shall go with them to see this well.'

'The well is blocked except for a narrow tunnel. But if you wish this foolishness, we shall do it.'

He signalled to several men and gave them instructions. They shuffled off to find the rope and bucket, followed by five others who mumbled they would look for containers.

The Storyteller turned to Soraya beside him.

'Soraya, tell the children I need three stone bowls about this size,' with his hands spaced about thirty centimetres across. 'They must hold some kerosene without it flowing out. They must find some and fetch them for me.'

She at once ran to several of the older children, who drew back as she approached. But when told with an air of total authority what she wanted, they ran away to find the stones.

'Now, Fatima, fetch the pots and kerosene.'

She went forward to speak to the women, the men in front separating into two groups as she walked along confidently and proudly, head high.

Then, three men returned with a bucket and ropes, and the Storyteller strode off around the Mosque, so they followed.

'Where is this well?' he asked the one with the bucket.

'Follow me.'

The group went ahead. Having rounded the Mosque, it was apparent where the well must have been. The rubble of the destroyed Mosque spread across the sand, but at one point, a small clearing in the wreckage had the remains of a circular wall with a piled stone peak.

'There.'

The Storyteller looked at the ring wall. He lifted his staff twenty centimetres above the ground and spoke.

'I call on Allah the Almighty to bring water again to this town so that the people may drink, wash and cleanse themselves before they pray for the forgiveness and protection that He gives to those of a pure heart who ask for his protection.'

He lifted his staff higher and stamped it hard on the ground with a resounding thump. Less than a second passed, then a rumbling noise and a vibration felt through the feet started to build. The earth shook, and then the pile of stones on the well disappeared down the well.

'Now, take your bucket, draw water, and take the containers to the people.'

He turned to find that the *Hajji* who had initially opposed him stood behind him. The others had run back until the rumbling had stopped; now, they were returning cautiously.

The *Hajji* looked at him and said, 'We shall do so, but first, I think the men should give thanks to our Lord.'

The Storyteller looked into his eyes, which returned his gaze fearlessly. 'I agree: You and Fatima will work well together.' He turned and strode back around the destroyed Mosque. Passing by some more men with containers, he gestured for them to continue.

The *Hajji* gave an order to the assembled men, 'Draw one bucket of water. We shall wash our hands, feet and face. Then we shall pray, giving thanks for Allah's gift. Then, we shall fill the containers. As soon as one is full, carry it to the others.'

The Storyteller found Fatima examining a collection of cauldrons and baskets. She selected three and two baskets as he arrived. Soraya's children had brought stones, so he chose three with an even sole for stability and a dished upper surface.

'Fatima put these three in a row, the largest at one end, the smallest at the other, and then support the pots above them with stones. Pile up several stones at the small end to make a stable platform for the baskets, a bit above knee height.'

The children scrambled for rubble to support the cauldrons above the chosen hearthstones and the makeshift platform for the baskets; then, the first man returned with a water container.

'Pour the water into all three pots and return for more,' the Sage said.

'Now, Fatima, pour a tiny amount of kerosene into each stone, carefully in the middle, and light it.'

She did, and all those looking on waited to see what happened, expecting the single flame to die away as it consumed the fuel. A murmur among them grew into a babble as the flame grew into a fire hot enough to heat the pot of water.

More water came, the pots filled up, and then the Storyteller told Fatima.

'Place two or three more pots in front, on stones, fill them with water, and tell everyone to fetch a cup and drink as they wish.'

The crowd was so thirsty that they didn't need encouragement. Soon, everyone was drinking fresh, clean water or sharing a cup of it. The excitement was such that no one noticed the pots beginning to bubble until someone cried, 'The water in the pots is boiling.'

The Storyteller beckoned to the elder who had led the

prayers and had now returned from the well. Then, he strode over to the pots, opened the woven wool bag on his shoulder, and took a small handful of what the crowd saw as dried berries or beans five times. They saw him sprinkle them into the water of the three pots in turn, then into the baskets.

He turned and faced the sun, lifted both arms above his head in a wide embrace, raised his eyes to the glaring sun, and spoke, 'We shall pray to He who has given us water to give us food.' The crowd kneeled. Some quickly and others with difficulty, and he continued when they had all bowed their heads to the sand, *'I call on The Force of Allah the Almighty for his children here, who join with me in this request, to fill these pots with food and to keep them full until all here have grown strong and healthy and can fend for themselves. Look at the faces of these women and remember them as your servants. Protect them from evil and those who would harm them and their families, especially their children.'*

He turned to Fatima, who was close, 'Fatima, in this pot,' pointing to the largest, 'will be rice, in the next fish, and the last vegetables, in the baskets, will be bread and fruit. This place is Allah's Kitchen. You will arrange for a group of women to be permanently here. The fires will not die, and the pots and the baskets will not empty for thirty days and nights. People may eat and drink anything they want. You must ensure they all understand He wishes them to eat fruit and vegetables, not just rice, fish, and bread. Especially children.' She nodded, speechless at the wonder of what he said.

Turning towards the *Hajji*, he added, 'Between you and Fatima, to whom Allah will grant the power to punish anyone who transgresses your agreed rules, it shall be your task to ensure that when the pots empty, this town shall not go hungry.'

The *Hajji* nodded, 'I agree, Lord.'

'No, not a lord, a Storyteller, and after everyone has eaten, here in this square, to these people, for the first time, I shall tell the story I have come to tell.'

He continued, talking to the two of them, 'Men have severely damaged this world. It is time for women to manage it with the help of men. It can become a world where women and children can live and grow without fear. Fatima, there is always a man who insists on coming before women and children; if such happens, point your finger at him and say, *"No Clothes."* The punishment of ridicule is more effective than anything else for a man.'

The *Hajji* nodded his head in agreement, 'Your words are wise, Lord; perhaps it is time for a change.'

6

At the western entry to the town, far up the road, the invading Jihadi group had their main headquarters. More extensive than the eastern post, it boasted a roof. They had forced the townspeople to clear the rubble and sweep it. The thirty-one soldiers, plus the captain and his lieutenant at the east end, had arms for a hundred. The captain was in his comfortably decorated headquarters, with a desk and chair, some carpets, and a secluded resting place. He was a Saudi who had been a member of Al Qaeda until the attraction of wielding a weapon in the Jihad had proved too strong.

Unlike Lieutenant Mahmoudi, whom he had not hesitated to assign as far away as possible, as he had at once recognised him as dangerous, the captain was an intelligent and educated man. He had attended Quranic school, avidly read the Quran, and studied other texts. A self-disciplined man, he washed and carefully shaved each morning before saying prayers. His parents had dreamt he would rise in a religious hierarchy until his diversion into the terrorist Al Qaeda movement and disappearance.

When eight exhausted men, one half-naked, ran into the headquarters, he looked over his desk with no expression except a raised eyebrow.

After examining them briefly, he asked, 'What is this all about?' The babble between deep breaths as they all spoke at once was incomprehensible, except for the word *'Djinns,'* which occurred multiple times.

In exasperation, he stood and yelled at them, *'Go!* Drink and recover your breath, and when you can speak clearly, you'll come one at a time and see me.'

They staggered away, bumping into each other, and Sidi sat down worriedly.

Twenty minutes later, the first man returned timidly, pushed to be first by the others who were highly aware of the situation and didn't want to face the captain.

'Where is Lieutenant Mahmoudi?'

'I don't know, Sir.'

'You and the others ran off and left him behind?'

The soldier realised his predicament and at once tried to justify his actions.

'We had no choice, sir. Our guns turned into snakes and tried to attack us, so we had to run.'

'Start at the beginning, please, tell me what happened from the first thing that you saw.'

'Please, Sir, you must ask Muhammar; he was the eastern end guard this morning and saw the *Djinns* first. Then there was Mohammed, who went to look by the lieutenant's orders, and Corporal Ahmed, who led us out to confront the *Djinns.*'

'Then go away and send me Muhammar.'

Ushered in was the man who had arrived barefoot and half-naked. Sidi told him to report from the beginning, and he did so. Mohammed, the second soldier, added his experience of seeing the *Djinns.*

'Now send in Corporal Ahmed.'

Ahmed told the second half of the story.

It left the captain with no doubt that he had a problem. The only man missing was Mahmoudi; as he despised him, he would not take any precipitate action in the hope of saving him. He decided to proceed cautiously. He called in his two best scouts, seasoned soldiers with extensive experience from recent skirmishes. Sidi knew survival was a matter of luck in guerrilla warfare. Still, war honed some animal instincts. The more intelligent soldiers were the majority among the survivors.

'You two will go down the road and discover what is happening. Do not let anyone see you. Do not fire on anyone unless you are fired upon first. I want a report back, not a corpse.'

The men left, and with forethought, he decided breakfast might be an excellent idea.

In the town centre, people lined up, with children first, then women, and finally men, while the Storyteller watched.

The Storyteller looked up at the other side of the road where a small group of people had collected: two or three men, some women, and a few children. They were staring but not coming forward.

He noticed the *Hajji* had also seen them and was walking over to them.

The *Hajji* reached them, and a quiet conversation ensued; then, they all came over, led by the Hajji, to join the crowd. He had a few words with the men at the back as they approached, and then the women and children came forward quietly to join the others, who accepted them without difficulty.

The Storyteller was smiling as the *Hajji* came to him and said, 'They have suffered more than most; they are Christians. Today, we can openly support them without reprisals that hurt our families.'

Fatima and two other women stood by the food pots, and a third by the breadbasket. The front ranks watched hungrily, lecturing those behind on the progress as the cauldrons filled with food in the bubbling water.

'I can see the rice!' exclaimed one crone.

'I can see fish!' said another.

Fatima and each serving woman stirred their pots, and then Fatima gestured to Soraya.

'Come, you may be our taster.' She glanced at the Storyteller, and he nodded.

No woman or child would have dared dispute Soraya's right to be the first served, but one of the men, with a stern face, as predicted, pushed forward in front of Soraya, held out his plate and said, 'No woman or child will come before me.'

Fatima didn't hesitate; she pointed at him and exclaimed, '*No clothes.*' The man found himself naked as the day he was born, without even the plate he had been holding.

Someone in the crowd tittered, triggering a burst of laughter that spread throughout the entire assembly. Clutching his genitals, the man turned and pushed his way through the group, now in paroxysms of laughter. It grew until he passed through the crowd and scuttled off to find some clothes.

The *Hajji* was smiling as he said to Fatima, 'We shall have trouble with him.' She nodded but beckoned to Soraya, to whom she gave a small helping of everything. 'Eat it slowly, Soraya; you have had so little food that eating fast will make you sick. It should be enough, but you can return if you need more.'

Soraya went to sit on a concrete block with her precious personal spoon at the ready and started to eat.

Thirty minutes later, the scouts returned. The captain was finishing the last of some dates.

'Well?'

The taller of the two men pulled out a portable phone. 'I have some pictures, sir; these are of the crowd in the town square. I could not approach any closer without them seeing me, so some photos use zoom; they are grainy.'

He looked at the photos. 'What are they doing?'

'They appear to be cooking food, and they all go to the pots, fetching food and water to drink. We saw no sign of any weapons or guards.'

'The women all seem uncovered, and the men are mostly old.'

'That seems to be correct, sir.'

'Did you see who was leading them?'

'There is one woman and an old man at the pots; they seem to be supervising the food distribution, and there is a man with a staff standing to one side, guarding them. Who is the leader? I cannot tell.'

'Call in Mohammed from the East guard.'

Mahommed returned and looked at the photo. His response was confident.

'The old man with the staff and the woman at the pots are *Djinns*. I know the man helping by the pots is the oldest man in the town, who sometimes leads prayers. He has an education.'

The captain remained silent, and the soldiers remained stiffly at attention while he reflected on the information, trying to decide on a course of action. He was a courageous man who would willingly lead his men into battle, but this was a situation he had never encountered before.

Finally, he looked up at the two scouts.

'You two will follow me down the street, hidden as before and at least a hundred metres behind me. We must take no action until we know what we must face. The remaining soldiers will prepare for an attack but remain alert. You will not intervene unless I give you a signal.'

He stood and removed his uniform, then pulled a *thawb* from a pile of clothes on a shelf behind him. He donned it, removed his boots and slipped on a pair of sandals. From his desk drawer, he lifted a tiny automatic pistol, checked its loads, set the safety catch on, and placed it in the voluminous pocket of his *thawb*.

He then walked out and paced slowly down the middle of the road towards the ruined Mosque.

Preoccupied with the food, no one except the *Hajji* noticed the Storyteller ease himself to his feet and walk over to the centre of the roadway, looking westwards. He went over to join him.

'Someone comes.'

The Storyteller strolled forward until hidden from the crowd surrounding the food. As the figure in the *thawb* came closer, the *Hajji* remarked quietly.

'It is the rebel group's leader; they call themselves the Jihadis.'

'We shall soon learn what he wants,' replied the Storyteller.

They waited until the captain stopped three metres in front of them.

'*As-Salaam-Alaikum*, Sidi bin Abbas,' greeted the Storyteller.

Startled when greeted by name, he recovered quickly. He bowed and replied, '*Wa-Alaikum-Salaam*. You know my name; I do not know yours.'

'I am Allah's messenger; how can we assist you?'

His words disconcerted Sidi; it had been a long time since a confrontation with anyone in this town had not generated signs of terror. He thought for a moment.

'I am the authority in this town; I demand to know what is happening.'

The reply shocked him. 'The people of this town have never chosen you as their leader; no one in the nation has appointed you, and you have taken your position by force. This town and its people are now under the protection of Allah. When they have eaten, I shall tell the people the story Allah has sent me to tell. You may wait and hear it. Then you will leave this town with your soldiers and may take all the arms you can carry.'

Sidi had difficulty holding his temper: 'I can bring my soldiers and impose my will; you have no weapons.'

'Neither do you. Take that ridiculous thing from your pocket and examine it.'

Staggered by the reply, Sidi removed the pistol and looked at it. It appeared unchanged at first sight, but then he realised it was much lighter as it had become a single piece of soft rubber. He dropped it on the road.

The realisation dawned on him; forces of incredible magnitude confronted him. In a single flash of thought, he *knew* the sensible thing to do was return home to his country as rapidly as possible. His survival instinct told him to be polite.

'I shall listen to the story.'

'Then please sit out of sight; I cannot answer for the people's reactions if they see you. You will hear my words without difficulty.'

The Storyteller, followed by the *Hajji*, turned and walked back to the crowd, now all eating.

'Serve yourself, Fatima, and eat. I shall wait. But do not serve more to anyone. They must wait an hour before eating again; otherwise, they will experience nausea and vomiting. They may eat again after I pass on Allah's message.'

It was then that the unseen satellite began its passage over the country. The CIA collects information in many ways; satellites are just one of them. The data collected may follow a tortuous route through the massive organisation, but eventually a report with correlating data arrives at the desk of the Director of Analysis.

Meghali's mind convinced her she should ask Patrick to join her for a welcome dinner. She had no idea what had prompted her to invite him, for she never questioned her mind, and her mind liked it that way.

'Hello Patrick, has boredom set in yet?'

'Not for a long time, Meg. I'm investigating the CIA to determine where you and I fit amongst the hundred or more committees. It's fascinating, especially the Committee for Research into Alien Phenomena.'

'We must be alike in many ways, Patrick; I did similar research when I started. It took some time to understand the committee, because although the name was accurate when it formed, it evolved into something else instead of closing. I'm sure you could imagine a movie script covering its history. That's not why I called. Are you free for a welcome dinner this evening?'

'I'm not. But as you are free, how about joining me for a thank-you-for-giving-me-this-job dinner?'

'Patrick, I invited you first, and you've admitted you're available.'

'True, but my reason is far more important.'

Piqued, Meghali asked, 'Do you need a reason?'

'No, Meg. Unless it's hunger. I feel we don't need a reason. Let your feelings speak for you, and we'll take turns choosing a restaurant.'

'Then, your reason is more important. You choose tonight. Say seven-thirty? You can collect me.'

Two minds congratulated themselves on a successful strategy.

Patrick's dinner with Meghali was at a vegetarian restaurant near her apartment.

'Patrick, you have an expensive condo, and this restaurant is not cheap. How can you afford it?'

'Meghali, I've traded on the stock exchange for years; I'm not a big player and rely on my software to buy and sell. I make a good income from it. It took a lot of work to build up the data and the programs, but now that the fun of trying to beat the odds is over, I accept a steady return. As I don't have many other expenses, no cars, and no staff, I can afford a large apartment for the computer, instead of an office, and good restaurants when I have guests. I work because I want to.'

'That explains the big apartment for a single man; I had imagined a huge bedroom with a hot tub, an enormous bed and a mirror on the ceiling.'

Patrick grinned at her. 'If that's what you like, I shall install a mirror tomorrow; the hot tub may take a few days.'

Meghali didn't take the bait. 'No, I would like you to explain why you said my mind is weird.'

'Not true, I didn't say that – but it's unusual. Have you identified any dark forces threatening our world?'

'No, but I have a gut feeling that the world has taken the wrong direction, and someone will step in to change it. For better or worse, I'm not sure. I'll keep looking.'

The food became the subject until Patrick took her home.

7

Soraya was the first to notice, but didn't question it after the morning's events. She had a pair of sandals on her feet, simple thongs with decorated straps. Soraya thought they looked beautiful. She looked at Fatima's feet; Fatima had similar sandals, but she hadn't noticed. Soraya was about to speak when she realised Fatima's *abaya* was fading. As Soraya watched, fascinated, it slowly faded until it was invisible, leaving Fatima dressed in a penetrating white dress with an embroidered top. When Soraya looked down at her shift, she found it to be fine, shining white cotton.

She looked at the Sage; he smiled and winked at her, beckoning her to him.

'Soraya, I shall tell my story. You will stand on my right side, Fatima, and the *Hajji* will stand on my left. After the story, I shall leave. If you wish, you may come with me.'

With wide eyes, she nodded.

Fatima finished eating, oblivious to all but the delicious food, instead of the scrounged scraps she had eaten for three years. She put her bowl down carefully and then gasped as she saw her sandals and the white dress. Frozen from shock for several seconds, she saw Soraya wearing a shining white shift beside the smiling Sage, who beckoned for her to come to him.

Fatima reached him as the *Hajji* arrived. The Sage instructed,

'Fatima, please stand on my left; I shall climb on this block; *Hajji*, stand next to Fatima.'

They moved into place but didn't see him climb onto the block. When they turned to look at the crowd, he was already on top, lifting his arms.

Peering from his hiding place, Sidi bin Abbas understood the scene's impact on the crowd. How the woman and the girl had changed clothes without leaving the group was inexplicable, but the group would think it miraculous.

With his arms raised, one hand holding the staff, the Sage was an imposing figure; with the woman and girl on either side of him, it was a stunning scene.

'People of this town, I have come to tell you a story; this is what I must say.'

The crowd sat or stood in total silence.

'It was a long time ago.

'Allah was studying his Universe, a vast space He had created like a giant balloon in which millions of stars floated and turned. Whenever He noticed a deep dent at a place on the inside of the balloon, a weak spot in the fabric holding His Universe, He would repair it, but His Universe was no longer growing. He was bored; nothing interesting was happening anywhere amongst the billions of galaxies, suns, and planets. Instead, He breathed into a weak spot; his breath is infinite energy, and a new balloon grew from the old Universe and separated from it. Allah's power expanded the balloon just like you have seen a balloon blown up using a gas cylinder, extremely fast at first, too fast for the eye to follow, then slowing. It is still growing.

'As it grew, the expanding energy's speed dropped in the new Universe; tiny whirlpools made the atoms, the building blocks of our Universe. But always, wherever you are in the Universe, some of His force remains. He ignored the new Universe for billions of years, for He knew what would happen and would return to look later. He has others to watch.

'Then, in the Universe, the atoms joined to form molecules and combined with others as they collided. They swam not in a liquid or gas but in the force field of Allah's breath. It didn't push them one way or another, but every piece of matter, like the grains of sand in the desert blown by the force of the wind, moved and sometimes joined with others.

'When they grew, like desert sand roses, they grew further; when big enough, collapsing into balls of molten iron and rock that continued to grow until they became suns. And the suns captured other balls that crashed into or began to circle them.

'So, our Universe was born from the breath of Allah.

'More billions of years passed, and balls cooled and became solid planets, circling suns, but always with Allah's force in the growing Universe. His Force still pushed atoms and molecules around. Even the planets took part: heat and gravity, electric forces from lightning, winds from gases, and eventually rain from liquids when they had cooled enough. On the surface of hundreds of thousands of planets, the molecules formed more complex fluids, and they gathered into themselves a little of Allah's force; they had life; they were His children, and He was pleased when He looked at his new Universe. It would interest him to see what happened.

'You know what happened. Life has evolved and populated your planet, as it has done on many others. Eventually, a brief time ago, compared with the time it had taken, people walked the Earth and still have His force in their cells.

'Some planets didn't progress; some succeeded but collided with others, broke into pieces or formed new planets. Your world was lucky; it suffered many impacts, at least two of which nearly wiped out all life on Earth. If the moon, a wanderer between the stars, had hit this planet, it would have destroyed all life. But the Earth captured the moon. Others died; of the millions of worlds which might have lived to form great civilisations, only tens of thousands remain.

'Allah never visits, but occasionally He sends an observer to report, and sometimes He sends a messenger.

'He has sent me because, amongst the tens of thousands of planets continuing to develop a civilisation, this is the first one where the inhabitants are destroying their world. Allah finds it shameful, but seeing what happens is of great interest; the knowledge may help save other planets.

'These words are Allah's message: *"You are destroying your planet, and one day it will be a dead world like your neighbour, Mars."*

'Before beginning my task to tell you this story, I have observed the life on this planet with interest, for there are other flourishing civilisations here; you call them ants and bees, and I have decided to tell you what I have seen. The ants and the bees have females leading them, and the males work beside them. Men rule the humans, and women are subservient. The men destroy; they do not have the female's caring instincts to look after their home, children, and the planet.

'I remind you that Allah invites both women and men to *Hajj*, and the rules of *Ihram* prohibit women from hiding their faces with a niqab, a burqa, or even using their hands. During *Hajj*, everyone must reveal their faces to the Lord. Only when necessary should people cover their heads.

'Allah does not intervene; if you pray, you pray to His force within you; you can help yourself by listening to your prayers and the force in you. If humanity can change, if women can impose an effort to care, this world may recover. When the world is a cold ball in the cosmos, Allah will no longer send a watcher or a messenger. There will be nothing to see.

'Think deeply about what I have said. I shall not return. If you allow women to make decisions, there is hope for the world; if not, you have heard what will happen. Your destiny is yours to decide.'

Turning to his disciples, he said, 'Walk with me until we're outside the town.' He jumped lightly from the block and walked through the fawning crowd, accompanied by the three.

Sidi bin Abbas knew fighting meant defeat. He slipped out of his hiding place and ran to the headquarters. His orders were emphatic: 'We abandon this town at once. Quickly, fetch the trucks.'

Three minutes later, a Jeep in the lead, with two trucks behind, drove west from the town.

Thirty minutes later, the entire crowd walked down the street following the Sage, Fatima, Soraya, and the *Hajji*, but at a respectful distance. When they reached the edge of the desert, Fatima took one of Soraya's hands, dropped to one knee and then hugged her. Soraya put both arms around her and her head on Fatima's shoulder as Fatima said, 'Soraya, I know you must go; it is your destiny. I have loved you as mine, and I will remember you until you return to visit us. There were tears in her eyes as she kissed Soraya and reluctantly released her.

'One day I will, Mama, I promise.'

The Sage turned to Fatima and the *Hajji*. 'I have done all Allah permits; it is now up to you.' To the *Hajji*, he said, 'If called on to lead prayers, repeat the story I have told, no more. You will never forget it.' To Fatima, he said, 'If you must stop a truck, pray for Allah's help, point at it and say, *"No tyres."* Allah will remove the tyres from the vehicle.'

Taking Soraya's hand, he stepped out along the road while the others watched. After fifty paces, a breeze sprang up; dust swirled, and a conical whirlwind grew. After a minute, it hid them from the spectators. Then, it died away to reveal an empty road.

The CIA gathers intelligence in multiple ways. One is IMINT, their acronym for Image Intelligence. In a dimly lit basement room at Fort Belvoir, USA, rows of IMINT specialists sat examining satellite photographs on the screens before them. As one left, another took his place. At five am, the National Geospatial-Intelligence Agency room was quiet; the white noise generator's background hiss, unobtrusive during the day, intruded on the silence. The specialist for the Middle East was on the early shift, from midnight to six am, sitting at a specially constructed desk with a large square screen directly in front of him and narrower screens on each side. The primary screen size matched the photographs he studied; the photo series had just arrived. When the reconnaissance satellite passed overhead in orbit at 27,000 km/h, the series of images taken came to his desk for analysis from the NRO, the National Reconnaissance Office.

He paged through them, pausing for several seconds on each one, a bare desert with nothing unusual in the pictures. When he came to a photograph including a small town off-centre, he stopped and checked the photo's coordinates. A list on the right-hand screen had not moved while he scrolled through the empty images until the last, when it jumped to an entry. A table on that screen displayed the coordinates and descriptions of all fixed objects identified over the years of analysis. It scrolled automatically to the coordinates shown in the picture. He clicked a button, and all the known items changed into black shapes on the screen. He checked the remaining desert-coloured area for anything. Just before the black areas filled the screen, He noted some new shadows to the west and placed a crosshair marker on them. He then switched off the black colouring and examined the town in greater detail. He zoomed in further and scrolled, exploring the alleyways lit by the sunlight and the building's flat roofs. He placed no other crosses until he came to a patch with a gathering of people. A Ctrl-key-click on the building's ruins beside the people forced the table to scroll to an item labelled Ruined Mosque. A double-click added a name in a box outside the picture, along with an arrow pointing to the ruins. He placed a crosshair on the people and continued. He found nothing else, so he returned to the first crosshairs using the F1 key and zoomed in further. He noted two trucks and a Jeep heading out of the town. He counted thirteen terrorists in each vehicle, then added two hidden by each cab and the two he could see in the Jeep. He typed onto his report pad on the other screen:

> Thirty-two Jihadis left the town, one missing from the previous complement of thirty-three – the reason for the unusual evacuation and missing jihadi is unknown.

Feeling he had done his job for the day and that others could investigate further, he added the image reference to the report, ticked the box labelled [*Analysis Required*], and then dispatched it.

8

Meghali saw the report when she arrived for work at eight. She would have forwarded it to one of many analysts a few days earlier. However, her mind stepped in, and interested in how Patrick would react, she forwarded it to him and then went to his cubicle, where he was lying on his modified chair, staring at the ceiling.

He sat up and then levered his chair to a normal position when Meg rapped on the panelling and pushed open the glass door.

'Am I disturbing your morning snooze, Patrick?'

'No, Meg, I was running some scenes through my mind; the white ceiling is the best place to play them to avoid distraction.'

'I apologise for distracting you; I sent you a satellite image, and I want your reaction.'

'Then take the chair beside mine, and we'll look at it on the screen.'

'Where did you get this huge screen?'

'I asked for it and bought my own when I couldn't get authorisation. I find immersing myself in the picture easier than peering through a keyhole.'

After tapping a few keys, the Satellite image appeared, with the IMINT analyst's observations in a box to one side. Patrick read the coordinates and the time written below the picture.

'The Middle East, the shadows confirm late afternoon. An excellent time for a desert picture.'

'Why?'

'Midday, there's heat haze to filter out, so the detail is lost; a bit later, the diurnal wind East to West will grow and carry dust.'

'Patrick, have you done this before?'

'Looked at images, yes, thousands, and when the moviemakers don't get it right, I must scrap the photos as they don't represent reality. It doesn't bother the audience that the lost soul staggering westwards is walking into a sand-laden headwind, but it does to me. It's not right.'

He repeated it; it must be right. 'So what do you see in the picture?'

'What the analyst saw, but there may be more than that. He must have had a worry about the crowd by the mosque to place crosshairs there. I'll zoom in.'

The crowd filled the screen until the picture became grainy.

'Meg, can you ask for a different data set from Geospatial-Intelligence?'

'What do you want?'

'The Satellite transmits the image in a compressed format; the software removes all touching duplicate pixels and, upon arrival, decompresses it and adds the missing pixels with the same colour as the first. I want a picture with the missing pixels bright red.'

'What will that tell you?'

'We can't see a slight change in colour of one pixel; if those white dresses in front of the crowd are all identical pixels, they will become red.'

'Okay, I'll ask. If this tells us anything, you will appear before the IMINT analysts to explain your method.

'Now tell me why.'

'If those dresses are a pure shining white, something unusual is happening. It's a desert town, and there won't be white clothes anywhere. It's a sandy white at best and streaky. Ask for a previous image of the town and a copy with the missing pixels in red to compare.'

'That makes sense.'

Meg called Geospatial Intelligence, and then Patrick asked.

'Now tell me what you see in the image?'

She replied, 'To me, the departing Jihadis, with one missing, is the key factor. Something has driven them out and may have killed one of them. I can't remember anything that suggests what that something is; it could be a disease or starvation. Whatever it is, it was a threat to the Jihadis and may be a threat to us. There's no sign of recent building damage. The image comparator would have highlighted that, but it did highlight the trucks.'

'Why haven't you considered that their bosses ordered the Jihadis to leave?'

'Because we have no intel of any movements elsewhere.'

The white dresses became bright red.

'Are you surprised, Patrick?'

'Of course. I suspected something, but didn't believe I would be right. Let's compare it with the earlier red pixel image.'

'There are a lot of little red patches. What does that mean?'

'The smallest ones are two or three pixels, and we should ignore them. The others, I don't know, I'll overlay the normal image.'

'Patrick, it looks like the red pixels are on people. They are women wearing abayas, so the pixels show the colour of the abaya.'

'I'm sure you're right; the women are not close to each other. We can see more of their abayas.'

Patrick is excited.

'Meg, I'll return to the first red image... The women are in a packed group in this picture, but why are there no red pixels on their heads?'

Now I'm excited. 'Go to the first image and zoom in on a woman's head.'

'Meg, there's no red because she's not wearing a hood. *That's her hair!*'

'Check the others.'

'They are all the same, Meg, no hoods, so bareheaded. Whatever drove the Jihadis away has had a bizarre effect on the townspeople.'

'I shall authorise an investigation. If the town has a telephone connection, we'll try to ask someone there. If not, we'll place an operative on the ground.'

'They won't have comms, Meg. The Jihadis will have destroyed any aerial. The best you can hope for is a hidden satellite phone. Do you have enough clout to get info from the satellite companies?'

'We might not need anything from them. I'll ask the SIGINT guys what they can do.'

'I'm new to this business, Meg. What do the SIGINT guys do? What's an operative like?'

'They intercept and copy phone calls and radio transmissions; they call them signals. When I select the right operative, I'll send you the CV. They are people of both sexes who fit in wherever we send them.'

'I'll get to work, Patrick; I'll see you later.'

Patrick read the CV as soon as he received it.

> Akeem al Ghamdi is a third-generation American; his grandfather settled in America for reasons he never learnt. He was raised in the Islamic faith and spoke

Arabic in the family since childhood, so he studied languages at college. Naturally, he had added Arabic to his list, along with Farsi and Turkish. His college results were the highest in his year due to his aptitude for languages and his childhood in Delaware, where he lived with his family in a diverse community that spoke several languages. He has no difficulty speaking all four languages, with accents that match those of his tutor's native language.

With family ties to relations in several places in the Middle East, he spent school vacations in various countries. During his college education, he leveraged his family ties to immerse himself in the languages spoken by his family.

Fully screened before recruitment for foreign surveillance, he is a twenty-six-year-old, tall, handsome man with defined Arab features, who can pass as a Saudi anywhere.

Patrick lay back horizontally, and five minutes later, he thought, *I wonder where the Jihadis were going.*

Sidi bin Abbas reported to the garrison commander in the next town, then stated that he would proceed further up the line to a more senior officer. He must have taken a side road; no one saw him again. However, three months later, in his Saudi Arabian hometown, a new Imam with very liberal ideas supported women's progress.

The garrison commander ordered five trucks and a hundred and forty soldiers, fully equipped with mortars, to clean out the town where the reported enemy had taken control and to blow the place apart.

Patrick was right; a civilian with a satphone called his cousin in Fatima's town to inform him about the invasion force. The cousin told the *Hajji*. He called on Fatima, and then they walked from the village and climbed a dune on the side of the road. Dunes grow beside roads when tracks disturb the wind flowing across the desert. Wherever man goes, even without intent, he upsets the balance of nature.

They had a view of eight or ten kilometres and had to wait for half an hour while calmly discussing the town's government. Fatima wanted to recruit young women. 'Because women with a child under twelve are the most caring and protective.'

They saw the trucks on the horizon after the Jihadis had driven thirty of the forty kilometres between the towns. Fatima stood and prayed, *'I call on Allah to protect us, the people who have heard his message from those who come to harm us.'* Then she pointed her finger at the trucks and firmly ordered, *'No tyres!'*

The driver of the first truck suddenly had to wrestle the steering as the now tyreless wheels dug into the sand and brought it to a halt. Suddenly, thrown forward, cursing and yelling, the soldiers piled up against the cab. The truck behind was less fortunate; the driver, half-asleep, had not realised his tyres had gone, had seen the front vehicle's brake lights, so had turned the wheel before colliding with the front truck. The wheels dug in further, and the lorry turned onto its side, spilling the Jihadis onto the hot desert. The other trucks stopped just in time, with the soldiers piled up against the cab like the first.

The front vehicle driver had just descended from the cab

when Fatima pointed again to order, *'No Clothes!'* He found himself naked and barefoot on the hot desert sand.

It was too much. All the others quickly followed the first man to start running back along the road, although, after two hundred metres, they stopped, wondering what to do next.

The captain, now wearing a uniform like the others, but without any covering to conceal a noticeable paunch that partly hid his appendage, had no authority. After an intense argument, several said they would not chance the unknown and started walking towards their town.

The others then joined them. There remained three older men; once the Jihadis were out of hearing, one of them said, with a gesture of his head towards the truck, 'Water.' Before the Jihadis had shot and eaten their camels, they had been herders in the desert.

The other two nodded and returned with him to the trucks. They knew the necessities of desert survival. They created shade with a truck tarp, cut another to make cloaks, and filled water bottles for the evening, when the desert cooled.

The first soldier staggered into the second town five hours later with bloody feet, severe sunburn, and heat exhaustion. The garrison poured water over him, covered his genitals, and sent trucks down the road to collect the others. They found the last dying man after eighteen kilometres; some, dehydrated and delirious, had wandered off the road, leaving tracks that showed where they had gone. Of the one hundred and forty, twelve survived. Three remained missing. The trucks and a twisted mass of useless weapons became a memorial to stupidity.

Once dark, the three that remained behind began to walk, guided by the stars, not along the road but in a straight line. When they reached the town shortly before dawn, they slipped quietly past a drowsy sentinel, collected clothes and personal things, food, and water, and then left to follow the stars to where no one knows.

Fatima made her first request, 'Place a sign some distance up the road to inform visitors: If they carry weapons of any kind, rejection will be immediate and severe.'

The satellite continued to pass over a similar area every ninety minutes, but the Earth had turned enough by the next pass, so the photo sequence didn't show the town.

Twenty-two hours later, another satellite passed over, and the analyst in Fort Belvoir sent in a report. In this one, he reported that the town's residents had returned to normal, except that the photo's sole woman was not wearing a black *abaya*. The first and second reports carried the Geographical reference, but with a count, – /1 and /2.

He also marked it as urgent because he found five trucks, eight kilometres out of town, heading toward it from the west, one lying on its side, and no Jihadis.

The first report had not caused a stir, but the second did. Something was happening in the area. A satellite request for daily passes over the town, its western neighbours, and the road arrived by email at the NRO.

The report was routed through *channels* and arrived in Meghali's email inbox in a designated subfolder. She studied it, and because it included a photo, she sent it to Patrick.

Patrick had spent four hours staring at the ceiling in his cubicle office. He was thinking about two items his AI system had reported. They were odd enough for him to think seriously about them.

When he finally concluded that he should wait for more data, he saw the message on his screen and opened the second report. Seeing the reference /2, he loaded /1. In his mind, he had two successive scenes from a movie. But what was the film about? And who was the editor? He couldn't imagine any connection to the AI-reported items, but instead of discarding them, he added them to his mental movie, *The Future Starts Here.*

Then Meghali arrived.

'Patrick, do you have any idea what those satellite photos mean?'

'No, Meg, I suspect they are the opening scenes of a movie we know nothing about. I'm unsure whether the scene is a flash-forward or a long ride, though I favour the latter.'

'You're confusing me again. Explain, please.'

'There are two favourite scenarios to begin a movie. The flash-forward is a short scene from further into the movie, like *Jaws*, which starts with the death of a young woman. However, the editor chooses to cut it at the point where he feels the anticipation reaches its peak.

'Given where our satellite took these two pics, I favour the second, the long ride. You must have seen a movie that opens with a beautiful, peaceful picture of a valley with mountains; it could be a canyon.'

'Yes, and a black dot in the distance slowly grows as someone rides into the foreground. So, you learn a bit about him.'

'There's more to it than that. Next time, study the scenery. Most people notice it but don't *see* it. First, trees, rocks and a dusty track give the impression of distance and justify the delay; otherwise, the viewers would become impatient. The music starts at a low volume and increases as the horse approaches. Secondly, there are other static indicators. There might be a tepee or puffs of smoke above the horizon, indicating there will be Indians. A rise of ground nearby with a tombstone or two means shooting, and one or more people will die. A low-budget movie might feature a dilapidated sign reading *Boot Hill*.

'As the man rides towards the audience, they can judge his horse, clothes, and weapons. It's a classic introductory scene, although in today's two pictures, an undefined group of terrorists has left town and failed to return, creating a mystery and intriguing the audience. The five trucks with no people have increased the mystery. The inverse of the long ride is not the hero arriving but the baddies leaving. We will do what the editor intends: investigate it. So, he has attached the audience, and we anticipate more.'

'Patrick, you're good at making it plausible.'

'Not me, Meg. *You've* recognised what I've described and feel it's plausible.'

'So what's the next scene?'

'Meg, I don't have enough data. It could be anything, but I'll offer a vague gut feeling. After the opening scene, the hero who rides in must show he has guts and is a good guy. He might rescue a woman in a store from harassment and might have to beat up the guy. It's too early for shooting. He might have a badge showing he's a Marshall or a Ranger, and some guy picks a fight and gets a beating. Is there a town further west? That might be where it has happened, and the trucks are a consequence.

'I don't think it's a war film; we've had no sign of battles or explosions, but I might be wrong.'

9

When Soraya opened her eyes, she felt like she had slept for many hours after the excitement and the filling meal the previous day. Then her eyes widened as the whirlwind died, and she saw a different town a hundred metres ahead. It looked similar, but there was more town and less building damage. A guard, a Kalashnikov hanging from his shoulder, stood in the road ahead, looking to one side. As they stepped forward, he turned and saw them where there had been no one seconds before; riveted by the shock, it took him several seconds to react. The guard grabbed his Kalashnikov, raising it to aim at them, and showed bewilderment as the barrel bent down in a graceful curve. Bereft of any understanding, the survival instinct took over; he dropped the gun and ran into the town. After the first twenty metres, he began shouting.

The major commanding the Jihadis had learnt a lesson the previous night when he lost a hundred and twenty-five men. He had no idea what he would face, but had placed snipers in two high places facing the road. He would have positioned more, but two snipers were among those who had died while walking back. The first sniper watched the road as the morning light spread over the desert; then, when the crescent of the rising sun breached the horizon, it shone directly in his eyes. He had to turn away, temporarily blind, groping for his sunglasses.

When he looked back, he saw the Storyteller and Soraya, then saw the sentinel drop his AK and run. He had his orders, so he raised his sniper rifle and aligned it carefully on the Storyteller, and found the telescope dropping steadily. He was a trained soldier; he knew when a retreat was a better option. He left the rifle with a bent barrel, descended from his rooftop position, and returned to the transport compound through deserted alleys to the opposite end of town. He hid behind a truck, knowing it was the only way to leave town; he had a terrible desire to be elsewhere.

The second sniper was in the Mosque's minaret; the Jihadis had not destroyed the Mosque, and the minaret provided an excellent elevated position for observation. He watched from the window where the *Muezzin* called the faithful to prayers. He had to lean out because it wasn't the best position to watch the road, so he had steadily stared at a building, a flat-roofed house with a high perimeter wall like all the others. The woman who lived there used a bucket of water to wash in the morning, unaware that a watcher could see her from the minaret.

When the sentinel's shrieks began, they disturbed the sniper's hope for an illicit view. He leant out and saw the shape of something in the road. In the heated air, the angle of view distorted the form made by two people. His reaction, fuelled by guilt from not covering the road, was unthinking; he ignored the sniper rifle, grabbed his AK, switched it to fully automatic, and leant out the window. He didn't have enough time to register the bending barrel, as without aiming, he triggered a full burst of fire in the direction of whatever was there. The first bullet, trying to force its way down a bent tube, heated up and then welded to the barrel. The AK exploded, and the headless soldier, leaning well out the window, tumbled to the ground, a victim of his recklessness.

The townspeople had received accounts by phone calls from

Fatima's town throughout the night; those who had no phone learnt from others. They were awake and hidden, waiting expectantly for something to happen. Every dark shadow and deep alcove had someone inside.

The Major had drawn his remaining force into the eastern post, for the invaders would come from the east. Some were awake, others still lying down, when they heard the guard shouting.

The Storyteller told Soraya, 'If you see any soldiers with guns, point and remove their clothes.'

The Jihadis, woken by the shouts and the exploding AK, leapt from their carpets, grabbed their guns, and rushed out to do battle. Who with, they had no idea. Those who tried to see what they were fighting, Soraya turned into naked dancers occupied with fighting Kalashnikovs that had turned into attacking snakes. A few stupidly reacted as untrained fighters often will, running into the road and with their guns on fully automatic, firing in the direction they thought the enemy lay. They didn't fire a single round, but died in the explosion of their weapon; twice, one was too close and died as well.

Once again, the survival instinct took over. The remaining Jihadis, the major in the lead, turned and fled up the road towards the transport compound.

The town's occupants had suffered untold horrors for months, many tortured, fathers executed, wives and daughters raped. The sight of naked Jihadis without weapons sprinting up the road encouraged one man to throw a brick. Hard. He could hardly have missed; the man he hit might not be the one aimed for, but the Jihadi stumbled and fell. It was enough. None of the

Jihadis made it to the transport compound; they died on the road, stoned to death.

The soldier hiding behind a truck, hearing the shouting, had peered down the road and saw the carnage. He leapt into a Jeep and drove to the next town without waiting for his comrades. It was fortunate he didn't wait, for there were none.

The Storyteller and Soraya continued their walk and then stopped at the Mosque, where they calmly sat down on a stone block and waited. A *Hajji*, wearing a *taqiya*, the Imam of the town, appeared, walked over to them and bowed deeply.

'Lord, are you Allah's Storyteller?'

'I am.'

'What are your commands, Lord?'

The Storyteller had decided not to fight the title; it was immaterial, but it helped people seeking a leader.

'First, make sure every corpse is taken into the desert and buried before disease sweeps through the town. Then search everywhere, especially the Jihadi quarters, for food, and if you find any weapons or ammunition, have them brought and piled here. If you find a satellite phone, confiscate it and keep it safe.

'Tell me about the food stocks, then gather the town's citizens, including the women, who must wear no headscarves or headcover in the sight of Allah. I shall then pass on His message.'

The Imam went to do his bidding.

While the Storyteller and Soraya sat waiting, a small boy came up the street alone, little more than a baby, perhaps three years old; he came to them and stood in front of them, a curly-haired child in a thin, stained but clean smock too big for him, his thumb in his mouth. Soraya extended a hand and asked, 'Hello, what's your name?'

He took his thumb out of his mouth long enough to say, 'Med' before replacing it. He took a hesitant step, followed by another as Soraya held her arms out. When she picked him up and sat him on her lap, he turned and looked at the Sage, who smiled at him. Reaching into a pocket Soraya had never noticed, his hand came out with a biscuit. He held it out to 'Med', who decided it might be better than his thumb as something to suck.

As he took the biscuit, the Storyteller said, 'The woman who cares for him comes.'

A young woman ran into the plaza and slowed as she saw them sitting before the Mosque. As she reached them, torn between her need to recover her baby and awe of the Storyteller, he said, 'Rima, he is safe. I have monitored his movements since he left your house. He is young to seek adventure, but quite fearless.'

'That is my problem; he has tried to go outside several times.'

'Then, do not stop him; you can now go out safely, so show him the world he wants to see.'

She suddenly realised he had called her by name. 'How do you know my name?'

'As I know the names of all I meet. You, I have wanted to meet for some time.'

'Why? Why me?'

'Sit with Soraya, she'll tell you about the town to the east, and you will learn.'

Soraya told her story to Rima.

The Imam returned two hours later to report the men had buried the dead; it takes little effort to dig a shallow grave in soft sand, and he had found a satphone. The food stocks tallied; they had more than enough to last thirty days, and they had water. The guns and ammunition began to arrive, thrown down where the Imam pointed, followed by a pair of mortar tubes, three grenade launchers, and ammunition for both. The men who brought them stayed, and then other townsfolk joined them until people murmuring in muted tones packed the plaza. The women wore no head coverings.

When the Imam said everyone was there, the Storyteller stood and said, 'Rima, take your child and stand on my left with the Imam.'

To Soraya, he said, 'Dispose of those weapons, say *"snakes"*, then return.'

Soraya stepped confidently forward to the pile of arms. Two metres from it, with the entire population of the town looking, she straightened her arm and hand, then, with a finger pointing at the pile, cried, '*Snakes!*'

The exclamations of amazement were loud and excited as the weapons twisted themselves into a dense ball, enclosing all the ammunition within. When Soraya returned to the Storyteller, the people on either side hurriedly drew back to give her a clear path.

As they took their places, Soraya was pleased to see that Rima's dress had become much whiter. The murmuring stopped as everyone stared at them, and the Storyteller raised his staff.

'I am Allah's Storyteller; I have come today to pass on His message; it is my task to tell the story and no more. Then I shall leave and never return.'

He told the Story.

He then said to the Imam and Rima, 'Come, we shall walk to the end of the town.' As they walked, he spoke to the two of them, '*Hajji*, if you repeat my message at prayers, it will meet with the Lord's approval. You will then say His words mean the town must choose a woman to lead it. You will propose Rima, who stood beside us, as the leader. Ensure both men and women hear your proposal and agree. Rima will gather other mothers to help her, those who care for their children as Rima cares for the orphans, and who have enough love to share by caring for everyone in the town. But she'll not give orders to the men; she'll tell you what she wishes, and if matters require judgment, you will consult with her.'

'I shall obey, Lord, but how will the town fight the Jihadis if they return? We have no weapons.'

'You will have no problem. You have a telephone. Rima, call Fatima in the town to the east; they will tell you they fear no soldiers and about their signs. Now we shall leave you.'

The crowd behind the Imam and Rima saw the Storyteller and Soraya walk down the road hand in hand; the whirlwind formed and then grew, gathering sand and dust until it hid them from view, then died away, leaving an empty track.

At evening prayers, the town unanimously agreed Rima should be the town's leader, especially after the Imam had confided to several men that Rima had powers like Soraya. As Soraya was such a young girl, it didn't need much imagination to suspect Rima might have even more extraordinary powers. The Imam had heard the Storyteller issue the 'snakes' command to Soraya, so he alone thought it was the Storyteller who wielded the power.

The next day, Rima started on the town's clean-up; she asked the children to gather small rubble and place it in piles on the main road for collection by men with carts. The Imam organised the rest.

A day later, Rima, with the Imam beside her, saw one of the men strike a twelve-year-old boy collecting stones with others. She was about to shout at the man when something stopped her. Instead, she said to the Imam, 'Ask why Abdullahi hit his son, then come and tell me.'

Later, he reported, 'Abdullahi had told his son to go home, then the boy said he would go when he had finished moving stones; his father struck him for disobedience.'

It surprised the Imam when she said, 'At prayers tonight, I wish you to tell everyone, men and women. I am the person who will keep this town safe from violence brought by outsiders, and I cannot tolerate violence inside the town between its residents, whether adults or children. Tell them if any adult, man or woman, hits a child in anger, Allah will allow no further children to be born to him or her.'

'I shall do so. Allah chooses well.'

10

The following night, the specialist in Fort Belvoir received a fresh image to examine. The town to the west was in the picture. None of the terrorists known to occupy it were visible. Earlier images had shown them on strategic rooftops. The report he compiled was even more puzzling. No armed men were anywhere, yet the transport compound had one Jeep. He was thorough. He checked the last identified number of vehicles, deducted the wrecked lorries on the road, and added the two trucks and Jeep previously photographed leaving the first town. He concluded one Jeep was missing; it was not visible in the photo. The townsfolk were visible, the women didn't wear *abayas*, and there was a new graveyard outside the town. He counted two hundred and three graves. A check on the previously known terrorist count showed five were missing. This third report was significant. Someone had killed two hundred and three terrorists.

A meeting between specialists who had studied the three IMINT reports came to a singular conclusion, expressed by the most senior.

'We don't know what's happening, but something sure is. We must ask the CIA to provide HUMINT, but keep the satellite passing.'

When he asked the CIA, he was surprised to learn that a HUMINT order was already in place. It was not surprising when the senior analyst, with three years to his retirement, said, 'And send the reports to the CRAP bunch; maybe they can come up with an idea.'

Meghali and her newest recruit read the third report and the conclusion.

'Patrick, do you foresee any threat to the US?'

'No, not at all. Those three images are introductory scenes, but I can't tell you what the movie is about. This editor is a master; it's not a basic long ride; it's the most difficult version, the participation long ride.'

'Explain, please.'

'That black spot that seemed to come closer and closer has stopped moving. The camera will begin a zoom-in to impart a sensation that the audience is moving and will participate, and as we get closer, your HUMINT will reveal what he's doing. Wait. I'm sure more will come. I'm also sure that there's a subliminal message hidden in what has occurred.'

'Explain again, Patrick.'

'There's a rule in movie stories: Punishment is due if the baddies attack and lose. That's what audiences believe. If it doesn't happen, the audience wonders why the baddies got away without punishment. I think the Jihadis in the second town attacked the first town and lost, and then something else rocked up and wiped them out. Is there a town further west?'

'Why, Patrick?'

'In some movies, the opening scene drags on, the good guy visits one town after another, building a reputation that then goes ahead and rallies the bad guys until there's a shootout, but I'm doubtful. It's not more than fifty per cent.'

Meghali added a line to her report to the CIA Director.

'No perceived threat to the US.'

Whereas Meghali thought she had insufficient data, Patrick's mind came to a different conclusion.

Yes, something has intervened, but it is not human; it possesses the unlimited power of an editor, like a movie film where an editor, who does not act in the film, cuts and splices pieces of the action, changing sequences or events at will. The producer or director has decided to change the script, and the editor has edited and spliced it.

Editors have their likes and dislikes; Patrick thought he knew something about this editor, but had yet to imagine the script.

The two items his AI had sent popped up in his mind again.

They might be experimental scenes intended for later inclusion; if so, I have a good idea what this movie will be about.

He waited for the following report.

Akeem Al-Ghamdi flew into Oman and then took a bus to Abu Dhabi, where he switched passports to one with no US stamp and flew to Damascus.

The passports issued to him for his latest job were Saudi, with all but three pages filled with stamps, showing that he had travelled extensively over the last four years between Middle Eastern and North African countries. He described himself as a businessman.

In Damascus, he rented a car and drove to Palmyra. Several kilometres before arriving in Palmyra, he passed a train of camels, three with men riding them and the others led on ropes. He stopped long enough to don a dusty desert *thawb* and a *keffiyeh* he wrapped around his face. The camel closest to him had knelt while the man held it; he mounted, took the prof-fered whip, and the camel was up and walking in moments. The whole operation took three minutes without a spoken word. The other man stripped off his *thawb* and, wearing pants and a shirt, drove the rental into Palmyra, where he made a tour of the ruins and returned to Damascus to check in the vehicle. The camel drivers rode into Palmyra, where they negotiated the sale of the camels they had led. Then, they bought food, filled their water cans, and disappeared into the desert. No one took any notice of them.

Three days later, three men rode their camels to Fatima's town. They rode in after spending two hours observing from several hundred metres, using powerful binoculars, during which they had not seen a soldier or an armed guard. They dismounted in front of what appeared to be a makeshift cof-feehouse. Three tables cobbled out of blocks from ruined buildings, with others positioned to sit on. The three camel drivers sat down at a table and unwrapped their face coverings as the proprietor came forward from a small alcove in the rubble. He gave them an effusive welcome and offered them coffee at a price, as well as food and water at no charge. The offer left the three of them speechless until Akeem recovered enough to ask, 'We shall drink your coffee with great pleasure after a gruelling ride, but how can you offer free food?'

'The food is from Allah's Kitchen, a gift from Him; I cannot charge for it. If you wish to give something to the boy who fetches it, it will be more than enough.'

'Then bring us coffee, then three plates of food with water. Then we shall have more coffee; we invite you to join us and tell us about this wondrous thing you describe.'

The proprietor disappeared and called a young boy, who sped off carrying brass trays.

Two minutes later, the proprietor returned with three small cups of thick black coffee and a sugar bowl. The three men spoke quietly to each other, observing the people as they moved busily on the street. They were clearing the rubble; even children carried small stones and bricks, placing them in piles along the middle of the road. They could still see no armed guards or weapons anywhere.

Akeem said they must look carefully at what was happening in the town, for it was most unusual.

Two young boys arrived with the food and glasses of water, and they began to eat. The food was delicious, and the water was pure. When they had finished eating, the boys carrying the trays came to collect the dishes. Akeem had readied two one-thousand-pound notes and gave one to each of them. He wasn't sure the boys knew what they were, but they thanked him politely. The café owner, returning with four cups of coffee, saw what Akeem had given the boys; he bowed to Akeem and said, 'Lord, you are a generous man. It will help their mother enormously; I thank you on their behalf.'

Sitting on a block to one side of the table, he said, 'What would you like to know?'

'Everything, we understand nothing. What is Allah's Kitchen? Where does the food come from? What is happening?'

The café owner described what had happened when the Storyteller came, doing so in graphic detail while Akeem listened without interruption. When he finished his story, Akeem asked, 'So you say a young woman now runs the town? How can this be?'

The café owner, who thought Akeem probably had the traditional attitude to a woman's place in society, tried to explain tactfully. 'Yes, it is true, but our Imam, who was but a *Hajji* before, is the one who gives orders to the people. She makes the decisions as the chosen of Allah; no one will refuse to obey them.'

'It still seems impossible. You speak of a Message; what is this message?'

'Come to the late prayers in two hours, held in front of Allah's Kitchen, as our Mosque is a pile of rubble. You will see the wonderful source of our food, and I shall introduce you to the Imam. He'll repeat the message at the prayers, as God requires.'

The three walked around the town, amazed at the activity and noting all the new walls identifiable by fresh cement. They found Allah's Kitchen, where the three cauldrons filled with food still bubbled slowly, and the baskets filled with bread and fruit, attended by two women who were not wearing a headscarf or an *abaya.*

Akeem noted the water pool and the pipes used to fill the containers, and asked his two colleagues to investigate what had happened to the water disappearing into the ground. Then, he went to find the water source. The well behind the mosque's ruins had a crude manual pump with a long handle; as a man leant on it, a gush of water came from a spout into the basin, with an outlet pipe to the pool. There were two men taking turns to pump. Akeem spoke to the one resting in the shade of the block. Learning the unlikely story of the well's opening took several minutes, but Akeem didn't say anything; he tried to look impressed.

'This must be arduous work. Have you no other pump?'

'It is demanding work, but it is work ordered by the chosen of Allah; we do it willingly. She says she'll find a pump.'

'You have no motor pump? Or is it no fuel?'

'We have no fuel, but she'll not use fuel as it is against God's wish; she seeks another way.'

'How deep is the well?'

'To the bottom, I do not know, but when we installed this pump, the water was nine times the height of a man below ground level.'

Akeem estimated about fifteen metres. He thanked the man and returned to the cauldrons of food, where he met the café owner standing with the much older Imam. The café owner introduced him.

'Lord, this is our Imam; I've told him about you and your colleagues.'

Akeem was extremely polite, not because, since childhood, being courteous to Imams was a habit, but also because the Imam impressed him. The greetings over, he said, 'We travel to our homes after selling camels in Palmyra. We would not have called here, but as we saw no sign of terrorists, we came to see why. We are amazed.'

The Imam replied, 'It is the will of Allah; we follow his instructions. The prayers will start. I shall repeat God's message, told to us by his Storyteller, and you'll understand.'

The Imam left him to take his place in front of the gathering crowd as Akeem's colleagues arrived to tell him of the work done to carry the water to the four corners of the town, saying, though unfinished, it was progressing well.

The Imam started the prayers. As a follower of Islam, Akeem enjoyed the prayer routine; it took his mind off the extraordinary situation for a while, although the presence of women without a head covering mixed in with the men was disconcerting until he remembered his pilgrimage to Mecca, where he had experienced a comparable feeling.

Akeem had a tiny pocket recorder and switched it on; it was the latest spy technology, capable of picking up a voice at over fifty metres. He recorded the story.

Then the Imam began to speak. He reminded everyone of the coming of the Storyteller and how he had driven out the terrorists by stripping them naked. He then reminded them of Allah's gift, supplied so the town could recover, and finally, he repeated the Message.

After prayers, the crowd drifted away, and the Imam approached them with an attractive young woman he introduced as Fatima. She blushed as Akeem studied her face; raised in America, he did so without feelings of transgression and didn't look away.

He bowed and addressed her politely, 'Your Imam has told me you have a heavy responsibility placed on you by God. I've seen what is happening in the town, and I congratulate you. There is much to do, but I see little with which to do it.'

The reply, delivered with a smile and sparkling eyes, was simple: 'What you say is correct; we need a solar well pump, and our children need a school, not just religious teaching, but all the knowledge the world can learn. We need high-speed internet to achieve this. I am confident the Lord will provide.'

Her smile, which showed strength and confidence, captured him as he replied, 'Do you have anyone in the town who knows about such things?'

'We have a young man who kept our mobile phone mast working before the Jihadis destroyed it; he studied in Damascus and has told me what we need. I must discover where and how to obtain it.'

Akeem used a typical reply, *'Bukra inshallah.'* Tomorrow, if God wills it.

He bowed to Fatima and said he must go; he and his colleagues had many kilometres to travel. Minutes later, they were riding the camels out of the town.

11

In Town Two, for two days, the Imam didn't notice the young man with the exercise book and a pencil; he saw him when Jamal sharpened a pencil during his repetition of God's message. Jamal had several pencil stubs in his pocket but had run out of sharpened ones and had to improvise. After prayers, the Imam called him over to reprimand him, but first asked what Jamal was doing. Jamal explained he was writing in the book everything he knew about the Storyteller and what he had said and done.

Jamal told the Imam he had heard stories from the other town. The Imam decided he could not reprimand the writing of holy words, but he did say no photograph or drawing should appear in the book. Jamal replied, 'Of course not, but it would seem impossible, for although many have seen him, and many have cell phones, no one has a picture of him.'

'That confirms what I've said; a picture is against the wish of Allah.'

Jamal added a section titled '*Rima the Blessed's Decree against Violence.*'

Akeem had left a low-powered beacon at their previous night's camp. They had enough time to pick up the signal before dark as they retraced their incoming tracks. They hadn't travelled more than six kilometres before dark overtook them; they followed the signal for the last two kilometres to the campsite used the night before between two dunes where they had buried survival supplies under the sand.

While the others hobbled the camels and prepared food, Akeem removed some equipment from the packs and climbed the highest nearby dune because he had no idea where a satellite might pass. It was hard going, for the sand, heated by the sun during the day, was loose, and for two steps up, his feet slipped back one step. By morning, the sand would have packed hard as the air between the grains contracted. Once on top, he set his communications equipment on the dune. It could connect to a satellite and send a compact burst of encrypted data in seconds. He opened his small notepad, drafted a report, and then downloaded the Storyteller's recorded message from his recorder as an attachment. After encryption, he clicked connect. The prompt popped up on the screen. It read:

Satellite passes in 5 minutes 40 seconds.

He lay back on the sand and thought of the unusual findings of the day; the image of Fatima in his thoughts made him smile. Then, he reviewed his requests at the end of the encrypted message.

1. Request immediate airdrop of a solar-powered bore pump package with panels and wiring for support of the current movement, deemed necessary for the continued destabilisation of terrorist activity. The estimated depth is sixteen metres to the water level and a volume sufficient for the town's population.
2. A package to supply high-speed internet to the town, including mast, aerial, solar panels, and equipment, all desert-rated, with a connection to our Comsat.
3. Provide instructions for both in Arabic – no identifying marks. The above is a gift from God.
   I suggest a container made from artificial stone, with con-

> tents packed in rough cloth and natural fibres. No identifi-
> able markings, please.
> 4. Drop a2:nj:bg-b7:pw:ka.
> 5. Notify date and time.
> 6. Need one *Hajji* with a camel. The identical position on drop
> night. Can meet and support. Notify instructions. His task
> is to inform the town of the dropped gift.

The coordinates were double encrypted; locations could be dangerous.

There is no ping for covert activities; they are silent. Akeem saw the pop-up box change to *sent*.

Akeem's message arrived seconds after he sent it. First, a computer decrypted and then translated the story, which a language expert then checked. The story was added to the file within thirty minutes, as it was an active operation, and dispatched to the officer handling Akeem. After digesting the contents for thirty minutes, he requested an immediate meeting with key persons. While waiting, he wrote his recommendations. The meeting began two hours after Akeem pressed the connect button. Meghali was present.

It was a short meeting. The senior official summed up by saying.

'We have a better idea of what happened than the IMINT provided. We have no idea who the *Storyteller* is, nor any clue as to where he came from, but we have a detailed report of what the place is now like. The terrorists have left. Others who tried to invade from the next town are dead; those are the wrecked trucks on the road. The people there must have killed the remaining terrorists, as there are none visible in the second set of IMINT images, and there are new graves.

'Our asset on the ground will try to clarify the situation. However, we have a request to support the movement that Akeem believes God's message has motivated. We agree that it needs analysis and evaluation; however, it is in our interest to help counter the Jihadists.

'Can we find a man on a camel with a drop beacon to meet our asset and ride to the drop zone? Then can we organise the equipment drop off quickly?'

The operations specialist took the lead. 'The first is not a problem. We drop the beacon from a supply truck at the nearest base, and one of our covert operatives will pick it up and meet our asset. Akeem's request includes a battery-powered blower; I assume we must purchase one and test it to ensure it works for covering tracks. I estimate we can organise a drop in four days; a C130 can do it as part of a routine supply mission to one of our bases. The transponder signal at maximum power will blanket radar reflection from the dropped equipment. We can route it from Diego or Akrotiri. It will be a night drop. Now, where do we buy the equipment? The pump and panels should be no problem. Buy them in Europe and fly them to Diego or Akrotiri by jet. Internet equipment might be more difficult. We must ask the communications experts.'

'Okay. Ms Azzaro, do you agree?'

'I do.'

'Okay, guys, please do this; next meeting in twenty-four hours.'

Patrick read Akeem's report; his reaction differed.

He immediately labelled the editor as friendly and classified the story as the message the film would convey. He expected the editor to add a scene to reinforce the first two. The introduction was incomplete.

Meghali was, however, bewildered; she thought of organisations; power was proportional to an organisation's size, so this one must be huge, and yet they had no clue. She decided to review her data banks for anything unusual until further information arrived. Starting with anything Patrick could tell her.

'Patrick, what do you think?'

'The introduction isn't over, Meg. There's more to come. The editor is an expert, and he chose the perfect place for the first scene.'

'Then tell me why the Storyteller spoke his message to a small group of people in a desert town instead of Times Square, New York.'

'Meg, if he had done so in London, on Hyde Park Corner, the English might have listened and then walked away shaking their heads at the thought of another nut case on the loose. In New York, someone would have at least tried to steal his staff, and as no one is aware of the person next to them, he could have stripped people naked, and the sole reaction would be from a stranger to New York who might ask why the guy had undressed. New Yorkers and all big city dwellers must focus on distant objects to avoid claustrophobia; they don't *see* people nearby.'

'But why does he have a young girl with him?'

'Meg, would you be more wary of a man alone or one with a young daughter?'

'The man alone, but Akeem doesn't say she's his daughter.'

'That's immaterial. Female and about ten to eleven years old, makes him appear harmless.'

'So did she come with him?'

'We don't know, but she left with him. Ask Akeem if she is a child from that town.'

'Is she harmless?'

'Yes. Consider three scenarios. In one, the storyteller strips the Jihadi. In the second, the young girl does. And in a third, a dog savages the Jihadi. How would someone react in each case?'

Meghali tried to imagine the scenes. 'If he did it, people would be afraid of him. If she did it, they would believe it was an act of God, as adults wouldn't be afraid of a young girl. If the dog attacked, they would want to kill the dog.'

'Exactly. The girl is a harmless prop and may reappear in future scenes. That was an introductory scene – be patient. Building followers is relatively easy once a few people believe something. People have a herd instinct. He's gathered a few devout believers. Now he will grow the numbers.' *I'll bet the editor's expecting us to help.* 'We will assist.'

The next night, having moved thirty kilometres, Akeem received a reply. It was short. It gave coordinates, a date, and a time. He and his companions arrived with twelve hours to spare and set up camp. Twelve hours later, two camels, one carrying packs and the other a *Hajji* joined them. The four mounted and left for the coordinates Akeem had put in the first message.

Four days later, after the moon set, Akeem set the beacon in the sand on a dune and activated it at the designated time. It transmitted a UHF signal in a narrow vertical cone that the aeroplane registered three minutes before drop time, enough for the last course correction. Akeem left the dune as he didn't want a container to land on his head. He rode away and stopped a kilometre away, where the others waited.

They could hear the faint whistle of the turbines. It died for half a minute, then rose again. Akeem identified a signal six minutes later when the package touched down and switched on its low-powered beacon. He and the others rode to the dropped container, deflated the black landing cushions, and detached them from the black-painted box to load onto their camels. They rolled up and loaded the matt black parachutes, leaving a sizeable, dull, black artificial stone box on the sand.

No one had thought black would have any significance.

As the sun rose, Akeem used the battery-powered blower to blow the loose sand to hide their footprints and all but one row of camel tracks in and out.

The box sat on a pristine desert with a camel's tracks to and from it. They packed their camp, and three of them left, agreeing on a meeting point with the *Hajji*, who mounted his camel, led another, and rode into the town, asking for the Imam. When he found him, he said, 'I've come from the desert to the south. I saw a large black box in the desert this morning, *alhamdulillah*, so I came to tell you.'

The Imam decided to go with the *Hajji* to see it. The *Hajji* gave him the camel with the saddle.

When he saw it, he looked for tracks to reveal how it had arrived and saw nothing except the camel tracks that the Hajji said were his camel's. So much had happened since the Storyteller had come; he could believe it came from God, especially when he thought it resembled a smaller version of the *Kaaba* in Mecca.

The *Hajji* went back with him to the town, then, leading his second camel, said, 'Allah *ma'ak*,' 'God be with you,' and rode back into the desert.

The Imam recruited a crew of men and some tools to open the box.

Over the next few days, the men installed the solar pump, and the young man who looked after the mobile phone mast erected the Wi-Fi mast with the help of many others. A week later, the town had high-speed internet via a satellite link. The young man had followed instructions. He didn't need to know who owned the satellite. Or that a copy of every message went to a CIA computer.

The image of Akeem's face kept intruding into Fatima's thoughts each time she saw the pump and the internet mast. She remembered the Storyteller vividly; he had brought about the change, and she couldn't help but believe that Allah had sent Akeem. She recalled telling him she wanted a school to educate children correctly. She now had internet; she would do her part.

12

The sole survivor from the Storyteller's second visit fled in the jeep to a third town about forty kilometres away. A stranger could easily mistake one village for another; the ruined buildings and rubble piles made them appear identical. The Jihadi garrison was small, thirty-five men, with a captain who managed to terrorise both his soldiers and the townsfolk.

The jeep had rocketed into the town, where the soldier reported the events in the village he had left.

With closely spaced small eyes and a round face, the captain had grown fat from a lack of exercise. He rarely left his desk unless it was to terrorise someone dragged into his office. The soldier's story generated fear and rage; his immediate worry was whether people in the town had heard something similar. He called for two of his soldiers and instructed them to patrol the streets and report back; he wanted to know if the people were behaving differently from the previous day. They returned to say there was nothing new. The entire garrison, except four guards on duty at the town's extremities, had heard the story by then. The captain called them together and said they would not mention it to anyone. He would personally execute anyone who did. They knew he meant it.

When nothing happened for several days, the captain relaxed. The people knew that something had changed due to the daily patrols, so they continued as usual, taking extra care.

Then something changed; the patrol returned and reported that the town was exceptionally silent; it seemed all the citizens were hiding. The captain had ordered cellphone confiscation when he took over, but for some time, he suspected a hidden satellite phone existed. He ordered two men to fetch the hag he knew couldn't resist passing on shocking news; it was all she had to draw attention to herself.

When she came into his office, dragged between two soldiers, he could sense her fear; it gave him a feeling of pleasure. The soldiers also had a small boy with them.

'Why is he here?' he snapped.

'He was with the hag; we thought it best to bring him; else he would tell others.'

'Good,' the logic satisfied him, so he looked at the hag in silence for a minute, noting she trembled, then smiled a thin, satisfied smile. In a menacing tone, he growled, 'You will tell me who has a hidden phone.'

As he expected, she claimed she didn't know, as no one told her anything. The captain levered himself from his chair and rounded the desk to confront her; her increased terror was a ball of pleasure in his gut. When she wailed, 'I don't know,' his open palm struck her hard enough on the side of her face to throw her against the nearby wall, where she collapsed on the floor. Cringing under his gaze, she could see his boots.

She expected a kick in the face when suddenly he barked, 'Bring the boy here.'

He grabbed the boy's arm, oblivious to his crying, and twisted the arm behind his back. 'Listen, you old hag, either tell me who has a phone or who provided the latest news you heard. Otherwise, I shall break every bone in this child's body and dislocate his joints while you listen to his screams.' He twisted the boy's arm until he screamed.

She could sense his pleasure in the idea; she knew he would do it, so she surrendered.

'Muhammar.'

'You will take me to him.' Turning to a soldier, he ordered, 'Fetch six men, then hold this woman and the boy; we will go to find this Muhammar.' A vicious smile played on his face momentarily as he said, 'Put a rope around her neck, lead her like a dog.'

The captain with a holstered pistol and the eight soldiers carrying AKs, one dragging the woman by a rope and the other marching the sobbing boy in front of him, walked down the road, past the Mosque, to a jumble of rubble-strewn buildings on the far side. The hag gestured to a path between fallen blocks and said, 'He lives there.'

'You three, fetch him,' ordered the captain.

They heard sounds of shouts and violence; then, the three men came out, dragging a man in his late twenties, whom they threw on the ground at his feet.

'Ah, Muhammar, I believe you can assist me,' said the captain, in a tone everyone understood as threatening. Muhammar shook his head, but before he could answer, the captain continued, 'I shall not waste my time beating you. Until you tell me where you hide your phone, I shall proceed to break every bone in this boy's body.' He grabbed the boy and twisted his arm behind his back again. He stopped when the child screamed and waited for Muhammar's reaction.

No one had noticed a young woman without an *abaya*: Khadija, Muhammar's sister, who had followed the soldiers dragging Muhammar. All were staring at the captain and his victims, so Khadija moved slowly to avoid anyone seeing her, but had a full view when the boy screamed. After months of living under a regime where the least resistance brought a beating or death, her reaction was completely irrational; something snapped. She ran forward until she had a clear view of the captain, stopped, flung her arm forward, pointed at him, and yelled, *'PIG!'*

The captain's first reaction was a delighted smile, replaced at once by puzzlement as he saw his hand holding the boy's arm had turned into a cloven hoof. Then he screamed. The soldiers, who had turned to see a furious Khadija with an extended arm, had heard such a scream many times when the captain had tortured a captive. They whirled around to see an enormous boar standing on its rear feet. A cartoonist could not have drawn an astonished expression on a pig's face any better. The soldiers instantly understood its origin as it wore a captain's uniform split open at its seams, with the captain's hat on its head and a pistol in a holster slung around its neck. The pig, clearly confused, fell onto all four feet and then accelerated down the road towards the headquarters in a mad charge. It was too much for the eight soldiers; perhaps it was an instinct to follow the captain, more likely driven by the terrifying thought of becoming a pig. First one, then the others broke and ran in an extended line.

The townsfolk, hidden and alert, took a few seconds to react; the first brick stunned the last of the eight, and then many more knocked the others down like pins in a bowling alley. Still following the pig, the leading soldier was the last to fall, hit by a brick fifty metres before the headquarters entrance. The guard saw the pig hurtle by and recognised the captain's epaulettes on the pig's tattered and torn jacket still around its chest; then, he saw the last soldier fall. He ran back into the headquarters yard, shouting, *'Evacuate! Escape!'* Then, he headed straight for a truck and climbed into the cab to start the engine. The other soldiers threw themselves into the lorry through the open back without a second thought.

The man who had stunned the last soldier with the brick he threw had served in the military when young; he ran to the downed soldier, picked up his fallen AK, clicked off the safety, and shot him in the head. They had raped and then killed his wife months earlier. Engine roaring, the truck swung out of the headquarters gateway, swerving dangerously to point out of town. The man switched the AK to automatic and, keeping the aim low as his training sergeant insisted, fired a long burst at the truck. Before the barrel had risen far enough to wound or kill the soldiers in the back, it blew out all the tyres except one. The last bullet in the magazine killed the driver. The hurtling vehicle didn't complete the turn but ran into the building opposite. The soldiers didn't escape. Within two minutes, the truck's rear was a lorry load of broken stone and concrete.

The victorious men returned to learn how it had started. They found the Imam, Muhammar, his sister, the boy and the crone. The Imam had just arrived and asked, 'Muhammar, what happened?'

'I don't know; I was on the ground; I could see the captain's legs, then the boy screamed, and a woman's voice yelled *"Pig!"* Then the captain turned into a pig.'

The crone told how Khadija had pointed and said, *'Pig!'* She had not had time to add the embellishments she usually did, but Khadija gained an aura or a halo when she told it the next time. By the fourth telling, lightning had sparked from Khadija's eyes.

Khadija had checked out the boy's arm; he had one nasty bruise. After she comforted him, he stopped crying. Muhammar was unhurt, although he had a bruise and scraped knee. Khadija listened to what the men told the Imam about what had followed.

'Khadija,' the Imam asked, 'did you point at the captain and say "Pig"?'

'Yes, he was hurting this child.'

'Well, it was a brave thing to do, but what do we do next?'

He was surprised when she said, 'Bury all the dead in graves outside the town before disease brings further misery to us.'

They did what she said, and later, when the Imam came back, he noticed she was still not wearing an *abaya* and asked, 'Khadija, why do you have no covering?'

'I don't know; I just feel it is wrong to put it on.'

'Did you know what you were doing when you pointed and said "Pig"?'

'No, I didn't do it myself; an Angel, a young girl in a shining white dress, with blonde hair down to her shoulders, came with a message from Allah's Storyteller. She told me to point and say 'pig' if I felt it necessary.'

At the evening prayers, the Imam spoke, 'We are free from the clutches of Satan; our freedom is the gift of God. We shall pray.'

At the end of prayers, he said, 'You have all heard that Khadija pointed at the captain and turned him into a pig; many of you saw the pig, but few of you saw it happen. You may believe it impossible for a young woman to do such a thing, and you would be right if it were an ordinary woman. But Allah sent a messenger to Khadija, a young girl with long blonde hair wearing a shining white dress, an Angel who told Khadija to do it. I've heard of the Angel; she travels with the Storyteller who recounts the Lord's message, and he says all women must uncover their faces, as required during *Hajj*, not so men can look upon them, but for Allah to see their faces. According to His message, I shall work with Khadija to improve the future of this town. If I can learn the right words, I shall recount the Lord's message tomorrow.'

When the news spread, the terrorist movement found its soldiers vanishing. It was one thing to die gloriously in a battle for God. But not if God turned you into a pig.

Jamal's exercise book has a chapter titled *'Khadija the Blessed's Curse of the Pig.'*

13

In Fort Belvoir, days after he had compiled report /2, the specialist scrutinised the photos from the last satellite pass. When his computer highlighted a change outside a town west of the second report, he zoomed in to look and counted thirty-six graves. His search of the village brought a now-familiar conclusion. There were no armed soldiers, and the women were without scarves or *abayas*. A check of the known list of Jihadis showed an extra grave. When he saw an additional jeep, he thought he had the explanation; it was the jeep from the second town, and its driver would account for an added grave.

The operations meeting didn't take long, summarised by its chair, who said, 'This whole thing is nuts. We had three small towns controlled by the terrorists. The towns suddenly manage to kill the entire Jihadi force without any help from outside, and now behave as if they are safe from further Jihadi invasion. Furthermore, the women have thrown off their *abayas* and are walking around as if they were in Washington, DC.

'Tell the CIA we need more HUMINT, and let's push this up to the Joint Chiefs, with a suggestion we should prepare to protect these towns and others close by if we learn of Jihadi threats. They are doing a much better job of eliminating the terrorists than anyone has achieved to date.'

Meghali received the meeting report, forwarded it to Patrick, authorised the HUMINT expenditure request, and then went to find Patrick; he was in his cubicle, lying horizontally on his back, earphones on his ears, looking at the ceiling. The computer screen scrolled through a list of movie titles, each annotated with a row of numbers.

'Sorry to disturb your nap, Patrick, but we must work.'

'Oh, I'm not sleeping, Meghali; I can imagine pictures and scenes on the ceiling much easier than with my eyes shut.'

He levered his chair into a sitting position as she sat in the spare chair in the cubicle. 'What's up?'

'What's scrolling on the screen?'

'Movie titles and correlation coefficients to four factors. I want to see if one has high correlations.'

'Okay, have you read the last report? And I want to know what you think of the Middle East events.'

'Something is screwing up a small piece of the world, but it's not a danger; it likes women and hates psychopaths.'

'Why do you say something?'

'Because I can't define what it is, although it's behaving like an editor.'

'Why then do you say it's not dangerous? That it likes women and hates psychopaths.'

'The reported *story* proves it likes women, and I'm sure the Jihadi who disappeared was a psycho; that would fit into the screenplay.

'I believe it's trying to persuade people to watch a movie and is succeeding. And so far, it has done as little as possible in the cutting room of our film *Civilisation*. It likes women because it frees women from their *abayas*. Also, the Storyteller recommends promoting women to positions of responsibility in the story.

'It's not dangerous because, if you haven't already concluded, it's the most skilful attack on human interpretation of religious writings I could have dreamed up.'

'I did notice the story mentions *Hajj*. Why do you say skilful?'

'There is no attack against Islam; the Storyteller essentially said women should behave as they must during *Hajj*, which is a sacred state. No religious argument is possible, but it will undoubtedly draw considerable attention and spark heated debates between the Imams and lay leaders. I checked on the rule, Meg. Guess who was the first to announce it?'

'If it wasn't Muhammad, I don't know.'

'Saint Paul, in AD 54. – The Bible: 1 Corinthians 11:4-16. Five hundred and sixty-eight years before Islam. But only for women praying in church and for their hair. He never said it was a message from God, and men have extended that rule to suit themselves. The Quran verses, Surah An-Nur (24:31) and Surah Al-Ahzab (33:59), require women to dress modestly. Islam, not Muhammad, used St Paul's rule and distorted it.'

'Why did St Paul make the rule?'

'Meg, I wasn't around then; I can guess if you wish, but assume it's a low probability.'

'Please do.'

'Long hair has always been a genetic indicator of femininity. In a primitive society, the so-called weaker sex needed to broadcast the need for physical protection from wild animals. Covering hair would hide the sign and make both sexes equal before God.

'The other reason may be as simple as lice; they spread easily between people when packed together in prayer. Lice have been a problem for centuries; that's why mothers told their daughters to brush their hair a hundred times daily, and bald heads and wigs became popular among both sexes. We know some of the Ancient Egyptians shaved their heads.'

'Okay, that's as good a guess as any. But what future do you predict?'

'I can't. I need another scene or two. The scenes will play because the editor must build up to a big scene. If it were like an early cowboy film, the Indians still wonder what's happening and whether they should attack. They will lose fighters, and desertions rise when an army loses, but they need provocation. It will be something that increases desertions by the rank and file.'

'Patrick, you sound as if you want it to happen.'

'Meg, think of it as a movie you watch; what do you want to happen next? The editor will give it to you because that will please the audience.'

'My god, you have a weird mind.'

'Unusual, but no weirder than yours. Join me for dinner tonight, and I'll tell you why.'

Patrick's dinner with Meghali was at an Irish restaurant. 'Meg, I found this restaurant two days ago. The Irish stew is great, and they make real soda bread. It stimulates memories of my childhood and a trip I made to Ireland. Have you tasted Guinness? I have a glass with my stew.'

'So will I, Patrick; do you have relatives in Ireland?'

'I must have. There are hundreds of O'Connors, so I immediately felt at home, but they are all distant cousins. I'm a sixth-generation American.'

'Me too, although my cousins are from northern Italy. Now, explain why you think my mind is weird.'

'Not weird, Meg, I said unusual. I shall provide you with a few facts; then, you must ask me for more data to fill in what you think is missing.

'One: Various governments and the WWF report human deaths in game parks. After making corrections for the number of staff working in the game parks, excluding tourists, the number has remained constant within statistical deviations over the last twenty years. The number of human deaths this year is above the average but within limits for a typical year.

'Two: CITES, which controls the sale of endangered species, reports rhino horn sales have dipped in China, and the price of rhino horn is peaking. The change is within historical variance.

'Three: The WWF has removed poisonous snakes from the endangered species list.

'Four: CITES reports elephant ivory sales have dipped like rhino horn.

'Now ask.'

'Question: Historically, do ivory and rhino horn sales correlate?'

'Answer: Not at all.'

'Question: Is there a change in the deaths by snakebite?'

'Answer: Yes, they have more than doubled and are increasing faster than the snakes. Now give me your analysis.'

Meghali replied, 'I don't know why the number of snakes is increasing, but logically, the number of poachers shot and killed by game guards has dropped. Instead, the snakes are killing them, probably more than were caught last year, but *before* they can do any poaching, which has affected the trade in both rhino horn and elephant ivory.'

'And you're the second person to conclude that. Although hundreds have the facts available, you asked but two questions.'

'Who's the first person?'

'Me, but my computer gave me facts that could link. The AI asked the questions.'

'So, I have an unusual brain?'

'One that accepts relationships a normal brain rejects as impossible.'

'Do you know why the snakes have multiplied?'

'No, but movies can portray fantasy; I think the editor likes elephants and rhinos, so hates poachers.'

'Why?'

'Because it does. Our world will not allow the shooting of poachers unless they are caught with a kill and resist arrest; they are humans, while rhinos are animals. We don't judge the value of a living creature using adjectives like bad man and good rhino. If the Editor killed poachers, we would be angry, but we're quite happy when snakes kill them. Ask any scriptwriter; he'll tell you that. Shall I describe a typical scene?'

'Please.'

'The elephant peacefully pulls branches from a tree and stuffs them into its mouth, preferably showing pleasure.'

'How can a movie display that?'

'The branch has fruit, and the elephant carefully picks it from the branch it pulled down and puts it gently into its mouth. Although an elephant, it's a frequent movie scene in which a sexy man eats something juicy, lasciviously, with a dribble of juice down to his chin. One of the best scenes was in a 1963 film titled *Tom Jones*.'

'Okay.'

'A baby elephant eating the fruit slobbers even more. The audience thinks it's lovely.'

'They would.'

'There's a hunter with a rifle creeping through the bush; he's unshaven and dirty, possibly with a bald head.'

'Why?'

'There are fewer bald men, so there's less likelihood an audience member will identify with him.'

'So, then a snake bites him?'

'Not so fast, Meg; you must see the snake; it's probably shiny black or has vivid markings, with evil glistening orange eyes. They appear evil because the pupils are vertical, shiny black slits devoid of expression. The Gaboon Viper is an obvious candidate, and it's lying in wait, its forked tongue flicking in and out as the hunter creeps forward, his attention fixed on the elephant. Then comes the flash routine. The editor builds the audience's anticipation by switching views with steadily increasing rapidity from snake to man to unsuspecting elephant. You *want* the snake to bite him, but you don't know if it will do so in time before he fires. A good editor includes a one or two-second close-up of a finger tightening on the trigger before the snake bites.

'The audience will say he deserved it, and it was a great film.'

'Patrick, I think it's you who has a weird mind. It will take time to learn how your mind works.'

The two exceptional minds thought this was an excellent time to prolong the contact. They tickled more hormones, and Meghali said, 'Come to my place for a nightcap. I want to learn more.'

'Meg, you once asked why ads differed by country.'

'I didn't, you said it.'

'Well, I said you must come to my apartment so I can show you why. If you want to learn more, come to mine.'

She did.

'This is luxury, Patrick. The view is fantastic, but you need more decorations and furniture, not a ceiling mirror.'

'I'm still trying to decide the mood I want to generate, and I don't often have friends over; you're the first.

'I'll start a video of an ad on the wall screen. Say if you've seen it before, and I'll stop it.'

...

'I recognise it.'

Patrick stopped the video.

Meghali remarked, 'That's a Viagra advert. When the grandma walks to the bed in a nightie, the grandpa goes to the bathroom and takes the last Viagra pill from a box, and then loses it on the way to bed.'

'Then what happened?'

'Oh, the pill flew out of his hand when he tripped on the carpet, out the window and into the open fuel filler of a parked car, and then he ran downstairs to find the pill. I thought it was a stupid ad, especially when the car grew into a monster. It didn't relate to Viagra; cars don't have erections, so I stopped watching.'

'You've proved my point, Meg. That wasn't an ad for Viagra.'

Meghali played back her memory. 'Was it for the car?'

'Yes, the message was, "We've pumped up our new model as Viagra pumps you up." It tanked in the US, first because the message is to men and second because it started with a Viagra tablet; it confused you. In another country, a vitamin pill worked. That proves the viewer's culture has an enormous influence. Now, I'll admit to something.

'When you employed me, did you check who I worked for?'

'Yes, a conglomerate with thirty or so subsidiaries.'

'Did you notice one manufacturer makes and markets an intimate gel?'

'I did. A well-known brand. Did you do an advert for them?'

'No, but I did suggest when they presented a new ad to me and asked if it would work. I said no and told them to change it. Let me play the version that went live.'

– Patrick paused the playback.

'Why did you stop it?'

'Because I want your reaction up to this point.'

'Although the grandpa looks different, the bathroom is different, and the grandma has a frilly nightie and looks like she's full of fun, it's like the first ad up to where he's about to trip on the carpet.'

'What's different?'

'The grandpa took a pill and found a gel tube in the cupboard. The way he held it made the logo unmistakable. He's carrying it with him to the bed.'

Patrick ran the remaining seconds of the video.

'*Oh wow!* What a marvellous ending; when the grandpa showed the grandma his tube, and she produced one with a huge grin, I knew it was a superb product. Did that work in other countries?'

'I'll show you the Brazilian highway billboard.' Ten seconds later, the picture filled the screen.

...

'I don't understand it, Patrick. I can see the product name at the bottom right; it appears to be too small. The photo is beautiful, with the sunset over the bay and the mountains on either side. Is the quayside with the four mooring bollards supposed to be phallic? They aren't tall enough for that, and the woman sitting on the quay edge with her back to the camera is just a black shape. But what's the message?'

'Use your mind, Meg, look at the facts and conclude.'

'– Patrick, it's suggestive, rude, and impossible. The woman is sitting where a fifth bollard should be.'

'Suggestive, yes, ads are suggestive. It's possible, Meg; she's sitting with the bollard in front of her. You made the rude assumption. I had nothing to do with the ad, but the Brazilians loved it, and sales soared. It's a case where cultures differ. You make a good guinea pig.'

'Although that's not a flattering term, do you have more?'

'A different reaction, two ads for competing products that

could work in one country, and only for a short time.'

'Okay, what are they?'

'A drunk driver on a winding road by the sea drove his luxury saloon off the road and a hundred metres down the cliff to the rocks. When the rescue team came, they found him uninjured. Newspapers had photos of the road, cliff and car.

'The motor company made an ad two days later by pushing a new car off the edge where the first one left the road, and announcing they made the safest car in the world!'

'That's a *safe* assumption.'

'The competitor made an ad three days later; their car screeched around every corner on the road, and the ad announced, "*The car that stays on the road!*"'

Meghali laughed. 'Two opposing views for two market segments?'

'No, Meg. The first company pulled its ad a day later, as the perception shifted from being safe to safe when you crash. The second one pulled their ad because the consequences of a future crash would make the ad appear false.

'In every ad I've shown you, it's human perceptions that bring a reaction, which is why I say movies, which must satisfy those perceptions without trying to change them, are the best indicator we have to forecast the future.'

'Patrick, I've learnt enough; my hormones are bubbling; drive me off the cliff.'

Their hormone levels went sky-high....

Then, two minds decided not to miss an opportunity and found deeply buried memories.

'Meg, why are you feeling my bum?'

'I'm trying to find your scar.'

'Who told you about it?'

'The FBI report included your medical history.'

'It's faded away, Meg. A girl bit me.'

Meghali grinned. 'She didn't, Patrick; the report says you fell backwards onto some rocks, and the gash needed stitches. As you had no pants, she might have pushed you.'

'We were both seventeen and helpers at a kids' summer camp, and when I returned from the hospital two days later, she had gone, so I never learnt if she pushed me on purpose, but why can't I find your tattoo?'

Surprised, Meghali asked, 'How do you know about it?'

'My AI looked up your past and found you paid a tattoo artist, but where is it now?'

'I was also seventeen, a virgin with a crush on an older boy. When I decided he was the one I wanted, I visited the tattoo parlour and had *Charlie come here* tattooed on my pubis below my bikini. Then I flashed him by pushing down my shorts.'

'Did he come?'

'Yes, once, then I decided he was a dead loss, so I had it removed. It's the kind of thing young girls do. But if you look closely, you'll see the scar.'

'Then I shall.'

...

14

Akeem received new orders. He had at least two more towns to report on, so he rode away to the second town with his two colleagues. Before arriving, he received a further instruction. It read:

Internet aerial in operation. Classified major asset.
Establish a possible method for identical installation
on other sites.

At least, he thought, he would have no trouble obtaining two more.

Like Fatima in the neighbouring town, Khadija sat in her small office, a cleaned-up space that had once been a shop. There was no door. Where the roller shutter had been, a makeshift wall of scrap boxwood closed half of the opening, and a cloth curtain sewn from several sacks hung over the other half. There was no window, but it didn't matter, for a hole in the roof in one corner, the result of a mortar bomb, allowed light to enter.

She studied a list of items needing repair in the town and a list of all the solar panels that they had found to be working. The young electrical repairer, who, like many others in the country, had never had formal training but had learnt through years of an informal apprenticeship in an electrical repair workshop, had done some calculations. If she understood correctly, they showed the number of solar panels the town needed to give everyone a small amount of light every night and charge phones and computers. It was the last item, the calculation of storage batteries; she understood the least.

Suddenly, she felt that someone was present, a sensation that everyone experiences at times. She looked up to see who. Soraya stood in one corner of the room.

Shocked initially, it took a moment for her to say, 'I didn't hear you come.'

Soraya spoke, 'Hello, Khadija. I have a message from the Storyteller. He says I must tell you how to call for Allah's help if you need to punish a man for a specific crime.'

'Please explain.'

When Soraya told her, Khadija realised why she had not heard Soraya come, for she faded and vanished.

Late in the afternoon, the Imam came to see her; his distress was visible as he told her.

'A man has raped a young virgin. Her parents caught him as he left her room, for they heard her moaning. He tried to escape, but her father shouted, and two men outside their house grabbed him and then called me. A crowd was collecting, and I could see the anger. To stop them from beating him to death, I told them you would give the judgment of Allah.'

Khadija knew from Soraya's visit what to do. 'Take him to the plaza in front of the Mosque, tie him to a pole, with his back to it, facing the crowd, and tell everyone, especially the men, to attend. It would be better for children if they did not attend; send them elsewhere.'

An hour later, the Imam returned. 'All is ready.'

Followed by the Imam, she crossed the plaza to the Mosque

steps; on the upper step, Khadija stood with her eyes closed, looking skyward. The crowd fell silent as they saw her praying.

She lowered her gaze to the crowd, descended to the plaza, and crossed to stand before the man bound to the pole. She said nothing, but he looked at her and screamed, 'It was not me; I would never do such a thing.'

She replied, raising her voice, 'You deny the crime; everyone here must know the lie.' With a straight arm and a pointing finger, she cried, *'No Clothes!'*

Instantly, he was naked. One or two may have turned away, but when an elderly woman at the front shrieked, 'I see it, I see blood on his penis.' Everyone turned to look. Then a man condemned him, 'He lies; he has a virgin's blood on his thigh.'

A rumble of anger flooded the crowd; Khadija raised her arm and pointed again. She paused while silence returned; not even the rustle of feet disturbed the silence as they waited for the Lord's judgment.

'Sometimes, a woman falsely accuses a man of rape; if this happens, the man carries no blame, and punishment of the woman must follow. But today, the proof is clear: this man is guilty. Not even the lowest animals in this world rape young females; this is not a crime committed by a man or beast but by a demon equipped with the genitals of a man. Allah decrees that all convicted rapists shall cease to be capable of such a crime from this day forward. *Eunuch!'*

The crowd saw it happen; the man's genitals, penis, and testicles shrank, then disappeared, leaving a tiny hole to urinate. The silence continued as they absorbed what had happened. Khadija turned to the Imam, 'Cut him down and let him go; the Lord has punished him; it is not for others to judge further.'

She returned to her office with the Imam, while the crowd dispersed silently, and they discussed the punishment. None of them disagreed.

Khadija told the Imam in her office, 'It is hard to do the work God requires.'

'It is hard for all, but few have the courage and the load you carry. You can count on the town's support, especially from all women. My Lady, today's actions will have consequences; I foresee all women worldwide will hear and obey the Storyteller's words. The men, I do not know.'

The story reached the scribe. The scribe added it to the exercise book with the heading. *'The Judgement of Khadija the Blessed.'*

With *'Rima the Blessed's decree against violence.' 'The Instruction of Fatima the Blessed.'* and *'Khadija the Blessed's Curse of the Pig.'* The book was the key to a future revolution in the Catholic Church and all other religions.

Akeem and his colleagues set up camp within view of the second town, fixing their camel hair tent to the poles their camels carried. Akeem and the others walked the short distance into the town once the camels were hobbled and allowed to browse.

Akeem noticed it was much bigger than Fatima's village, with more than one principal street. The second street, primarily lined with shops, was a hive of activity; two or three shops were already displaying their wares for sale. In others, they saw people cleaning them out, and the typical roller shutters were under repair in front of several. The noise of hammers was deafening. The townsfolk were all clearing rubble and sweeping sand and dust from houses in the rest of the town. Many of them had suffered minor damage, primarily explosive damage from bullets; it would be visible for years. They found a block of offices with workers removing a Jihadi sign, passed in front of the mosque, and finally found a café in a side alley. There were no customers, so they chose a table; one leg didn't match the others, but it was steady. The three stools were also different, clearly a collection of what was left. The owner bustled over, and Akeem ordered coffee.

'*Thlath fanajin qahwatan min fadlik,* and bring one for yourself. Join us; we want to know about the town.'

They discussed what they had seen until the coffee and the owner came.

Akeem opened the conversation, 'We passed through the village to the east and met the Imam and Fatima. It is an impoverished town; the people have little, but they possess great courage. We are merchants; we trade camels.' Akeem grinned and added, 'It is easy to transport camels, but other goods can be more profitable, and carriage is free if we use the camels. Tell us about your town, what has happened here, and if there are things we could supply.'

The owner was eager and proud to tell how the town had freed itself. When he finished, Akeem asked, 'Are you not afraid the terrorists will return?'

'No, we know God protects us; we pray at the mosque for His guidance and protection. Our Imam recounts the story told by the Storyteller. My Lady Rima, who guides the town, will ask for Allah's help. You should visit the Imam to see if there are things you can supply for the town, but visit the shops on the street of the carpet sellers for other goods.'

After confirming that the street with all the shops was the carpet sellers' street, Akeem remarked, 'Many of those shops are still not ready; perhaps we shall stay for several days. We will pray at sunset and return tomorrow.'

They did. The following day, Akeem found the Imam in a freshly cleaned and whitewashed office in the building sporting a handwritten sign. *Albaladia.* He thought a municipality with two people was pretentious, but it showed pride and ambition. He asked to see the Imam, and a minute later, the guard ushered him into the office. The two men followed the usual greeting protocol. The Imam noted the Saudi accent of his visitor, then excused his inability to offer coffee as he had just moved into the office.

Akeem waved it away as unimportant. '*Numbritna*, I'm a merchant; I'm impressed by your town and the energy of the people here. I travel with my colleagues to trade camels, but the camels can carry goods, so we have a profitable business with free transport. We will visit the Street of the Carpet Sellers, but I came to ask if the town needs anything.'

The Imam replied, 'I shall take you to see My Lady, and we shall discuss it.'

They walked down a corridor to a similarly whitewashed office where Rima sat at a desk, puzzling over some written reports. Although a man was taking measurements, there was no door, so the Imam tapped on the wall. Rima looked up and smiled. Akeem fell in love.

There were no chairs, but on one side, there were two mattresses on the floor and some cushions. The Imam went to one and gestured to Akeem to join him, as Rima rose from her chair and sat on the other, facing her visitors. Akeem waited while the Imam explained why they had come to see her; he could see she had a good figure, a beautiful face, and eyes with depth and intelligence, but the air of quiet confidence, when faced by a stranger, captured him completely. When the Imam finished speaking, she answered the question Akeem had asked.

'We have driven off the terrorists, as have the two villages east and west of us. We must collaborate with them to ensure our future. We cannot do this well with our satellite phones. I do not understand why, but I've learnt that satellite connections limit us. Fatima says she has a new aerial, a gift from God. I can pray to Allah for similar help, but I would rather the town does it. Khadija, the guide in the village to the west of us, also needs something. If we are to coordinate our development and safety, it is imperative.'

Akeem asked, 'What happened in the town to the west?' The Imam told him about Khadija and the incident involving the pig.

Akeem had made notes and then asked, 'Is there nothing else you require?'

Her smile thrilled him as she replied, 'The list is too long to worry over. I must think of priorities. I've discussed them with Fatima and Khadija, and we've agreed that communication is the most important item. We have water from three wells. We must clean a fourth outside the town, but it is not essential. I'll check with Khadija; she may have more water problems. The next thing we have agreed on will be to set up solar panels in the desert or windmills to provide light at night without burning oil or candles. I have no internet, so I cannot learn what is available or write up a project and a budget to buy such an installation.'

Akeem answered, 'I don't know if there is enough wind for windmills. Has anyone tried?'

The Imam replied, 'There is a house with a windmill; I asked the owner if it worked. He said it did when the wind blows from west to east in the early morning and from east to west in the late evening. He told me he had read of windmills working from the sun's heat during the day but not at night.'

'I shall learn,' Akeem said. 'I have many contacts, some with the Sheikhs of Saudi Arabia and the Gulf. If this is a project for the glory of God, then perhaps some will sponsor it.'

Rima warned, 'The Storyteller passed us Allah's message.' She knew it by heart. '*You are destroying your planet, and one day it will be a dead world like your neighbour, Mars.*'

The conviction in her voice and determined look made Akeem admire her even more when she added.

'I cannot allow any project where machinery burning fuel comes to the town. It would be against the wish of Allah, and we would lose his protection.'

After wishing her success and agreeing to return tomorrow to learn of Khadija's priorities, Akeem and the Imam left together. Back in the Imam's office, he faced Akeem and asked bluntly, 'You're Saudi?'

'I was born Saudi, although the wandering spirit has taken me far since childhood.'

'Then, perhaps you can help us. I shall do all I can to aid My Lady and this town for the Glory of God, but she and I are not experts in technology and many matters. We need help to avoid exploitation by those who are evil. If they carry guns, we will know them, but we will not understand those who don't.'

They returned the following day to learn Khadija needed a second well pump; she had one working bore. Akeem returned in the afternoon for the promised answer to his question about the well's depth and how far down to the water.

They left in the afternoon; Akeem's two helpers had spent their time with the shopkeepers taking a list of orders, but, during their conversations, stimulated by 'What will you do next?', had learnt of Jamal writing the *Book of the Storyteller.*' One of the two had promptly found Jamal and managed to photograph all the pages he had written. When Akeem read the story of the *Gift from Allah*, he was pleased to learn that the proof of its origins was that it was a black box, like the *Kaaba*.

They also learnt of the rape in Kadijha's town and what had happened to the rapist.

It took Akeem three hours after they camped to compose his report, including reading Jamal's text. Considering what Jamal was doing, he thought a little help might have positive results. He could not guess what. The encrypted message took seconds to leave his outbox.

15

Within seconds after Akeem pressed the *send* button, a computer read and translated Jamal's text and sent it to a human translator. The decrypted version of Akeem's message, without the message identifiers, date, and position, which remain secret, reads:

> Town-Two: [A detailed description of events, and then:] The town has water; the citizens are cleaning up the damage caused by bombs. They have the same problem with comms, and they will accept aerials. See recommendations.
>
> Town-Three: As reported to me in Town-Two. [Detailed description.] They will accept communications and a borehole pump.
>
> Photos: The sequence of pages from the Book of the Storyteller is attached.
>
> Further news from Town-Three: [There followed the description of the rape and the consequences.] The book includes the story. Refer – Rape may become a rare crime, at least among Muslims.
>
> Analysis:
> The towns are stable, safe, and protected by significant forces I do not understand. The residents believe in Divine Intervention. They seem confident in repelling

or destroying attackers, but have done so up to ten kilometres from town; hence, I recommend that they receive early warning.

The first steps in normalising life have begun; however, no pre-terrorist artisanal small-scale manufacturing facilities exist, so no income sources are available.

Supposing that the belief in Divine Intervention spreads, and there are other similar acts, visions, or appearances, this area may become a significant religious centre with a large population. There may even be pilgrimages like Mecca. In that case, the income sources will primarily be from tourism, pilgrimage, or donations. However, as the Storyteller recounts, the strict adherence to rules to save the planet and devotion to His Message will prioritise everything. I cannot forecast what will happen, but I suggest it is worthwhile to be here on the ground floor with established credentials if it happens, and I believe it will.

Recommendations:
1. Installation of the internet ASAP, followed by full-time monitoring of activity related to Jihadi activity to identify potential attacks on the towns. They will not require help to repel an attack, but an early warning is imperative.
Package the container contents in separate cloth bags with jute straps for attachment and transport by camel.
2. An effort to support an early return to an income stream for the towns.
3. Personal request: A three-hundred-page manuscript-sized book. High-quality heavyweight paper, off-white. No markings, binding tooled dark red leather. Gold engraved title 'The Storyteller from Allah,' Classic Arabic with suitable ink and pens. It is a gift to the writer of the attachment. Intention: Reinforce the belief in Divine Intervention. Suggest an initial drop of two aerials, the book, and a pump, as per the attached specs – an implementation plan to follow.

End of Message.

The agent managing Akeem read it and called for a meeting. He copied the report to Meghali.

The department head had two things to say.

'We asked our agent to place Sat Comms in both towns, and he's organised it. Arrange the drop, including the pump and book. He says his plans will follow. Ask him for his ideas urgently.

'Sidonie. Select three agents and instruct them to conduct surveillance of the area. He may be right, and we must warn him if an attack against the towns is likely.'

Patrick had finished reading Akeem's report moments before Meghali knocked on his cubicle wall.

'Good morning, Patrick. If the scenes in the report are the ones you mentioned, what happens next, and why?'

'Am I converting you into a movie lover?'

'No, but you said in your speech when I met you that if there's an apple each day, there will be one tomorrow, and so far, you've given me several apples.'

'I did say the mother might make an apple pie at any time, but I'm sure she won't for a while. I'll give you the background. Millions may believe the Jihadis are a separate tribe of people with incomprehensible motives, unacceptable morals, and cruel behaviour. That's not true. They are just a segment of humanity like all others.'

'I won't argue that for now,' Meghali murmured.

'They consist of three groups, each with a different motivation. Like most politicians, their leaders want power, adulation, and money and will lie to achieve their aims. They take advantage of a leadership vacuum in the countries they occupy, usually because the country's leaders are more interested in lining their pockets than helping their people. Those leaders pay for a small military force to look after the leaders, not the people, who they leave at the mercy of the Jihadists.

'Then, the fanatics and nut cases. They are a deranged few, just as they are few in the world's population, although they will be more numerous among the Jihadis. The most dangerous are the mentally unstable. To commit suicide by blowing yourself up must be due to mental derangement.

'The vast majority, over eighty per cent, are mercenaries. Drawn from the poor and disadvantaged, often young and orphaned. Life as a Jihadi provides them with food, companionship, a salary and, although forced, sex.

'The scenes Akeem describes spell out the death sentence for the Jihadi leadership.

'I said provocation would follow. The rape and the judgment will remove sex from the rewards available; being changed into a pig makes their life far less attractive, so the leadership now expect their forces will evaporate and must act. The equivalent in a cowboy film is the pioneers shooting the buffalo; without them, the Indians will starve, so they attack.'

'Do you understand more about your editor?'

'Yes, it's not human, but I'll use He, not it, despite His affection for women that might indicate She. He can't be human unless you tell me how a human can turn a man into a pig. I'll change my definition if you do.

'As He has the power to turn a person into a pig, He could have made all the Jihadis disappear. He could also have stopped the rape. My data correlations show two persons directly affected by Him, both, I believe, were psychopathic; People killed all the others.'

'So why didn't he stop the rape?'

'He said in his message, *"God does not intervene"*, but assisting a human to punish another, if justified, seems possible.'

'If He's not human, what is he?'

'Meg, have you read the Bible?'

'No, but I heard the bits read to the class at school. And you?'

'I had Sunday school Bible classes for confirmation, but much later, I read the Bible from cover to cover. It's a fascinating study.'

'Why did you ask, Patrick?'

'The equivalent to turning a man into a pig, or transforming a man into a eunuch in public, is described in the Bible.'

'The miracle stories?'

'Yes, there's a direct parallel between the miracle of the loaves and the fishes and what the Storyteller did to feed the people of town one, although it seems he has more knowledge of vitamins and a balanced diet. He must have spent some time studying us.'

'So you think the *Who* I'm trying to identify is God?'

'I'll be precise, Meg. No. It's not the God that religious leaders describe, but behind the word lies something we cannot and do not understand. Remember the words of the Storyteller: God does not intervene...'

'Patrick, it will take much more than that to convince me otherwise.'

'Then stand by for an event that will convince you.'

'So what comes next?'

'The Jihadi forces will gather and attack the towns. Like all films, there must be a comeback. It's the opportunity for a big scene where thousands of Indians appear suddenly on the horizon. They will lose spectacularly; I don't know how, but keep an eye out for it. It's a desert area; I can imagine the Jihadis swallowed by quicksand, but I'm probably wrong. In the *Mummy* series, the evil army of the Scorpion King turns into black smoke at the last second. I don't know what scene the editor will cut in; there are several possibilities.'

'Why, Patrick?'

'Think about it in movie terms, Meghali. What would ninety-nine point nine per cent of the movie audience, seeing the Jihadi forces coming over the hill, want to happen?'

'I suppose you'll say for the Jihadis to lose.'

'If you had watched the *Mummy* movies or others where a crowd of bad guys outnumber and attack the good guys, it's always the baddies who lose. The scriptwriter knows it is what sells cinema seats, especially if he can make it spectacular. It's what the audience feels should happen.'

'But why must this something follow a movie script?'

'Because the audience, that's us, is human. The editor wants publicity and wants us to like him and his screenplay. When I read the description of the Storyteller, I couldn't help but think that the editor must have watched the movie *The Jewel of the Nile*. Did you see it?'

'No.'

'Then maybe you should; I have a copy in storage in my apartment.'

'You're still weird. But why?'

'I'm unsure, Meg; there could be several reasons. Remember, every ad needs an audience that will believe the ad. He's building the audience, but what the ad will be, I don't know.'

'Okay, Patrick, we'll see.'

Akeem received the drop message and two short sentences.

> Early warning implemented.

> Send implementation plans ASAP.

He replied:

> Financial backing from sources motivated by religion
> may be forthcoming.

Meanwhile, I suggest support for an artisanal income stream. A list of goods is attached.

I shall establish a seed business in town two.

End of message.

Patrick read it and said to Meghali that night, 'I suspect the scriptwriter has included some romance in the current scene and will delay the attack. I don't know if it will play out or the editor will cut it short.'

'Romance between who?'

'Akeem and Rima.'

'Patrick, are you a secret romantic?'

'No, Meg, look at the facts and the inference in Akeem's last message.'

....

'He's doing something not in the CIA manual; he's participating, not observing.'

'Exactly.'

'But why Rima?'

'He could set up his business anywhere but chose Rima's town.'

'I suppose it's possible, but I don't believe it.'

'We might never know, but watch for a moment when Akeem takes a risk he doesn't need to take. I'll bet Rima is close.'

The drops occurred. Nine more camels and three men to care for the camels joined Akeem, and the first camel train, loaded with bags like all camel trains crossing the desert, came into the town and knelt in a row along the street in front of the office building with the *Albaladia* sign. While a crowd gathered outside, Akeem entered the office to see Rima.

Her welcoming smile was almost too much, but he controlled his emotions and bowed to her, then, with a broad grin, said, 'My Lady, I've brought you what you need.'

She stood, walked around her desk to where he stood, and looked at him thoughtfully. 'You brought me support and assistance before; I could not ask for more and will be forever grateful. What have you brought me now?'

The Imam interrupted them as he rushed into the room. When he saw Akeem, he exclaimed, 'I thought it was you, Akeem. What do you have on those camels?'

'What camels, *Hajji*?' Rima asked.

He was like an excited little boy. 'There are twelve camels with packs on the road; come and see.' Then turned and rushed out. When Rima and Akeem came outside, the sight of a tall man wearing desert garb, a *keffiyeh*, and a black *agal*, standing beside a beautiful young woman with long black hair, impressed the crowd. Someone clapped, and then the crowd erupted in applause. The Imam asked Akeem, 'What is in the bags?'

With a smile, Akeem replied, 'Mostly radio and internet equipment. Please tell the crowd not to touch anything; we must unpack it carefully; now, please come and discuss matters with our Lady and me; we have much to decide.'

Rima and the Imam listened while Akeem laid out his proposal. Then he asked, 'Do you agree to my terms?'

Rima looked at him for a few moments; he noticed her eyes were twinkling. 'You have not heard mine.'

The Imam wasn't sure what was happening when he heard Akeem reply, 'My lady, what are your terms?'

'First, you bring nothing to this town contrary to the wishes of Allah; second, you do nothing affecting the people of this town without consulting me; and lastly, you come regularly and tell me what is happening and what you are doing. I was once one of the first people to know of events; today, I'm the last and will only learn what the Imam tells me. Agree to my terms, and I agree to yours.'

With a matching sparkle in his eyes, Akeem said, 'I agree, and when I have settled everything, I'll take you to ride a camel around the town to see what it looks like from the desert.'

'Then it is settled; I suggest the Imam tells the people at sunset prayers. Tell those outside the office to wait for the prayers. Now, choose your building.'

Once they found a building and the camels moved to it, Akeem's men unloaded the bags carefully, and he took possession of a small packet. He went to the mosque before prayers to find the Imam. He asked for Jamal, and the Imam replied, 'He'll be here in a minute or two; he's at every evening prayer with his book and pencils. But tell me, how is the unloading?'

'The men have unloaded the camels and are cleaning the rooms, but will be here for prayers; tomorrow, they will unpack and store the goods.'

Jamal arrived, and Akeem called him. He came to them, and Akeem handed him the packet. 'Jamal, what you are doing is for the Glory of God; these are the tools to make your work beautiful. You are to use them under the Imam's supervision; your writing must be beautiful and correct. There is no shame in practising until it is perfect.'

Jamal unwrapped the packet. When he saw the book, he lifted it reverently to his lips.

'Lord, your wish is my command; may Allah bless you.'

The Imam didn't know what to say. 'Lord, you honour Jamal and me. We shall pray for you tonight.'

The next day, Akeem told Rima he was going to see Khadija. As he stood to leave, she said quietly, 'You gave Jamal and our Imam a gift last night. I want to thank you, not on behalf of Jamal or the town, but as a woman. Jamal is an orphan; for many months after the Jihadis killed his parents, he didn't speak. Even now, he does not talk much. You have given him recognition and a task to fulfil. I think he'll improve; one day, he may be famous. You have made me extremely happy.'

'My Lady, I do not know why I gave him the present; I just knew I had to do so; I expected no reward except a child's happiness. But if I can address you by your name when in private, it will be a privilege greatly appreciated.'

She acquiesced gracefully, 'In private, yes.'

Khadija's town also received an internet package, and Akeem a wholesale depot.

Fatima welcomed him back. She also gave him a depot. He ordered goods for his business.

He was about to offer Rima a camel ride around the town when something else interrupted his plans.

16

Sidonie opened a file labelled 'Early Warning Reports.' The first reports came from HUMINT, referring to the multiple small informers who received payment for providing helpful information. They weren't spies in the employ of foreign powers; most did no more than report exciting things to the newspapers. If a woman gave birth to triplets or conjoined twins, the doctor would not announce it, but a nurse at the hospital would send a message and later receive payment from the person she informed. Many were almost professionals. The first to report the information earned income, so news travelled fast, but the more intelligent informers had learnt what information was worth the most to each newspaper. Some knew or suspected it was not a newspaper. Even small items could be worth something; it was not up to them to judge. Nothing of interest came for nearly six weeks, then at various places, a group of Jihadis climbed into a truck loaded with weapons and then drove out of town. At least one informer told someone.

The CIA computer collected the messages and filed them. Human operatives and analysts would read them later, in minutes or hours. The computer processor was faster, and the programs knew what to find. When fifteen different messages had similar words, like 'A truck,' 'Jihadi,' or 'Left town,' a pattern began to grow, and the computer raised the alarm. Within minutes, five analysts were examining the data, and one, in front of a screen, was programming the computer to display red flags on a map of the region, indicating the positions of the message senders.

Meghali joined them, and after a glance at the screen, asked, 'Do we have any intel on where they are going?'

'No, we have reports of a truck passing through a village, but the trucks don't carry identification, so we don't know which is which, and so don't know their direction. It should become clearer if we receive more reports, but if they disappear into the desert, we will be blind.'

'Call for satellite recon; we must discover where they are and where they are going.'

Nine hours later, they had photos and analysis. The destination was in the desert, approximately one hundred and eighty kilometres north of the towns where the recent events had occurred. The informer's count of combatants and the photo confirmations ranged between one and two thousand, growing.

Meghali called for an Operations meeting. The result was a message to Akeem. Because the Russians had noted that the Americans had moved a satellite, American and Russian satellites began to crisscross the sky. An hour after the Russian satellites started moving, the Chinese ones followed.

Akeem called on Rima; he was now a welcome visitor and an important man in the community, but an increasingly personal relationship was also at play.

He said, 'My head office has sent a warning. A gathering of Jihadis has begun about a hundred and eighty kilometres to the north. The office says the Jihadi group's intentions are unknown, but I should prepare to evacuate to the south if necessary. The office will warn me if they have further news.'

Rima smiled at him. 'It will not be necessary to evacuate if they decide to attack. Fatima, Khadija, and I shall ask for Allah's protection. We have kept faith with his words, and He will protect us.'

Akeem took advantage of the opportunity. 'Rima, I've no intention of leaving; I shall remain by your side whatever happens.'

When she understood the implications of his words, she blushed and looked confused. He thought she was adorable.

She took a deep breath and said, 'I must talk to Fatima and Khadija; please keep me informed of further news.'

It took the Jihadis a week to gather at their temporary camp and organise their attack. Then, in the early morning, about 250 vehicles left at dawn, heading south.

The continuously monitoring satellites overhead triggered a warning, and in minutes, Akeem received a message. He immediately went to warn Rima, and she informed the two other women. They had already agreed to go into the desert slightly north of their towns, but stay in contact via phone. Rima called the Imam, who arrived minutes later.

They set off to the dune Rima had picked. Akeem was amazed by Rima's confident, calm demeanour when asked what would happen. She replied she didn't know but doubted they would see anything, and the Jihadis would not harm them. Then she chuckled and said, 'It's a shame; to see a thousand naked men is a sight I would never forget!'

Arriving on the dune, the Imam called the Imam with Fatima, and Rima phoned Khadija. When the Imam nodded, she spoke to her phone, 'Ready,' and passed it to the Imam, who stepped back. Akeem switched on the recorder in his pocket and took two paces back.

The three women had agreed and memorised their prayer; Rima raised her arms to the sky and prayed.

'We, the leaders appointed by The Storyteller to fulfil
the wishes of Allah on this world, call on the Force of

Almighty Allah to deliver us and all those in our charge
to safety from the peril of those who come from the
north. May the force of Almighty Allah discard the unworthy in the sands of the desert, as those who would
destroy the Story from Allah would bury His words in
the sand.'

Rima lowered her arms and turned to the two men. 'It is done. We are in the hands of God. Let us return to my office and drink coffee while we wait.'

A kilometre north of Rima's town, from a small tent with a tethered camel, a man had crawled out with a prayer mat; spreading it, he knelt and prayed. Then, taking five steps, he stood with his back to the morning wind blowing from the west, lifted his *thawb*, and began to urinate. A few seconds later, he had to turn the other way as the wind changed to blow from the east. After dropping his *thawb*, he stood and listened with his eyes closed; then he returned to his prayer mat and prostrated himself in prayer. He knew the signs meant a terrible storm was brewing. He took the camel to the small tent, made it kneel, and then tied it to the tent. He would wait, lying on the lee side of the camel under the tent.

The satellites all captured the sandstorm, an unusual phenomenon for the time of year. It was completely circular and grew rapidly for three hours. With no visibility, in the centre of the storm, the Jihadi forces stopped and took shelter below their vehicles or sheltered on one side, covered by a tarp.

The satellites showed the storm intensifying further until, after twelve hours, it reached an intensity never seen before, one of the surveillance team said.

'If it were a hurricane, it would be Category Seven.'

Then, the sandstorm gained height; the satellites photographed it growing as a cone until the top reached the stratosphere. The surveillance man said, 'I can see it, but it's impossible.'

Rima, the Imam, and Akeem stood outside her office, looking north, where they could see the enormous conical tower against the clear blue sky; from a distance, it resembled a pillar of sand.

The Imam, his voice choked in awe, said, 'The Force of Allah is truly mighty. We must pray.'

They made their way to the Mosque, where all the townsfolk joined them. The Imam spoke the prayer.

In the other towns, the people said prayers of thanks. The sandstorm neither died nor moved for four days. By then, photographs from the ground, air, and satellites had gone worldwide. People with a television in every country watched the enormous cone of whirling sand for hours. Then, it broke in less than an hour, and the sky slowly cleared of dust. Sand from the vast area covered by the storm, drawn towards the centre, created a perfectly circular and rounded massive dune. No one has seen the Jihadi trucks or their occupants since.

The man lying by the camel crept out from under the tent, untied it from the camel, and shook the sand off. He laid out his prayer mat and offered thanks to God. After packing everything on his camel, he mounted. His camel's tracks were the first to traverse the now pristine desert.

Jamal, with help, drafted the story of the attack and the punishment meted out. The title is:

'The Prayer of Rima, Khadija, and Fatima the blessed.'

Unknown to Rima, Akeem had recorded her prayer using his micro recorder. He wrote it down for Jamal. The words terrify, for they precisely define what happened.

'May the force of Almighty Allah discard the unworthy in the sands of the desert, as those who would destroy the Story from

Allah would bury his words in the sand.'

He also sent it to headquarters.

The CIA always has an end-of-operation meeting to close a file and examine its mistakes. This meeting, held after Akeem's report arrived, took minutes. The chair summarised.

'We didn't do anything; we don't know who or what did or how, but we know those towns are fully capable of protecting themselves. Let's continue supporting them.'

Meghali added a comment to the report that went through *channels* to the Director. Once again, she wrote. 'No perceived threat to the USA.'

Meghali returned to see Patrick. He was again flat on his back but immediately sat upright when she entered his cubicle.

'Hello, Patrick.'

'Hi, Meg. It was a great scene. I learnt that the scene could last for days on a world stage. Do you now believe what I told you?'

'Patrick, I'm reluctant to do so, although your arguments are convincing. I've spent too many years learning that some people are always in the shadows.

'You said Akeem and Rima were a love interest. Do you still think so?'

'We warned him to go south before the attack, but he stayed. He must have been within a few metres of Rima to record the prayer the women spoke. You can argue that making the recording was part of his job, but the risk he exposed himself to was far beyond the call of duty. So yes, but I don't think the editor needs to expand on it.'

'Well, that time you were right; what's next in the saga?'

'Meghali, the Indians have attacked and failed; what will the cavalry and the pioneers do next?'

'I don't know; I haven't watched cowboy films for years.'

'It's easy to understand the scene sequence and reasons in cowboy films, but all films must follow the rules because the audience is human. The differences are incidental. Films reflect what people think should happen. Sometimes, it's easier to imagine how small children will behave; in this case, the bully came and lost. Children would see the opportunity to put the boot in and ensure he never returns. In a cowboy film, the pioneers might attack the Indians, kill some and drive them off their lands to punish them; the scriptwriter may even show them settling on the land if he wants another fight. In any case, the scene that follows is punishment. I don't know what or how, but it is likely to be something in the script that shows punishment for a failed attempt is inevitable. The audience must learn that the punishment will be severe.'

'When?'

'Soon. The editor will cut it in immediately. We'll have no problem spotting it when it happens. A hidden message would serve no purpose.'

'When does this movie end?'

'Not soon, this one is a blockbuster, not for many years, perhaps it will never end.'

The CIA Director called a meeting.

The meeting had the heads of every department in the room. The attendees were shuffling papers around, trying to look as if they knew what it was about, or having quiet discussions with their neighbours. The door opened, and the Director entered. He took his chair at the end, a larger and heavier chair that befitted an overweight senior official, with a backside that required it. He put a folder on the desk, then placed a hand on each side of the file and looked carefully at everyone in the room. The silence was palpable, for they all knew what the two-hands-on-the-table gesture meant; an explosion was due to follow.

'*What the hell is this all about*?' The words were even more menacing as he spoke in an even but emphatic tone. No one answered. It was the safest response.

Opening the file, he looked at a list of items. 'These are the events I've listed, for which there is no explanation.

'One. In a Jihadi-held territory in the Middle East, a mysterious man with a young female appears, alone and unarmed, and the town's Jihadis flee.

'Two: A terrorist group tries to attack the town and fails to approach within five miles of it, with a hundred and twenty-eight dead. With no battle, no weapons and no casualties from no opponents.

'Three: The mystery man and his companion appear in the second town; the townsfolk with no weapons annihilate the remaining Jihadi force, bury them, and the village returns to normal, with no guns, fighting, or injuries.

'Four: In a third town, there is no visit, but a woman has a vision of an angel, then transforms the terrorist leader into a three-hundred-pound pig; the town annihilates the remaining force again without arms and normality returns.

'Five: The CIA has supplied the towns with communications, but justifies this to collect real-time intel. We have also provided a blank book to a kid writing a new religious text, perhaps the new Quran.

'Six: We warn our asset on site of a Jihadi attack of over two thousand terrorists. They don't advance any closer than ninety kilometres when a sandstorm buries the entire force under a new dune.

'Finally, the analysts comment that there is no threat to the USA.

'People have died, and the casualty count shows it's a one-sided war, one that is escalating. In my book, it means a powerful adversary who could decide to attack anywhere. I see a threat. Why does the report say one does not exist?'

Meghali feared no man, especially one she recognised as a political pontificating appointee. 'Director, I wrote that line, and it says there is no *perceived* threat. To have a threat, you must have an adversary. Despite all the information we must analyse, and I can assure you all the agencies are looking, we have no adversary except three women who stood on a dune and prayed to God, asking Him to bury the invaders in the desert. If you believe I'm wrong, go ahead, tell the President that God is a threat to the USA.'

Several attendees looked down to hide a smile as the Director contemplated what she had said.

He snapped, 'So why are we supporting this crowd?'

'Because we are good guys, Director, we are on God's side. Besides, it enhances our intelligence and gives the USA a head start, potentially providing an economic advantage, should anything develop.

'If you think we should send in the Army, you can start a war, but be sure you tell the President the adversary is Allah and be ready for the crusade between Islam and the USA that follows.'

As the Director rose, there were more hidden smiles as he ordered, 'Okay, keep me in the picture,' and left.

17

The private jet should have flown from Northeastern Iraq to Mali. It didn't arrive. On board were three unregistered passengers, the leader of the Jihadi movement and his two lieutenants, who believed their movements were untraceable.

The captain filed the flight plan from an airport on the Northeastern Iraqi border, the day after the sandstorm broke; the destination was Hurghada on the Red Sea. It might have been odd, but the flight crossed Iraq to the Amman control area before flying south to the Egyptian FIR and across the Red Sea to Hurghada. A dog leg to avoid Saudi Arabia. The flight plan indicated that there were five passengers and two crew members on board the Beech 400. An observer carefully noted the five passengers at the departure airport and identified three well-known businesspeople in the gold market, accompanied by two assistants. However, the plane already had three other passengers on board; they had boarded at a private airfield with no immigration control, as it was an internal flight.

It didn't go to Hurghada, but three hours later, it landed at the nearby private El Gouna airport. When descending through five thousand feet on the final approach to Hurghada, the controller instructed the pilot to continue straight ahead and land at El Gouna, thirteen miles ahead, as there was an obstacle on the Hurghada runway. Immigration officers would drive there. The reception committee at Hurghada at once jumped into three large SUVs and rushed off to El Gouna; the observer at Hurghada just made it to El Gouna in time to film the SUVs leaving the airport and counted five extra passengers. The photographs showed they were identical to those who had boarded in Iraq. Fifteen minutes later, the Hurghada controller authorised the jet's return for refuelling, and forty minutes later, it returned to El Gouna without filing a flight plan for the thirteen-mile hop. The three extra passengers disembarked with the crew; the immigration officials had returned to Hurghada.

The CIA computer system added the flight, except the short fuelling hop, to its database, with the five passengers reported by the observer, but the other three remained unmentioned.

Two days later, the plane's captain filed a flight plan from El Gouna to Bamako – a long flight over the Sahara Desert. The flight plan stated Bamako was a refuelling stop; the onward flight plan to Kayes in Mali, within the Malian Gold belt, was attached.

The plane didn't land in Bamako. It arrived at Gao with a sizeable dead pig and severely injured passengers on board. The French military authority managing security at Gao airport pieced together a fascinating story.

The plane took off at one-thirty am, scheduled to land in Bamako an hour after sunrise. An hour earlier, the crew had arrived and prepared the plane. While doing so, the three unknown passengers had walked along the runway and boarded the aircraft. At one am, the sole observer was a half-awake controller, who checked the crew and the five passengers on the official general declaration, stamped and signed it, and then left for the tower. A complaisant official, who saw no reason to drive to El Gouna airport at an inconveniently early hour, had stamped the passports with an exit visa at Hurghada airport the previous evening. A *baksheesh* had smoothed the way.

The flight progressed steadily for five hours. The route took them into Mali, north of Niger, then followed a slightly northward course along the border with Burkina Faso to Bamako. It had no overflight permission for either Niger or Burkina Faso. A few minutes before sunrise, a passenger asked the captain to turn slightly so the aircraft's tail pointed directly at Mecca. He explained the passengers wanted to perform the morning prayer. The captain did this accurately by selecting Mecca on his navigation display and turning the plane to fly directly away from it. Simultaneously, for the course was slightly off the earlier heading, he throttled back and slowed the plane.

The passengers all lined up in the aisle facing the rear and prayed. The three unknown passengers were closest to the pilot's sealed compartment.

As they finished their prayer, the first to rise from his knees realised white light was growing from a source behind him, so he turned rapidly to see the Storyteller, his back to the cockpit's door, with Soraya in front of him. His shout brought them all upright, turning to see what the staring man saw. It left them speechless; Soraya pointed at the first man, the oldest of the three, and yelled, *'Pig!'*

While a large, totally confused pig was trying to figure out why it was in a jet at 38,000 feet, the Storyteller and Soraya disappeared.

The 150-kilogram pig, a remaining tendril of fear in its confused brain, decided to escape; it turned and dropped onto four feet, then charged. It smashed into the first man, crushed him into a seat, and hurtled down the aisle, knocking the men down like a row of falling dominoes. The last man managed to take a pistol from his shoulder holster, and as the boar hit him, he fired into its head. He missed the brain but severed the spinal cord. The steel-jacketed bullet came out of the pig's throat, passed through the man's foot and then the floor of the plane and the outer hull with little resistance, then continued to the desert floor where it threw up a column of dust as it buried itself into the ground several centimetres from a sleeping sandgrouse. The bird took off with a piercing shriek, waking an entire flock of sleeping grouse. When they disappeared skyward, a desert fox hoping for breakfast loped away.

The captain heard the explosion from the cockpit, and then seconds later, the *whoop-whoop* of a siren sounded, as a warning light indicated that the cabin was losing pressure. The captain and copilot reacted automatically, switching on the oxygen feed and clipping their masks on their faces. The co-pilot operated the radio and navigation system, checking on the nearest airport. Simultaneously, the captain switched off the autopilot, pushed the nose down, and throttled back further to lose height as quickly as possible. The injured passengers, unable to grab the oxygen masks from the seat pockets, lost consciousness within thirty seconds.

The cockpit computer indicated to the captain that 15,000 feet was a safe altitude, for the hole was small, so he dialled 13,000 into the autopilot, a survivable unpressurised altitude, and switched it back on. The co-pilot had found what he wanted and made two radio calls. The first was a mayday call on the emergency frequency 121.5 MHz; the second was to Gao control, the nearest airport to them.

The Gao controller was having an early coffee when the call came in. 'Mayday, Mayday, Mayday, November Nine Four Zero Papa, Gao control, do you read?'

He dropped his plastic cup on the floor as he reached for the microphone. 'Gao control, Mayday Four Zero Papa, go ahead five.'

'Four Zero Papa, losing cabin pressure, descending through two seven zero, will stabilise at one three zero. Beech 400, position four zero miles radial one six zero request emergency landing.'

'Four Zero Papa, landing approved, runway two five right at your discretion. The wind is light and variable, with good visibility. Emergency equipment is on its way. Do you have injuries onboard?' He switched the high-intensity runway lighting to its maximum.

'Gao Four Zero Papa will confirm injuries in one minute.' The captain nodded at the copilot, punched in the data to the nav computer, and left the autopilot to fly directly to Gao. He then watched the altitude, calculating the remaining descent. The copilot checked the cabin altitude. As the needle dropped to 13,000 feet, he unclipped his oxygen facemask, rose to open the cabin door, and peered out. The sight of the dead boar in the aisle diverted his attention; then, he noted the other passengers were in bad shape. There had been eight; there were now seven and a dead pig. He returned to his seat, shook his head at the captain, picked up his microphone, and pressed transmit.

'Gao, Four Zero Papa reporting, seven passengers injured, the extent of injuries undetermined, also one dead pig.'

The captain pressed his transmit button. 'Gao, Four Zero Papa, I have your lights in sight.'

'Four Zero Papa, land at your discretion. Please stop on the runway immediately, then open the door. Emergency crews will take over.'

The Gao controller turned to the military officer beside him. 'I don't know what he meant when he said a dead pig; he can't mean they have a real one in the cabin.'

As the officer ran out, he shouted, 'Well, we'll soon learn.'

Moments after the first mayday call, one of the emergency team members called his wife to tell her he would be late for breakfast due to the emergency. She phoned her best friend, knowing her husband was a reporter covering the military mission. He arrived at the airport in pyjamas and slippers as the jet stopped on the runway, with emergency vehicles roaring up.

The story went worldwide.

The authorities didn't charge the crew, but the passengers stayed imprisoned. One of the charges was the illegal slaughter of an animal.

Their names became public months later, but nothing can remain a secret when misguided fanatics are involved. Within days, the news of what had happened filtered back to the Jihadi high command. As none were fanatical enough to risk transformation into a Head Pig, the movement in the Middle East, lacking guidance, broke up into small groups, subsequently mopped up by various countries' anti-terror forces.

In Egypt, the authorities, possibly prompted by the UN, raided a house near El Gouna Airport, confiscated its contents, and then seized the house, which became government property occasionally used by high-ranking government officials for holiday accommodation.

In the CIA office, the Al Qaeda file lists the leader as missing, suspected dead from swine flu.

'Patrick, was that the punishment? Is it over?'

'Well, it was spectacular, but the farmers have not claimed the land.'

'What land?'

'The territory occupied by the Jihadis in North Africa.'

'How can they do that?'

'The editor will have prepared something; he's the best. I'll bet it's something unexpected that will, as the expression goes, put the fear of God into the terrorists there.'

In Africa, far from the Middle East, the terror groups were separate, rarely doing more than talking politely to each other; the spoils were too meagre to share, especially when they captured a group of young girls. Their motivations may be similar, but their politics are vastly different. On the ground, however, the fighters are much the same, if not worse. They travel considerable distances to hit remote targets unexpectedly, from bases hidden near Mali's borders in Algeria, Niger, and Mauritania. They believe that if military forces attack, they will have time to duck over the nearby frontier, thinking the military will not follow.

One such force was making its way across the desert, a column of six 4x4 vehicles, each with eight fighters, two in front and six behind, on either side of a mounted machine gun or rocket launcher. They travelled in the short twilight before sunrise, after sunset, or in the hour on either side of noon when the sun was overhead. The desert reveals shadows at other times, such as deep blacks on the yellow sand. At midday, the sand haze reflects the sunlight into the sky, making satellite observation difficult.

Two days after the forced landing at Gao, the request to rescue the prisoners arrived. The reward offered was worth a try, although the terrorists expected the prisoners to be well-guarded. Forty minutes after midday, the leading vehicle reached the top of a rise, rolled over it, and descended the sandy slope into a narrow valley. As the last pickup started the descent, the leading one reached the valley floor, where the driver slammed his foot on the brake. It almost created a pile-up of vehicles; they managed to miss each other by millimetres.

Sitting on a rocky outcrop, invisible to the terrorists, the Storyteller, with Soraya beside him, saw the vehicles. Soraya was looking at some exciting creatures gathered in the valley; she had no idea what they were, but they were enormous. More massive than anything she had ever seen, the Storyteller was teaching her what the Sahara was like eighty million years ago, when the valley had a river and a green forest. He said the bones of these creatures lay below the sand.

She had not questioned his ability to make them reappear in the valley; so much had happened, she knew he could do any-thing, but when the vehicles came down the slope into the val-ley, she asked.

'Who are they?'

'A bunch of bad men. We will see what they think of the beasts.'

Nothing happened for a few minutes; the terrorists seemed to be scrutinising the beasts, and then they gathered around the leading vehicle for a conference.

The leader, who owed his position to his physical size, was the heaviest man in the group, and no one would challenge him. But, now bewildered, he asked, 'Does anyone know what those things are?'

There were several replies.

'No, but they are bloody big.'

'They look a bit like giant lizards.'

'Funny lizards; the one on the right looks a bit like a kanga-roo.'

'I thought kangaroos were smaller.'

'I don't know; I've only seen pictures.'

'If it weren't impossible, I would say dinosaurs.'

'What are they doing?'

'I think they're digging for water.'

The leader decided. 'We can't camp here; we have fifteen

minutes before the shadows are too long. We shall drive around them to the left and find a place to camp further down the valley.'

The column started. Unfortunately for the terrorists, their leader was not a hunter of wild animals; his game was human. He would have chosen the right-hand side if he had been, for a light breeze wafted across the valley from left to right. Once the column had gone far enough, the scent of meat and water mixed with other smells drifted across to the beasts, and they raised their heads to look. When they saw moving prey, they burst into a run.

Kita, the startled leader, immediately yelled at his driver, 'Accelerate, maximum speed,' then, 'You lot back there, shoot.'

A rocking, swaying, jolting pickup, sometimes airborne, landing with a jarring thump, was not much good as a firing platform. The terrorists fired, wasting ammunition, but hit nothing, and the beasts continued to gain.

From the rock viewpoint, Soraya stood to watch, shrieking, 'Go, beasts, faster!' Waving her arm in the air to encourage them.

Kita managed to stand, gripping the roll bar, and then he looked back. The last vehicle was metres ahead of a giant two-legged beast; he thought it was about three times the pickup's height. He waved his arm in the air in a circling movement; it meant separate, a manoeuvre they had learnt to avoid air attack damage when a fighter strafed the ground in a straight line.

The last pickup swerved left, then rolled, throwing the fighters onto the ground. It supplied the diversion needed; the remaining vehicles tore straight down the valley at maximum speed when the beasts turned and headed to the overturned truck. The last Kita saw was the animals gathering around the inverted pickup.

They drove on for an hour, even though their shadows showed distinctly on the desert sands. They would not risk the animals catching them.

On the rock pile, Soraya asked, 'Are they eating the bad men?'

The Storyteller smiled at her. 'I seem to have a bloodthirsty companion. No, Soraya, they are not real enough to eat them. They will disappear now. If those men can walk, they may, but they have a long way to go. I think someone may rescue them. Let us go now.' He held out a hand, and Soraya took it; they vanished.

Kita and his men took stock while they camped. They had used over half their ammunition and lost the rocket launcher on the wrecked truck. Kita decided his men might not obey an order to continue, so he avoided giving it.

'We will return to base but take an alternate route. Every time we come to a crest, the leading vehicle will stop before becoming visible. Then we shall go ahead on foot to look for anything unexpected.'

They found more valleys with giant beasts and had to backtrack and route around them. Kita became worried about fuel reserves; he abandoned three vehicles and the mounted guns, putting all their fuel into the others, now with many more soldiers in each. Seventy kilometres from their base camp, he instructed the crew to camp and, taking one pickup with all the fuel, managed to reach the base, where he dispatched a rescue team to retrieve the stranded crew.

18

The specialist for the Sahara Desert, the area surrounding and including Mali, sat at an identical desk in the Fort Belvoir basement but at the opposite end of the room.

He paged through the stream of photos the last satellite pass had taken, pausing for seconds on each one, a bare desert with nothing unusual in the pictures. He didn't expect to see anything; this pass was seventy minutes after local noon, and he knew any terrorist movement would have stopped.

When he came across a photograph with several odd shadows, he stopped. He could not determine what they were, so he typed the commands necessary to overlay a radar image on the visual. Six of the shadows he could identify as vehicles, all in a line. The other visual cues, grouped on one side, showed nothing on the radar screen.

He paged to the next image and repeated the radar overlay, then went back and placed a marker over each vehicle, numbering them one to six. He rolled forward a photo and repeated the marking with each successive image until the pickups disappeared off the screen.

When he finished this, he carefully copied the sequence of images and wrote the following in his report.

Images, coordinates 18.018N-3.35W, six vehicles, initially
in a column, speed 40 km/h, accelerated to 70 km/h, then

split randomly in all directions. One vehicle overturned
and remains. No others returned, and the column re-
formed and disappeared to the southeast.

He then returned to the visual cues; the group in the first photo didn't show on the radar. They had also split up; they appeared to have run after the vehicles. When he calculated their speed, he couldn't believe it; they were running at about seventy kilometres per hour. He also realised they had all gathered around the overturned vehicle. It left him at a loss until he used the shadow lengths to calculate the size of what he assumed were animals. Then he was even more amazed; his calculations yielded a length of nine metres and a height of five metres.

As a professional analyst, he carefully recorded it.

A group of nine massive objects with no radar reflection broke up and chased the vehicles, with peak running speed estimated at 70 Km per hour. After the last
pickup crashed, the group gathered around the crash
site in a behaviour pattern like that of animals; the lack
of radar reflection confirms this possibility. I estimated
the animals' size from the shadows, with a length of 8
to 9 metres and a height of 4 to 5 metres.

Then he added,

The only known beast of such size capable of such
speeds is Tyrannosaurus Rex.

It had the effect he had hoped for; the mention of *T. rex* drew immediate attention. When a second analyst confirmed he could do no better, the request went out for a low-level photographic pass. With French military cooperation in the area, a photo was on the Captain of the French forces' desk within four hours, with a copy in Fort Belvoir.

The request made no mention of *T. rex*, but included the details of the vehicle. Two heavily armed military helicopters flew to the crash site and collected two bodies, four severely injured and two heavily bruised terrorists.

The interrogator's recording left no doubt; the two uninjured soldiers' descriptions, recorded in separate interviews, concurred. A *T. rex* pack had attacked them.

A routine meeting between specialists in Fort Belvoir studied the report data and the attached French military reports. Two specialists had been on the committee examining the Middle East data; one had an answer.

'We have eight terrorists; two are dead, and the others have disappeared. Search all the photos over a wide area around this site. I think we will find the terrorists have gone home; maybe we can discover their base, but they will have left. The pattern is the same as the other cases where the Storyteller from God intervened, except this time, he terrified them with dinosaurs instead of turning them into pigs.

'I like this guy; he's having fun and doing a damned good job for us. Find the base, guys, and destroy it.'

Although great fun to rape women and kill men, becoming lunch for a giant lizard three times the height of a car, especially one capable of running at seventy kilometres an hour in soft sand, is not a terrorist's idea of fun. Once the story circulated, the terrorists disappeared from the Sahara.

'You were right again, Patrick, not only about punishment but about it being unexpected. Now tell me what you think the next movie scene will be.'

'That's easy; in the Middle East, the rich rancher appears.'

'I don't follow.'

'The rich rancher is a standard cliché; the viewers expect him to appear. Although he has no right to the land, he sees no reason why a group of sod-turning pioneers should exploit land that the rich rancher can use to run his cattle, and he wants to stop it before their numbers increase.'

'And then?'

'Our hero defeats him, which demonstrates who is on the wrong side. The rancher would be shot in the cowboy film, although I doubt the defeat will be that drastic.'

'Who will it be?'

'You have more data than I have, can't you guess?'

'Apart from an increase in message numbers in the country's government, I've nothing new.'

'That's enough; the government will try to take control and fail.'

'And there's still no threat to the USA?'

'None at all. If there is any, it will come much later in the movie, and it won't be something we can fight.'

'Give me an example, Patrick.'

'My AI has flagged a news report from Brighton, England. The beach, probably the most well-known and popular in England, was covered with dead jellyfish on a Sunday morning.'

'Don't they have jellyfish in England?'

'Of course, from harmless to lethal, jellyfish are in all the oceans. The UK has about six common species. The Brighton ones were Box Jellyfish, a species common in the Caribbean. The last technical article proposes that the Gulf Stream carried them to England, and a pesticide from another country poisoned them.'

Meghali remarked, 'An invasion of jellyfish is hardly a threat, although I agree it's not something we can fight.'

'I agree, but consider how the people reacted. I'll add some other facts, Meg. The beach remained empty for a week; the hotels, which are normally full during weekends, were empty the following weekend, and the supermarkets threw away tons of fresh food. The trains from London were empty, and the postcard seller on the beach complained to the municipality that they hadn't cleaned the beach.'

'Okay, it's not the jellyfish that are the threat, but people's reaction to them. What if it had been a shark near the beach?'

'People hate sharks; scriptwriters have done an excellent job fostering hate, like the film *Jaws*, but, like humans, jellyfish must go where currents push them. They may sting, and one species can be fatal, but without a movie like *The Attack of the Jellyfish*, we can't think of them as a threat to our lives; they are fellow sufferers. The postcard seller would have asked for the capture or death of a shark, but capturing a million jellyfish is unthinkable. You might not believe it, Meg, but a shark would have created a bullfight scene.'

'Explain, please.'

'Thousands of people attend bullfights – one massive bull with sharp horns that not one of those attendees would dream of challenging. The bull faces a Matador and half a dozen Picadors and Banderilleros. The people expect the Matador to win, but secretly back the bull. A shark in the sea would have created such a scene; the town would become packed with people hoping to see the shark bite someone. The railway would have to double the number of trains from London.'

'Patrick, I'm just beginning to understand how you think. Are the jellyfish a scene in your imaginary film? And are we, the humans, the threat?'

'Not the jellyfish; that event may be a complete accident; if not, it's a well-disguised experiment testing how to damage an economy and weaken a government. The real thing will be something else on a far greater scale. As for the threat, I suspect we've been working on it for centuries. The Storyteller told the truth, and if I'm right, we'll have our worst nightmare rammed down our throats once the introduction is over.'

Meghali whispered, *'You are destroying your planet, and one day, it will be a dead world like your neighbour, Mars.'*

'Exactly.'

The saying 'military intelligence is a contradiction in terms' describes blind obedience to routine and orders. The President of Fatima's country, hearing alarming reports of events in his country that he had not sanctioned, ordered a military photographic survey. Three planes took off; one had the photographic equipment but was lightly armed. The dispatch officer ordered the other two fully armed fighters to escort it as protection. All went well until fifty miles from the target, when all three engines quit for unknown reasons. It took forty seconds for the pilots to try, unsuccessfully, to restart their turbines; by then, they had already lost height. A military jet with no engines is a flying brick. All the pilots ejected after announcing engine failure and landed safely in the desert. The pilot of one of the fighter aircraft was much brighter than the others. He gathered his parachute, folded it into several layers and cut a hole in the centre to make a desert robe. He cut up his boots until they looked like sandals, and with a part of his chute wrapped around his head, set off to walk to the road he knew was not too many kilometres to the north. The others waited where they landed.

A military rescue helicopter, also armed, suffered engine failure. Being a helicopter, it landed successfully in the desert. By then, the affair had escalated to the top level of the air force command. Displaying more intelligence than expected, the Air Marshal dispatched a second helicopter with instructions to follow a road and carry no arms. Only when within range of the downed crews could the pilot head towards the grounded pilots' locator beacons. One of the fighter pilots was dead. At least, the rescuers assumed so, for a large boar, wearing a flight suit and strapped into a parachute harness, showed signs of exhaustion from dragging a half-inflated parachute around the desert. When the news spread, the military personnel at the base remembered that the man had boasted after a bombing raid; he had fired indiscriminately at running human targets, laughing as he said it was like shooting rabbits.

The military might have covered it up, but the pilot who walked to the road walked on to the nearest town and, once there, borrowed a phone to call his wife, anxious to reassure her he was alive. She told her best friend, who told her husband, a Reuters correspondent. A flood of recriminating messages arrived from Islamic leaders and threats from Islamic countries.

The Prime Minister, recognising an opportunity for promotion, said to the President.

'Mr President, I suggest you resign and disappear before the army rebels and arrests you. I think you might face an Islamic court judgment for blasphemy.'

With the President's signature on a resignation document, he waited for two hours until the President disappeared, then announced the news and assured the population that a new election would follow within days.

The people's vote eliminated the ruling party and the opposition. Due to unexpected backing from the Grand Imam, they voted overwhelmingly in favour of a protest movement led by a woman.

She called Fatima, as she now had a job she had never expected to have. On Fatima's advice, she asked for a meeting with the last prime minister. After he agreed to follow her orders and do nothing without her approval, she appointed him to run the government. The announcement said it was a provisional appointment. Much to their relief, the army became an extension of the police force. Women didn't need telling; they discarded their veils.

Lying relaxed in bed with Patrick, Meghali said, 'I'll ask again. Has the introduction ended, Patrick? It appears your editor has cut out the Jihadis entirely.'

'Not quite. The church is still a ruin.'

'Explain, please.'

'In a movie, there is often a church in the middle of nowhere; most times, it's an adobe Catholic church, with a high gable above the door and a bell to ring before services or as a warning. Pillaging and battles have severely damaged it. The audience expects to see the god-fearing *peons* rebuilding it and some nasty guy, probably a Mexican Bandido, to rock up and stop them.'

'And then?'

'A good guy stops the Bandido. There is much drama, and then the movie ends; often, to make it a good ending, the final scene features the peasants rebuilding the church; they stand on the scaffolding, waving their sombreros as the good guy rides off into the sunset, leaving a lovesick senorita with tears in her eyes. There are two versions: either he never looks back, and the music fades away, or he gallops to the horizon with the music becoming louder, then it cuts, and as the sun is behind him, you see him turn his horse sideways. He's a black shadow as he waves his hat once.

'I can't guarantee the screenplay, but the first town has a ruined mosque.

'Then we must wait for the new movie, an extract of the world movie.'

19

It was inevitable. Fatima's town had become famous throughout the Middle East, and the visitors became a stream and then a flood, wanting to pray where the Storyteller had given his message to the people. Most were pious individuals, often hoping that such a pilgrimage would help resolve a problem or cure an illness. The town thrived, but the issues were growing. Fatima had declared visitors had to camp in the open desert; the small town didn't have facilities to house them. When too many people filled the space before the ruined mosque for prayers, she had to find a solution. She went out to look at the stars for inspiration. Someone, or something, watched her.

The next day, she asked the Imam if he could declare a large area out of town for prayer, starting from the part of the road where the Storyteller had disappeared in front of all the town's citizens, so that they could keep their mosque and Allah's Kitchen as a museum visit.

He did, convinced it was a direct order from God.

Some of the tented camps were almost like small towns, while others displayed signs of excessive wealth and comfort, as the wealthiest individuals in the Middle East sought to demonstrate their devotion. With an entire retinue of servants and followers, Emirs and Sheikhs came and set up their tents. And one of them asked to see the Imam. His proposition was simple. He wanted to build a magnificent Mosque on the site in memory of the Storyteller. The Imam personally thought it an excellent idea. He felt that his visitor must be a younger son, about thirty years old, with an athletic build and a handsome face, reminiscent of an Egyptian film star. But without agreeing, he explained he must discuss it with Fatima the Blessed.

Later that day, he explained the proposal to Fatima. She replied, 'This task grows more difficult by the day; it is not a decision I can take lightly. I cannot answer you now; I must have time to think and pray for guidance. Ask me in three days.' For three nights, she sat outside and watched the stars. On the third night, with a full moon in the sky, the Emir walked into the town with one of his employees, one of several men tasked with supplying information on what was happening in the village and other tents. Once they saw Fatima, her hair shining in the moonlight, sitting on a large block gazing at the sky, the employee said, 'Your Highness, there is Fatima the Blessed.' They watched for an hour, then left.

The next day, Fatima informed the Imam that she had made her decision. She asked him to write these words and deliver them to the Emir.

> The Storyteller told us Allah's message. We are a simple village. He said we are destroying our planet, and only we can save it and ourselves.
>
> I have the task of caring for this village, and to do so, I must ensure we allow nothing to conflict with Allah's message. Therefore, I cannot allow the construction of a large mosque using machines that burn fuel or cement made with fire. But building a mosque to celebrate Allah's message is a worthy task.
>
> Therefore, I make this suggestion. Build a mosque using no machines that pollute the planet and no ma-

terials that waste the planet's resources. As done in
the past – do it again.

Let there be many men; each may contribute in a joint
effort to glorify the words of Allah.

Construct this mosque from the town's stones and
materials, the bricks and stones on which the
Storyteller himself walked, sat and stood. Replace
the town's buildings with new materials, let camels
transport them, and rebuild according to a plan that
allows for visitor accommodation, water and sewage
systems, and electricity generation from a solar
farm in the desert.

Pestilence and death will result from a horde of visitors
without facilities, destroying this town just as we have
been destroying our planet.

When the Imam had finished, he read it back to her, amazed at
the wisdom of her words.

Despite several people describing her as a beautiful angel,
the Emir expected Fatima to be an older woman. He read her
words and was impressed for a different reason. He believed
God had given him a task.

He replied, 'Please tell the Blessed Fatima I shall do as she requires.'

He was to find he had started something that would take on
the dimensions of a crusade. And would find something else.

In a Shia-majority Muslim country, one of the Ayatollahs was a
religious fanatic, a believer in the oldest sacred texts he inter-
preted to the extreme; he imposed a fanatical discipline on all
who lived in the area under his control. In particular, he required women to remain in their homes. Men did the shopping,
and if a woman had to leave the house to see a doctor or visit

relatives, she had to wear a burqa and do so in the company of a male relative or her husband.

When he heard a woman had decreed all women should walk bareheaded, he knew she was a blasphemer of the worst kind, without the slightest doubt. That she was in a different country and of the Sunni religion made no difference. She had defiled the holy scriptures and deserved death.

With fanatical blindness, he didn't consider consulting with other Ayatollahs; he ignored any political consequences. In his mind, politics and politicians had no connection to religious affairs.

He ordered several of his more fanatical followers to travel to find the woman Fatima and kill her.

Fanatical though they were, they were cautious men, but one of them had a sadistic streak and had killed several times, always using knives, and would do so again if paid. The five men, who travelled without arms, knew the assassin carried several knives for such a task. They arrived a month later near Fatima's town on camels and camped out of sight in the desert. Five days later, they had each made a sortie on foot alone into the village to reconnoitre the layout. Then, they decided. The assassin would go alone at night. They didn't know where Fatima slept but had noticed she stayed late in her office, where the light was visible long after sunset.

The assassin almost succeeded the first night. Fatima exited her office and climbed onto a block to see the stars. She was a perfect target, but just before he moved from his hiding place in the deep shadows, he saw movement. Someone was guarding her.

The second night, he was luckier, and when no one had been in or out of her office for an hour, he slipped silently into the corridor and then into the lighted office where Fatima sat at her desk. He had taken two steps into the office, reaching for his knife, when he stopped, unable to move.

Fatima looked up from her work and stared at him. Without any surprise, she said, 'Well, well. What have we here?' Then she pressed a button to call an assistant. Summoned from his bed, the assistant took a minute or two to arrive and looked curiously at the frozen assassin.

'I have never seen this man before. What do you wish me to do?'

'Is the Emir here?'

The assistant knew she meant nearby and replied, 'In his headquarters camp, I hear.'

'Then tell the Emir I would appreciate his attendance urgently.'

It took fifteen minutes; the camp was over two kilometres away, and the Emir was asleep, but he came, accompanied by the guard sitting in front of his tent and his bodyguard.

While waiting, Fatima sat calmly, looking at the assassin in deep thought.

The assistant returned to say he had sent a messenger to the Emir, then sat in a corner to wait.

A young man, the Emir, had run part of the way, revelling in the chilly desert night air, but his guard was older and out of breath. Leaving the guard at the office entrance, the Emir and his bodyguard rushed in. When he saw Fatima sitting calmly behind her desk, he relaxed and saw the assassin.

'My lady, who is this, and why is he frozen?'

'Your Highness, I've no idea who he is. Why he is frozen, I can only guess.'

The Emir turned to his bodyguard and ordered, 'Search him.'

He found four knives that he showed to the Emir. 'Your Highness, these are long, thin, sharp, and easily hidden assassin knives. I've no doubt this man came to kill the Blessed Fatima.'

The Emir was about to say, 'Kill him,' when he thought of where they were and instead turned to Fatima.

'My lady, what are your orders?'

'Not orders, your Highness, just a suggestion. Take him away somewhere; tie and gag him first, as I think he will return to life once far enough away from this office. I'm sure he didn't come alone, find his accomplices, and discover who sent them. Keep them safe, then tell me. It is better to know your enemy before beginning a battle.'

The Emir bowed. 'As always, my Lady, your wisdom astounds me.'

He gave orders to his bodyguard. He then sat with Fatima for half an hour until a group of soldiers arrived with ropes, tied and gagged the man, and carried him away. While waiting, Fatima quizzed the Emir on the progress of the Mosque. During the discussion about the progress, he stated that the labour required was much more than expected, but he hoped to find a solution soon.

The next day, he returned. The man had spoken, and before sunrise, his guards had arrested the four accomplices while they were sleeping. They had all talked separately.

'My lady, the source of their orders is a Shia Ayatollah. I've heard of him; he's a fanatically religious man with no tolerance for deviation from his laws. The assassin has probably executed several people on his orders. Do you have a further –' he hesitated, then said, '– Suggestion?'

Fatima smiled at him. 'Your Highness, you said last night you needed labour. You may receive offers from wealthy individuals to send workers to you. You must refuse. Believers must build the mosque for the Glory of Allah, not for money. But I ask if they are Shia or Ismaili workers, will you refuse them?'

'My lady, they are all followers of God, as are Christians and Jews; all who follow the one true God are welcome, whatever they call Him.'

'Then I leave you to decide the punishment for the assassin; perhaps he may reveal other crimes to authorities in his country. The Ayatollah needs to learn the lesson of humility. I suggest you send the other four to the Ayatollah with this message.'

> You will find you can drink water but not eat for a hundred days after hearing this message, but you can eat with the workers as you labour to build our Mosque.

'Warn the messengers that the same fate will befall them if they do not deliver the message.'

The Emir bowed. 'My Lady, I shall do as you suggest. Your wisdom and mercy are boundless. I foresee many Shia volunteers.'

The Emir was right; one of the workers was the fanatical Ayatollah, who had a lesson in humility to learn. When his hundred days were up, he saw the project from the perspective of the devout workers. So many Shia workers were present that he decided to stay and complete the work to honour his God.

Jamal added a new section. *'The Punishment of Fatima the Blessed.'*.

20

In Washington, DC, Meghali asked, 'Has the movie in the Middle East ended, Patrick? From Akeem's reports, it appears that religious conviction now protects the towns in the Middle East; the Mosque will be magnificent, and the facilities for pilgrims luxurious.'

'I don't think so; the story of humanity is long, and what has happened is a minor drop in the ocean. What I've seen is just an excerpt of the whole. The scenes that have been rewritten and edited seem to me to be the beginning of more changes. I suspect that the last one had a romantic part.'

'Okay, you have had one romantic suspicion I know about; what's this one?'

'The Emir and Fatima. It fits too perfectly into the screenplay; I reckon the editor cut it. She would have made a superb tearful senorita as the Emir rode his camel over a dune on the horizon.'

'So, what is the next scene in the screenplay?'

'It's a change of scenery, the equivalent of a flashback or a flash-forward. Or the man on the mountain. Neither does any harm. They build anticipation that something will happen, but I think this time, it will be worldwide; the editor wants to tell all the viewers that something significant is about to happen. He's built a solid base in the Middle East.'

'What's the man on the mountain scene?'

'Exactly that, a strange man dressed differently, standing on a high ridge or mountain, looking down at the pioneers. The editor doesn't need to say who he is or what he'll do; he appears to raise expectations after the lull that follows the previous high. Zorro does it in every episode. *"Hello, audience, I'm here."* When it's a series, the editor sometimes ends each episode with the man on the mountain and choice words. Will you ever forget, *"I'll be back"*?'

Meghali's mind snapped to attention. 'Islam now believes in God's message. Is the next target Catholicism?'

'It would make sense, but I can't imagine what.'

They lay there thinking; Patrick stared at the ceiling, viewing movie scenes play out. Meghali let her mind wander through everything she knew about the catholic religion. When Patrick said, 'Symbols, movies are about symbols, people function with them, emotional or physical. Movies often use an object, such as a smile or a frown, as a symbol. A broken tractor missing a wheel or with flat tyres shows more about how long ago a catastrophe hit than a subtitle.'

Meghali remarked, '*Christ the Redeemer*. Probably the best-known catholic symbol in the world. The Vatican and Easter Mass might have a higher rating among Catholics, but nothing surpasses the Redeemer worldwide.'

'Yes, but what can the editor do without destroying it? If he defaced the statue, millions of Christians would direct their anger at him, and that's the opposite of what he wants.'

'What if he doubled its size?'

'That might do it. Meg, your thinking has changed.'

'What do you mean?'

'Before today, you sought causes for events; now, you have proposed an action for a hoped-for consequence.'

'Patrick, I never thought I ever would.'

'Well, just keep on doing so; it will help.'

The man and the young girl, a grandfather and his grand-daughter speaking Brazilian Portuguese, were visiting the sights of Rio de Janeiro, and they drew no attention as they walked between the hundred stalls selling replica statues of *Christ the Redeemer*. Statues from plastic, stone, alabaster, or marble, from three centimetres high, keyring included, to the size, delivery included – suitable for a church or hotel garden. Their walk took them to the Corcovado train station, where they boarded the *Bondinho*, a red-coloured cog train that wound slowly up the Corcovado Mountain through the forest for twenty minutes. Once on top, they followed the crowd to look at *Christ the Redeemer*.

Soraya had thoroughly enjoyed their walk and the train ride, but the sight of the statue drew a frown.

'Don't you like it?' asked her grandfather.

'Who is it?'

'It's a statue of a Storyteller; his name was Jesus Christ, and many people believe he was the son of God.'

'Was he a Storyteller, like you?'

'Yes, but it was a long time ago, and very few people could write when he came with his message, so no one knows what he said. Since he came, many people have mixed up his words.'

Scornfully, Soraya said, 'They couldn't even get the statue right.'

'What do you mean, Soraya?'

'He has no staff or *agal*, and his beard's too short. He doesn't look like a *real* Storyteller.'

None of the Rio citizens noticed anything; a tour guide was the first to notice it early the next day, and he had difficulty believing what he saw. He asked his companion guide, a young woman with whom he lived and worked. 'Rosa, look at the statue; it's changed.'

She looked. After half a minute, she said, 'It looks right, more *human.*'

The debate would rage for days over whether it was better or worse, while the government commissioned a research team to propose how to reverse it. The report mystified everyone, as the materials analysis and dating indicated that the age of the concrete and the soapstone covering of the staff and agal was identical. They had always been there. A new debate began: should the two items be removed or not?

Ten days after the change, hundreds of thousands of plastic and alabaster miniatures of the statue, for sale to tourists at every outlet in Brazil, were packed by the sellers into boxes or cases and replaced with new ones carrying a staff. A delegation of boutique sellers petitioned the municipality. Initially, audibly annoyed by their wasted stock, they quickly realised the sales of the new miniatures to replace all the models sold over many years would reap enormous benefits.

At the meeting to decide whether to reverse or leave the changes, Brazil's President was surprised when the Catholic Cardinal for Brazil attended, but understood shortly after why he was there.

The meeting was one speech long – the Cardinal's.

'Mr President, the Catholic Church has reviewed the technical documents describing the *Redeemer* changes. The Church is satisfied that the sole power that could have changed the statue in one night is God. The staff has a one-piece steel bar core; according to our consulting engineers, who are experts in building church steeples, this would require a tower crane to install, with or without its soapstone covering, as it is too heavy for a helicopter to lift. Furthermore, the steel bar sinks several metres into solid granite, which would take a mining machine many hours to drill.

'The Vatican will announce that God has changed the statue,

the Pope will visit to conduct a mass at the statue's base, and Catholics worldwide will not tolerate any act to undo God's will.'

The man and the young girl, clearly a grandfather and his granddaughter, visiting the sights of Rio, drew no attention as they stepped into the *Bondinho* to the Corcovado's peak. Once on top, they turned to look at the statue of *Christ the Redeemer*.

'Is it better now, Soraya?'

'Much better; he looks just like you. Can I have one of those small ones the man is selling?'

'Of course, then we'll visit somewhere else. We have a lot to learn about the people on the planet.'

A hundred video cameras survey the entire area around the statue, operating 24/7, with the key ones displaying their footage on screens in the security building. The software checks the images at night and triggers an alarm if there is movement. They are there because the government fears that if a terrorist or a madman succeeds in blowing up the statue, the government's members will have to emigrate. The people in one of the most devout of the world's catholic countries would brook no excuses.

Unfortunately, that meant all the cameras surveyed the approaches and the area around the statue's base. None of the security personnel had envisaged the figure's theft, so no camera pointed at it. Had it been a priceless jewel, there would have been. There was no recording of the change.

The CIA, naturally, received a copy of the camera feeds for a day on either side of the change. With four thousand eight hundred hours of video to review, it took time and cost a fortune.

However, Patrick had a different idea; he wasn't interested in how, but in who. His mind decided that the statue must now resemble the Storyteller; the descriptions were similar.

There were dozens of pictures of the new *Redeemer* from all angles; he fed them to a program and asked it to find a match in the crowds around the statue's base.

Patrick knew the Storyteller had been there when the software identified him before the change. Patrick requested the camera feeds for ten days, and his AI checked them. When it announced that he had returned to view the result, it reinforced Patrick's conclusion.

He noted the young girl with him and then looked again. His right brain said something didn't match. Patrick called for the first satellite photographs of Town One and zoomed in on the area that showed the white-clad figures before the crowd. The Storyteller was identifiable by his staff; the two figures on either side were female. Akeem had reported their names: Soraya, the young girl, and Fatima. He increased the zoom until the Storyteller and Soraya remained in view, and then he compared it with the second surveillance image from Rio.

Patrick was about to file the photos when he realised the girl in the Rio photo was taller than the girl in the first image. *Is it the same girl? If so, she's grown a head taller, and that's impossible in a year.* Then he thought. *No more impossible than turning a man into a pig. She'll be as tall as most men in a few more years. I'm sure she'll reappear.*

Then, he filed both zoomed images for future reference.

'Patrick, is that scene complete?'

'I believe so, Meg, but not the consequences. I underestimated the editor.'

'Explain, please.'

'The people in the Middle East, although few have seen the Storyteller, will see photos of the *Redeemer* and say he's the Storyteller. The *agal* is a physical link; the two religions may draw closer to each other over time.'

At McGill University in Montreal, Canada, James McCannon, an astrophysics professor from the University of Cambridge, studied a short text. A proponent of the Big Bang theory on creating the Universe, he was at McGill on a sabbatical. Research into the prehistoric Earth's atmosphere was his primary interest at McGill.

The text he studied was a translation of the Storyteller's Message.

Academics must seek renown. Constantly. It is their lifeblood, bringing promotion, funding, and income. There is but one way to achieve it: write technical treatises for acclaim by other academics and books for public praise. If lucky, the latter will also bring publicity from the media.

James decided to draft a short essay on the story's accuracy, relating to the knowledge that gave rise to the Big Bang theory and the theory of evolution. Before doing so, he considered where to publish it, for the audience dictated the style and the language. After running through a list of possibilities, he decided the University magazine was the right choice as a first step, for he was sure media reporters would read it. Furthermore, as a visiting Professor from Cambridge, priority treatment of any submission was ensured.

His essay was appealing to many and provided an opportunity for other scientists to join the fray. He carefully noted the areas he could not accurately interpret. He admitted to protestant origins and an enormous doubt, due to science, about the church's dogma.

He claimed the message didn't conflict with the Big Bang theory's proven data and that it solved its fundamental problem. *What was the source of the original point of concentrated energy that created our Universe?*

He said scientists had agreed for years that the universe was expanding, but had not yet decided whether the expansion rate was increasing or decreasing. He thought the message could be correct and intended to encourage research into the question. Then he touched on evolution, saying it explained the origin of life in a manner paralleling scientific research, claiming that life was an accident that occurred when the right circumstances allowed a collection of chemical molecules to capture a part of God's force. He said humanity would have to simulate a billion worlds and every variation in the combination of chemicals and the environment before it happened again spontaneously. Science could never create life. He ended by writing. 'All except the most bigoted know the truth of the one-sentence message; *you are the only form of life to be destroying its world. It should be a source of shame to all.* I shall leave the sociologists to argue the truth about the fairer sex.'

Naturally, it caused a stir; he became a TV celebrity for weeks until others produced comparable articles refuting his essay. Most of them were repetitive. Many said a human must have written the message because it agrees neatly with the Big Bang theory. Others argued it proved God had created life. If it weren't for the churches and the movements to save the Earth receiving a massive boost, they might have overlooked the simple statement about a dying planet.

21

Patrick's AI program, which scanned everything posted on Instagram and Facebook, was brilliant; it didn't bother him often, for most postings had nothing of interest and were classified as rubbish. However, one had popped up that morning. Most Facebook posts include many pictures, as the average person has difficulty stringing words together. However, Patrick's mind had no problem writing a screenplay, creating a scene list, and producing a video that featured a little boy on a beach, which he could project onto the white ceiling using the posted pictures. The AI then added a corroborating post.

When his video was complete, he felt satisfied; he knew what the future would bring. At least he understood the message.

That night, Patrick, by now spending more time with Meghali than he had ever spent with a woman, asked, 'Meghali, why have you never married?'

'Patrick, you're the first man I've ever spent a weekend with. I'm not ashamed to say there were many during my college years with whom a night was enough. I couldn't find one that interested me, but I kept trying until I finally decided to stop. None of them had anything interesting to discuss, but you do. Usually, within twelve hours, I feel the urge to throw a plate of food into their self-satisfied, smug faces. Now you've asked, I can ask that question.'

'Explain, *smug*, Meg.'

'A face that displays a feeling of self-achievement. You don't look smug after we make love. You won't know.'

'I'll guess that's probably the expression on many a man's face after successfully bedding a woman he doesn't care for. So what expression do I have?'

Meg closed her eyes to emphasise her memory, then shivered and had to tell her mind. *No, not my feeling, his.* 'I'll remember the next time, Patrick, but I can see tenderness. Now answer my question.'

'You can figure out the answer. Several girls tried to cook and do housekeeping; their utility kept them around for repeat visits. But most women seem to want a child at some point, and they left when they learnt I was a hopeless case. Haven't you had the desire for a child?'

'No, Patrick, somehow, it has never arisen, a lack of hormones or something else. I've always had better things to learn or do. My mother was a Child Psychologist; she was brilliant; she told me once that she had only to concentrate on the child, observing, I suppose, all the child's mannerisms and body language, to learn the child's problems. But I watched her for years, burdened by housework and cooking for us. My father was busy and let her educate me; they hardly ever talked, except perhaps after I fell asleep. I'm sure that put me off having children.'

'Are they still living?'

'No, they died when I was twenty-two. I know your parents died in a mud avalanche, Patrick. Your security clearance has the information; how did that affect you?'

'For at least a year, I blamed myself for not forecasting what would happen when a freak storm inundated the mountain. I had discussed it with my dad, and he said it hadn't happened in centuries, so why now? I hadn't studied global warming then; if I had, I might have insisted they move.'

He blamed himself for their death and pacified his remorse by perfecting his forecasts.

'And have you never wanted to be a father?'

'Not much; after the hormones kicked in, it was not fatherhood that interested me, but what I could do with my penis. Most men seem ready to trade years of their lives dedicated to nurturing children, but I've never thought that way, although I must admit that the thought of a son or daughter with mental powers that I could train has sometimes cropped up; I suppose a bit like having a human AI. Instead, I have my AI programs, like having many children. A child is unlikely to fall into the genius category. If the child didn't have a gift that fascinated me, the child would, I think, bore me.'

'Patrick, you have a gift for giving me ideas; I shall write a search for polymaths and discover how many have children, how many polymath couples have children, and what the probability is of a genius descendant. But let's debate the crux of today. What's the next scene in your movie?'

'We've had the man on the mountain; that was a brilliant change. Many depictions of Christ feature a staff and a crown of thorns; the *agal* is a symbol. The world knows the Storyteller is still here and is waiting for the next move.'

'What's that going to be?'

'If this were a movie, it would be the Batwing Doors.'

'Come on, Patrick, elucidate.'

'In cowboy films, the scene with the batwing doors is common in the sequence. It might start with the man on the mountain looking down at a one-street town with a saloon on a dusty street and half a dozen horses tied to the hitching rail. Inside, there's a roistering crowd of bad guys, a frightened bartender, and probably a dumb farmer. He's thrown through the doors or a window as the hero dismounts by the hitching rail.'

'And what does the hero do?'

'He loosens the Colt on his belt; he might have one on each side; they are dull gunmetal, almost black, with plain brown wooden handles. He wears a white hat, brown scuffed boots, and dull iron spurs.'

'Why?'

'It's what identifies the hero; the bad guy inside the saloon has silver guns with ivory handles, a black hat, a silver buckle hatband, and shiny black boots with silver buckles and spurs. He's the boaster; the good guy is modest, although a few cowboys have changed from one to the other in a movie.'

'Then, what happens?'

'He pushes the batwing doors open, and the editor cuts from an outside camera to one inside that shows him in the doorway with the light behind him. Then he steps forward and is recognised.'

'And?'

'It depends on the film; in most cases, the bad guy draws to shoot him, but the hero is faster, and one of the hired baddies tries to shoot him from an internal balcony. They always have a balcony inside the saloon, often with painted ladies who scoot off and hide when the good guy comes in; when they do, it tells the audience that violence will follow. He blasts the balcony killer as well, who then falls, breaking the balcony. It makes for a visual as well as physical impact.'

'The hero's hurt?'

'Rarely; most times, the rest of the bad guys gallop out of town because they no longer have a job, and then the hero rides off into the sunset. Other times, he proves how good he is by shooting a pistol from the hand of one or two others, and the bartender crowns a baddie with a whisky bottle, and then the rest surrender.'

'And you think this is a cowboy film?'

'No, he won't ride off into the sunset. The movie will continue.'

'So where is this scene going to play out?'

'I don't know. Look for a saloon on the other side of the world to Rio, with a baddie in it. I would guess a nut case dictator. The editor doesn't like dictators. They don't behave predictably. He must feel they stand in the way of what he wants to happen.'

'Why the other side of the world?'

'He needs a third religion behind him; he must align the faiths behind him. Islam and Christianity are in the fold. I would guess Buddha is next.'

'Not the Hindus?'

'Too many sects.'

'Okay, but why does he need the religions?'

'Governments, especially democratic ones, are supposed to represent the people, but have you ever known one, except a military dictatorship, which doesn't bicker and procrastinate? Dictators are often psychotic; they do what they want to do, not what's best for the people. Religions may change slowly, but they represent the people and don't make meaningless claims of innocence. Like Islam, which now believes in the storyteller, once hooked, a religion will give unwavering, resolute, and constant support.'

'Patrick, are you guessing?'

'Of course, I'm always guessing, based on as many facts as possible, and the batwing doors scene brings a radical change that's possible after the build-up from the previous scenes. The audience is rooting for the good guy; if he walked into the saloon and shot a rancher without it being clear who's good and who's bad, and that the rancher deserves to die, the audience would lynch him. The coming scene won't be peaceful like the *Redeemer.*'

'War?'

'No. The good guy has proved he's the fastest gun around; no leader will challenge him; they'll lie low. But watch for an event with worldwide publicity; Psychos love publicity, and screwing up the event brings even more.'

'What will it be?'

'Take your pick, Meg, something like a carefully orchestrated public launch of a new missile. The missile could reverse direction and blow up the palace. The editor won't write the event into the scenario; he will rely on a human to provide it, so I can't forecast it, but he will screw it up, and that will depend on the occasion. Look for a likely event and expect a spectacular rewrite.'

Patrick searched the Register of Births and Deaths for Azzaro. He found Meghali and her parents' names and looked them up. It shocked him, although he had suspected something: *Las Vegas, October 1, 2017 – the Las Vegas massacre.*

Once again, the meeting at CIA headquarters had all department heads in attendance. The CIA Director entered, took his seat at the end, placed a folder on the desk, then rested one hand on each side of the file and looked carefully at everyone in the room.

'I hope that no one will say that the CIA is in the hands of God.' The words were even more menacing as he spoke in an even but emphatic tone. No one answered. It was the safest response.

Opening the file, he looked at a list of items. 'These are the extra events I've listed since the last meeting, for which there is no explanation.

'Seven: A private jet carrying Jihadi leadership has to force-land in Gao. The movement leader, transformed into a pig at 38,000 feet, savages the remaining passengers.

'Eight: A group of terrorists in the Sahara reputedly meet a Dinosaur pack, including several *T. rexes*. The *T. rex* pack chases them; a vehicle overturns, two terrorists die, and the French military recovers injured terrorists. Then, a French military action destroys the terrorist base.

'Nine: The Middle East government sends an armed force of a reconnaissance aircraft and two fighters. They all have engine failure and crash. The pilots eject, and two survive, but all they have found of the third is a pig running around the desert in a flight suit, towing a parachute behind it.

'Ten: The government falls, the president vanishes, and a woman wins a snap election to become president.

'Eleven: An Emir from the Gulf is building a mosque in the desert near the first town with volunteer labour.

'Twelve: A fanatical ayatollah sends assassins to kill the woman in the first town; the assassin disappears, and the Ayatollah becomes a volunteer worker at the mosque.

'Thirteen: Someone modifies the statue of *Christ the Redeemer* in Rio overnight, and the Vatican declares it Divine Intervention.

'Fourteen: A Cambridge Professor from Britain, visiting McGill, authors an article that suggests this is the second coming.

'Now, I hear, a joint expedition of palaeontologists, sponsored by God knows who, is about to overrun the Sahara looking for traces of dinosaurs. Berkeley University has requested official American status and military protection.

'Can someone tell me what this is all about? I must report to the President. What do I tell him? The CIA hasn't the foggiest idea?'

Meghali, as the head of analysis, offered a reply, 'Occam's Razor, Director.'

'What the hell is that?'

'Something we learn at spy school, Director, it's a philosophical principle about eight hundred years old. It suggests that the simplest explanation is most likely correct if there are multiple and differing explanations for something.

'I can offer two possible answers. First, this is the work of a highly organised worldwide secret society with an unknown motive – one about whose existence we have never had any sign whatsoever, despite in-depth searches of recorded data. Second, the mystery man is what he says he is: God's Storyteller. No matter how unlikely, it is the simplest and, therefore, the most likely answer.'

'And if it is the answer, what do we do?'

'I can't answer you, but I can propose a strategy.'

'Go ahead.'

'What we have already done. As much support as possible without publicity, in case we are wrong. Then, we maintain surveillance but add to our task the identification of anything where intervention can assist in furthering the Storyteller's expressed objective to save the planet.'

'And you think I should tell that to the President?'

'What else, Director? I could add, like Kennedy, who dedicated America to putting a man on the moon, the President could dedicate America to saving the planet. It is probably the safest thing he could do if he wants a second term. It might keep the Storyteller from thinking up a stunt that takes place in America. Remember, the message from God says to give the management of the world to women, and so far, those events you listed have promoted four women into top positions.'

The Director didn't report the conversation.

22

Meghali called Patrick to join a meeting.

'What's it about, Meg?'

'I have intel on an event which might be your Batwing doors.'

'Ok, when?'

'This morning, at ten am in conference room six.'

Meghali was already seated in the conference room when Patrick entered and chose a chair at the round table. 'Hi Meg, who's coming?'

Meghali replied, 'Four specialists, Lu, – Far East intel, Captain Kelling – from the Pentagon, a weapons guy, Jonas – from IMINT and Carole – from SIGINT. It should be a short meeting, so everyone is up to speed.'

The four arrived a minute later. Patrick had already met the first three CIA staffers, and then Captain Kelling introduced himself. After handshakes all round, Meghali asked. 'Lu, can you fill us in on what you've learnt?'

'One of our Chinese operatives visiting a neighbouring country collected an item from a drop box. I'll display it on the screen.' Lu tapped an icon on his notepad, and the large screen on one wall filled.

> You will come to the party on the first of October to
> celebrate our Illustrious Leader's birthday.

You will wear the clothes specified and available from approved shops.

You will arrive at 11:30 and stand at a designated spot, T310:2765.

You will carry the state flag, purchased from approved stores.

You will cheer and wave the flag according to the orders you will receive.

Captain Kelling remarked. 'That's a relief. We've noticed an increase in heavy military movement in the last three weeks. That intel suggests they are preparing a weaponry parade.'

Meghali asked, 'Carole, have you had an increase in SIGINT traffic?'

'Nothing significant, but there's still six weeks to go before October first. If this is genuine, we will intercept an increasing message traffic as the organisers get to work.'

'Jonas?'

'Nothing exceptional, Ms Azzaro. We can plan our satellite surveillance and move one overhead. If we notify the NRO, they'll put up a drone; they have sufficient time to negotiate some lucrative contracts with the TV news channels, and we'll get better photos and a live feed.'

Patrick asked, 'Jonas, I must have seen news clips on previous birthdays, but I've never watched a complete film. Do you have one in your archives that I can view? I can remember wondering how they can have so many people of identical height.'

Kelling laughed. 'I can explain that. The soldiers march past in groups of five hundred. With the size of their ground forces, they can sort them by height and have groups within a centimetre or two. Then they adjust the heights with insoles or thicker boots to equal the tallest.

'Spacing the groups adds the illusion that it's identical to the one in front.'

'And the forced invitees?'

'The organisers sort them by height, shortest in front and tallest in the rear. As the tallest individuals are further away, they appear shorter in the picture, an effect produced using an elevated camera. The designated spot in that instruction list, T310:2765, is row T, number 310, and there's a pad 27,65mm high to compensate for a height difference.'

Jonas said, 'Patrick, I'll send you the latest video pack.'

Meghali closed the meeting. 'Ok, guys, stay on it. Message me if there's anything unusual.'

Three weeks later, Patrick had viewed five birthday parades, and Meghali arranged a meeting.

'Good morning, everyone. From the reports I've read, can we confirm that there's a parade and it's not a cover for something else?'

Captain Kelling replied, 'I'm certain it's a parade, Ms Azzaro. In one report, Jonas included images of their military bases with daily marching drills. Lu has reported an unusual number of tank pads delivered to bases. Tanks would not have rubber pads on their caterpillar tracks if they intended to use them in an attack; transporters would carry them. They will drive down the road. Like in other parades, the transporters will carry other machinery to provide proof of industrial capability.'

Jonas added, 'I'll send in a report tomorrow. I have images showing machinery and activity at their usual parade ground. My guys need a day or two more to be sure, but they say dozers appear to be increasing the area.'

'Why would they do that?'

Patrick answered. 'It's the Leader's fiftieth birthday; he wants a big party. I counted the crowd at the last one; it was sixty thousand. I'll bet he wants a hundred thousand at this one. Captain, you know more about organising a parade than I do. With that many standing for four hours, even though the temperatures will not be excessive, there must be hundreds who pass out. What happens to them?'

'They all have a water bottle with a tube by their chins that they can suck on to avoid dehydration, but it's a good question because they are civilians, not fit soldiers. If one collapses, he lies there until he can crawl to his left. No one helps. The man on his right takes his place immediately, so the row to his right moves one place to the left. There's a hidden group of replacements beside each row. Look at the video again. You'll see what looks like a walled building.'

'That's an extreme I never imagined. Thanks.'

Meghali asked Lu, 'Do we know which countries will send representatives?'

'Not yet, ma'am. They announce that a day or two before the event, for security reasons and because several times the Leader has announced a one or two-day postponement.'

'Why?'

Patrick replied, 'Every parade video I've viewed had a vivid blue sky clear of cloud. The weather in early October is variable but consistent; it rains for a day or two, then clears for three or four days. I suppose if his meteorologist says there will be clouds or rain, he postpones. I checked his birthday; it's June 27, so this is a celebration.'

That night, while eating an Irish Stew with Patrick in his favourite restaurant, Meghali asked.

'Have you spotted anything that suggests this is your Batwing doors event?'

'Yes and no, Meg. Yes, because it's a mega-parade, superbly orchestrated by a Dictator. The ideal scenario for the hero to screw up. No, because I can't imagine what the editor could do. I did consider him changing the weather at the last minute, bringing on a massive thunderstorm and spectacular lightning, but that wouldn't have the impact of a hero walking into the saloon, shooting the bad guy, and then holstering his pistol with a rolling movement that shows how good he is with a gun.

'He must appear, but if he did, there's so much security those men would try to take him down; they're not untrained Jihadis, it would be mayhem, not proof of how powerful the Leader is.'

'Could he come from behind?'

'There'll be a hundred soldiers behind the stadium where the dictator sits, all trained to watch in specific directions for anything unusual. They won't blink. And he can't pop up to say "Pig" and vanish. That would be over in seconds. In cowboy films, the audience has the time to see him ride up, hitch his horse to a rail, notice how he dresses, and loosen his guns in their holsters before stepping up to the doors. If this is the scene I expected, it will be a last-minute decision; We must watch the parade.'

'Where?'

'In the conference room where we have all the screens, each a feed from a different camera. Invite the others. The parade goes on for four hours, and we won't get to bed before three am.'

Captain Kelling was with them, watching the screens in the conference room, when the parade began after the Illustrious Leader sat in his throne-like chair on the podium, and the announcer started the commentary. The CIA supercomputer translation was a second behind the screen display. An hour and a half after the parade began, the captain stood. 'That's it for me. Industrial equipment will now follow the military hardware and soldiers. I'll get some shuteye before my team starts counting and classifying missiles. The Chinese and Russians will also. With the drone and that clear sky, the IMINT we have will show details.'

Thirty minutes later, the parade ended. The Illustrious Leader stood and approached the podium, and the crowd went wild. Patrick could almost feel the relief of the hundred thousand crowd, who had frenetically waved and cheered for two hours in a synchronised chorus each time the announcer paused.

When he raised his arms, the crowd cut their cheering in a second. And the screen, which had previously shown the parade path, zoomed out to reveal the entire breathtaking scene as the leader began to speak.

'Patrick, nothing's happened. Nothing exploded or fell off a truck.'

'No, but now I know the editor is there; there's a small cloud to the rear of the stadium at the top of the screen that we couldn't see when it showed only the parade.'

'That's a little cloud, hardly a threat. It may dissipate.'

'True, but I checked the weather forecast; it should not exist. I think it will grow. It's the beginning of the scene where something is arriving, and the audience doesn't know it's the hero.'

'It is growing, Patrick, it's also moving towards the stadium.'

'I still can't imagine what will happen.'

...

'Patrick, it's changing shape.'

...

'Meg, I think it's reforming as a Buddha.'

'I agree, and the crowd can see it; a few are turning their heads. But it's still hidden from the Leader by the building.'

...

'Meg, it's a Buddha, sitting in the sky with crossed legs and its arms on its knees.'

...

The Leader had just finished a self-eulogy about how generous he was to the people when a shadow blocked the sun's heat, and he looked up in surprise.

'The Leader has seen it!'

Perhaps a part of the crowd waited in the adoring expectation that the Illustrious Leader would, with a wave of his arm, banish the cloud to oblivion; the others, at the least, expected a reaction. The camera operator, following the leader's every movement and expression, reacted automatically. He swung his camera to film what the Illustrious Leader was looking at, so TV screens worldwide displayed a first-class picture of the Buddha Cloud and what followed.

Now closely resembling a Buddha, the cloud raised an enormous, unmistakably human arm. It swept down in a graceful sweep and, between thumb and forefinger, plucked the leader from the stage, now screaming in a much less illustrious tone but loud enough for the microphones to pick up the sounds. In seconds, it lifted him to a position where the cloud Buddha demonstrably inspected him. Then, after thirty seconds, with a flick of a finger in a gesture reminiscent of flicking a piece of dirt off a shirt sleeve, the leader became a vanishing streak, discarded to a cosmic dustbin.

The entire assembly remained frozen for over a minute until a woman approached the microphone and announced, 'Today's event is now over. Please return to your normal activities at once. Announcements will follow in the news.'

The cloud dissipated in a few minutes.

'My God, Patrick, you were spot on with the forecast!'

'It was a pretty good scene; if I had made the movie, I would have thanked the special effects team.'

'Why? I didn't see anything.'

'You weren't supposed to; a huge splash of blood or human parts flying in all directions generates a primitive level of disgust amongst the audience; however, if you propel a human being through the sky at supersonic speeds, you'll see nothing, and all the TV cameras recorded a contrail although there was no water-bearing engine exhaust.'

'Why was that important?'

'In movies, it's how you reinforce the message; this one told all the bad guys in the world, *"The cosmic dustbin is your destiny if you continue to be bad."* They believe they saw the leader take the trip. We'll learn what effect that scene had in the next few days.'

The Government, all men, found reasons to disappear. After seeing the punishment firsthand and without knowing what they could do to avoid it, they disappeared: A safer kind of vanishing than space travel without a spacesuit. The sole person left was the woman, a minor official in charge of the international press office, who was confident she had done nothing to reproach herself.

She called the Secretary-General of the United Nations – a woman who had watched the entire event on television in her bedroom. The instructions she received were immediate and definite.

'First, do not accept any aid or assistance from anyone. Inform whoever offers that the country is under UN control until further notice, so you can only receive help from the UN. However, you would be grateful if they could assist the UN.

'Second, I shall at once dispatch a UN team, including specialists, to disarm all nuclear weapons in your country and to dismantle and destroy them. If anyone asks, you have requested this to remove the threat of attack from other countries.

'Third, call your neighbour's president; she's a woman and will understand. Inform her of the first two decisions and state that you will remove the border and all troops and weapons between your two countries, allowing for free movement; inform her that the UN will supervise this.

'As soon as I have everything organised, I'll arrange a meeting between us with international press coverage.'

23

A week later, in the early morning, Meghali asked, 'Before I make breakfast, what's next?'

'The stampede scene, where the cattle are driven over the sodbusters to wreck their farms and maybe kill a few. No one blames crazed cattle for killing people. But there's always a warning stampede against one farmer before the big one.'

'Do you know anything more?'

'Nope, I can guess, but I'll send you links to several Facebook posts. So that you can form your own opinion.'

'Where?'

'I honestly don't know. There are several possible countries, but none have a significantly higher probability of being the correct one. If we knew the breed of cattle, we might guess.'

It took three years for the country to agree and organise free and fair elections under UN tutelage. Long before the elections, it became another example of a country with an ecologically minded government led by a woman.

'Five.'

'Five what, Patrick?'

'Five women promoted into positions of responsibility.

'How about a scene of our own, Meg?'

'What kind of scene?'

'One where I promote you into a position of responsibility.'

Mehali grinned. 'That might be a thrilling scene, but I'll need help.'

'I'll help; come here, you minx.'

...

'What's my expression, Meg?'

'Agony.'

'Not then, now.'

'Sort of happy and tender. What about mine?'

'I've never seen that expression before, so I don't know; you're smiling, your eyes twinkle, and I can see your teeth. I'll have to look up the smiley table for a name.'

Her smile widened. *I've never felt like this before, so I'll forgive Patrick.* 'Not what you see, but what you feel when you look.'

'Afraid, Meg, and I don't know why. – Uh oh, now it's tender.' He rolled so she was beside him, 'Kiss me.'...

In the CIA meeting room, a selection of photos, satellite, and TV shots lay on the table in front of each person. The video, a composite of both Satellite and TV output, displayed on a wall screen, had ended a minute earlier. The sequence covered the first appearance of the small cloud in the viewfinder to its final disappearance.

The Director spoke, 'Well, you've all seen it; you all have the photos. Has anyone anything to say?'

Meghali replied. No one around the table looked likely to speak...

'I've studied all the phenomena associated or thought to be

associated with the Storyteller as he's known. His story particularly impressed me; I've been through it line by line.

'No analyst has remarked on four words: *God does not intervene.* It seems to me that it is accurate, for apart from telling his story, which is not an intervention, few physical events have affected humans. Three terrorists became pigs, two of whom we know from accounts to be the direct result of a human female. Whether this is because Islam associates pigs with the devil, I don't know. From a Western viewpoint, we would all agree that pigs would be an apt description before they changed their outer shape.

'Jihadi terrorists were stripped naked. Their death was due to the townsfolk, although the ability, as reported, to turn an AK47 into a writhing snake implies a more straightforward solution was available; killing them or making them vanish.

'An army of a thousand Jihadis, entombed under a dune, is divine intervention, but I must emphasise it happened because three women prayed in front of witnesses, one of whom was our agent, and their recorded prayer request specified what happened.

'True, the Rio statue had a physical change, but it's a statue. The Catholic Church has declared it a divine intervention.

'Now, we have this last incident. Does anyone in the world outside of the Illustrious Leader's family circle consider his treatment undeserved? I don't think so. I believe this and the others have all been lessons, and I suspect they will end once the Storyteller thinks humanity has learnt them.

'I ask everyone here, imagine you were alone on earth with unlimited power; what would you do? I tried the exercise.

'I thought of changing all languages to one, so the world all spoke English.

'I thought of removing religious conflict by changing all religions to one.

'I thought of changing racial conflict by making everyone on the planet black.

'With unlimited power, those are minor tasks.

'Then I asked myself why he didn't and returned to the story. We have not paid attention to another group of words. Fortunately, the professor at McGill authored an article about the story. It stirred up academia for a while, but it focused my attention. He wrote:'

'All except the most bigoted know the truth of the message: "You are the only form of life to be destroying its world. It should be a source of shame to all."'

'The line is incomplete; it's an extract of this one:

"'This is the first planet where the inhabitants are destroying their world. Allah finds it shameful, but seeing what happens is of great interest; *the knowledge may help save other planets."*

'There is *only* one explanation. We, and all planets in our universe, are experiments, and the Storyteller cannot hinder our progress; he's trying to do the least amount possible to prevent us from destroying our world before God has fruitful results.

'Our world has no choice; we must do what the Storyteller says, and with all the power and facilities we can bring to bear.

'I then posed myself a question, and I can ask you all: what is the biggest threat to the planet's survival and civilisation?

'I find but one answer. Pollution. Whether it is nuclear waste, common chemical and physical pollution, or the heat that is warming the planet.

'I then asked what the Storyteller would do if we didn't comply with his message. I'll tell you what might happen. All carbon-based fossil fuels on Earth will eventually turn to stone or water, whether it is fuel oil, coal, or gas. The consequences for civilisation and governments will be enormous, but I suspect they will unfold over a few years. We should ensure that we cease using them as soon as possible to avoid any unwanted disruption. I suggest that the geologists check if the unexploited fields are still there; they may have already changed.

'Nuclear waste is something else. We have no technology to dispose of it, but imagine the political and social results if nuclear waste begins leaking into the environment. If we demonstrate maximum effort to find a permanent solution, we may be safe; without doing so, I think it may be a matter of time before the rain becomes radioactive, forcing it to happen. I could suggest a United Nations research program because it is a global problem.'

'A nice speech, Meghali, but what's going to happen next?'

'If you want me to play God, I shall. It will be worldwide, a message about pollution, and the first message will not be dangerous; I expect we are about to have the plastic bags our civilisation has discarded in the oceans returned to us.'

'How?'

'Rain, Director.'

'Shit, you want me to tell that to the President?'

'Director, say what you wish, but there is a pattern; I reckon this country comes next on God's list after one more country elects a woman president. Remember the line in the Storyteller's message, *If humanity can change, if women can impose an effort to care, this world may recover.'* If you don't want to wait for a hurricane to wipe out the South of the USA, I suggest you tell him. I hope we are not at the top of the list.'

'And make sure that when the plastic bags rain down, you have the minutes of this meeting to demonstrate the CIA is not sitting on its arse. Otherwise, you'll be sitting on yours in the wilderness.'

He didn't tell the President.

When Meghali arrived at Patrick's apartment that night, he could tell immediately that she was tense.

'Had a bad day, Meg?'

'I have one whenever I meet with a political appointee, but today was exceptional; one more, and I'll resign.

'I told the director that I hoped America was not at the top of the list and that when we are, we'll get our plastic bags rained on us.'

'Is that a guess?'

'I don't always know where my ideas come from. I informed the director that pollution was the greatest threat to the planet, and I mentioned carbon fuels and nuclear waste as key concerns. Your Facebook posts about the little boy collecting plastic bags might be why I thought of plastic bags. I'm sure you can get today's meeting minutes to read.'

'I shall, Meg, but your idea is exactly what the editor might write into the script for the next country. I'll suggest it won't be the US.'

'Why?'

'Because those Facebook posts were in Britain, and nowhere in the country is far from the sea. If there is a plastic rain scene, something must follow it, and the only clues I have are in Britain. But I have a reason that you will not believe. There is an election due in Britain in a few months.'

'What does that have to do with it?'

'In politics, it's known that the power shifts before the election to the electorate's opinion, and then returns after counting the votes to those of the winning party. The ecologists in Britain are already campaigning hard. It's the right moment to upset the applecart. Those in power must shift their public persona to reflect the electorate's opinion. Still, it's a delicately balanced shift; they must avoid pissing off the people they will need after re-election. A slight unexpected push can drastically change the outcome. If there's a chance that a woman could win the election, the Storyteller will intervene.

'But the editor can do whatever he wants. The Bible provides a detailed account of the ten plagues that afflicted Egypt. I have never thought any of them were divine interventions because scientists have suggested valid explanations. However, the Bible describes Moses as a prophet who, speaking on behalf of God, brought the plagues when the Pharaoh refused to allow the Hebrews to emigrate. We've had multiple demonstrations that the Storyteller is equally powerful. However, I suspect he's learnt more about this world than previous prophets did about theirs, so He's being careful.'

'Patrick, I'll finally believe you if England gets plastic bag rain, logic or not. Now feed me and then make me forget everything except tonight.'

'Meg, come into the bedroom, strip and lie on the bed; I can see your neck and shoulders need relaxing. Once you're loose, we'll eat.'

They ate reheated pizza slices *much* later while sitting naked on the bed.

Patrick read the meeting minutes and had an odd thought. *I wonder who else can read them?*

24

She was born in a small town in Wales, UK. After the ultrasound scan three months before her birth revealed the foetus had no penis, her parents had agreed that Susan was a nice name. With limited imagination but fervent patriotism, her parents instantly changed their choice to Charlotte Susan when she was born on the birthday of Princess Charlotte.

She grew up in her birthplace. An early sign of her character revealed itself when she first attended school. There were four Charlottes in the class, but Charlotte Susan was the only girl the teachers addressed as Charlotte. They used second names for the others, and no one ever tried to use Charly. With more intelligence than necessary to sail through school, she studied meteorology at university. When asked why she liked meteorology, her stock reply was straightforward: 'I walked to school and back every day for years. On a sunny morning, I would forget a raincoat or umbrella, and when I walked back home, unexpected rain drenched me. I've wanted to know if it will rain at four pm since childhood.' She knew the real reason; she liked integrating dozens of factors to build an image of tomorrow's weather.

She now worked for the National Meteorological Service in Exeter, which was close enough for her to make regular visits to her parents. Her home was a small house on Myrtlebury

Way, within walking distance of her work, along a picturesque path through a wooded area between two car parks. Although she was always confident in her forecasts, she was a practical person. She kept umbrellas in her office and home.

Charlotte had never married, for she rejected each suitor who asked, preferring an arrangement where she could return home from work whenever she wished to find a hot meal and the table laid. An ambitious suitor who failed to provide a tasty meal would find his suitcase outside the front door the next day.

Her forecast for Friday completed and posted to the Met website, Charlotte switched off her computer, shrugged on her coat – her forecast was light evening rain – and gathered her handbag; she was looking forward to the Thai red curry and white wine that Greg, her current guest had promised – she preferred *guest* to *lover* as she was not in love and rationed sex to when she needed a release. Her guest slept in the second bedroom. As Charlotte picked up her phone, it pinged. She opened the message, a news announcement from Reuters, titled *Plastic Rain*. Once she had read it, she switched on the computer again, then, while it booted up, removed her coat and sent an SMS to Greg.

I shall be late. Put the curry in the oven to keep warm.

The Reuters message reported that a few dozen plastic shopping bags floated down from the sky in a small town in the Netherlands, decorating the town square. – Charlotte looked at a map to find that it was east of Rotterdam.

As she had noted an unusual weather pattern earlier that day – an incursion of polar air into Europe that she thought might reach Britain, she decided to look again.

Like a long tongue, the incursion had advanced faster than she had expected. It appeared to be heading south of

Rotterdam and would cross the coast towards England, north of Belgium. If the airflow carried plastic bags, it would be dangerous to aircraft, so she decided to wait. An hour later, she called the Heathrow Met service office and spoke to Travis Grantham, who worked the night shift.

'Good evening, Travis, this is Charlotte.'

'Hello, Charlotte, nice to hear from you; what's up?'

'There's a polar air incursion on its way from the Netherlands; have you noted it?'

'Yes, but it's not too cold and very narrow; I don't think it will affect anything; we haven't done a TAF update for it. The Heathrow METAR is unchanged.'

'Well, a town in the Netherlands that it passed over has reported a few dozen plastic bags floating down. If it's carrying a load of bags, it might be a hazard to aircraft, so I called to ask if your radar has anything.'

Travis clicked the display button on his screen to show the current radar image to the northeast. 'It would be at extreme range, and nothing is showing, but I'll keep an eye on it and call if there's anything.'

'Okay, thanks, Travis. Call my cell; I'm going home for a few hours; the incursion should be north of you by three am.'

When Charlotte reached home, the curry was a warm, congealed soup, and Greg was not there. He had phoned the voluptuous blonde he had met two nights before in the pub. It took her four minutes to fill his case with clothes and place it under the covered step outside the front door. The door was like many others in cities, with two locks. One had a combination Charlotte could reset; she had the key to the second.

Charlotte picked out the best bits, reheated, ate, and went to bed.

Travis phoned at 03:12. 'Sorry to wake you, Charlotte, but you did ask. We have a dense radar reflection on a small patch to the north, a very odd phenomenon. London is still clear. At a guess, it looks like Birmingham might be affected.'

'Thanks, Travis; I'll go to the office and look at the radar image. Could you please share the radar picture with me? Speak to you later.'

She dressed in a tracksuit and ski jacket and jogged down the track, enjoying the cool night air that woke her senses. She fetched a coffee and biscuits while the computer system booted up and then sat down to review the data. After ten minutes, she called Birmingham airport at 03:27.

'Good morning, this is Exeter Met, Charlotte Jones.'

'Hi Charlotte, been some time. Lawrence Metcalfe here; what can I do for you?'

'Lawrence, there's a weather phenomenon east of you, approaching Birmingham. Do you have any flights coming in from the east?'

'Hang on, Charlotte,' she thought Lawrence was checking his inward flight schedule. 'Yes, I have a DHL from Frankfurt in twenty-five minutes.'

'Can you ask him if he has anything on his radar, probably low-level, and ask him to keep his eyes out for it as he approaches? Let me know if he does.'

Fifteen minutes later, at 03:43, Lawrence called Charlotte. 'The captain of the DHL flight has reported a very localised reflection at a low level that resembles a severe storm; he says he's never seen anything like it, but he'll pass over it.'

'Where is it?'

'A few kilometres east of Rugby.'

'If it reaches you, don't allow any aircraft to fly through it; it might have plastic bags and other stuff floating in it.'

Charlotte called the Rugby Central police station at 03:46.

'Good morning. Exeter Met Office here; I'm Charlotte Jones. We have a local storm showing on our system over the Rugby area. Can you tell me what the local conditions look like from the ground?'

'Hello, miss. Sergeant Pickle here; funny you should ask. It came over all dark a few minutes ago. I looked outside; the sky was very dark, and a thin drizzle had started. There's no wind, but plastic bags are floating down. The shopping kind. I picked up one; it has Sainsbury written on it.'

'Can you look again? Guess how many bags are lying in the street? I'll wait.'

She held on to the phone for three minutes until she heard the boots clumping, and the Sergeant spoke, 'There's a lot, miss, too many to count, spread out about one every two or three metres, all over.'

'Thanks, Sergeant; someone must pick them up, so you had better tell the authorities.'

She hung up, then called her contact at the BBC News desk. The BBC had interviewed her four or five times in the last three years.

'News desk, good morning. Can I help you?'

'Hello, Charlotte Jones, your favourite weather lady here.'

'Hello, Charlotte, why the call?'

'I thought you would want to know it's raining plastic bags in Rugby.'

'No joke?'

'No, I just talked to the police station.'

'Thanks, Charlotte; I'll send a photographer there immediately.'

Charlotte decided to run home, cook breakfast, and then watch the BBC's six am news. When she arrived home, the suitcase had gone.

The BBC News program riveted her. The photographer had done an excellent job, and the eerie sight of bags floating gently down, appearing from nowhere as they fell into the light of the street-lamps in complete silence, settling randomly on anything that caught them, fascinated her. The band at the bottom of the TV screen included 'By Charlotte Jones, Meteorology Consultant.'

She returned to bed, wondering what had caused it.

Her ringing phone woke her at nine am.

'Charlotte Jones.'

'Ms Jones, the Prime Minister's office here. Can you attend a meeting at number ten at twelve-thirty today?'

'I could if I were in London, but I'm in Exeter.'

'No problem, Ms Jones, if you can be at the Exeter airport at ten-thirty, an Air Force helicopter from St. Athan will bring you to London City airport, and a car will collect you there.'

She carried a small suitcase as she had no idea how long she would be away.

The car delivered her to number ten, and a porter showed her into a waiting room. She had already assumed her BBC tip-off had caused her invitation.

The Prime Minister had called for an emergency meeting, adding that he wanted Charlotte to attend. The Chief of Staff asked why.

'Because the whole country saw her name at the bottom of the BBC News, and unless we include her, it won't appear we are taking this seriously.'

Shown to a seat in the Cabinet room a few minutes later, she recognised the environment minister and then the Prime Minister. He introduced her to the Ministers of Industry, Home

Affairs, Science and Technology, and Agriculture.

The PM began the proceedings by asking her, 'Ms Jones, what can you tell us about the phenomenon that happened last night?'

'Prime Minister, a polar air mass flowed from the pole and narrowed into a thin tongue. Cold air sinks, so it remains low as the air mass above keeps it in place. It passed east of Rotterdam, curved to cross the channel, flowed across Norfolk, passed north of London, confirmed by Heathrow, and then petered out over Rugby, where it dissipated. I followed it from south of Rotterdam, and Heathrow also watched it because it might affect flights in and out of the airport.

'Somewhere, before Rotterdam, it picked up plastic bags because Reuters reported a short shower of bags, but I think it must have picked up more when it crossed our coast, for the Rugby police station collected a bag with Sainsbury's written on it.

'At no time was it a danger to air travel or people. That's all I can say about it professionally; anything else is guesswork and conjecture.'

'Ms Jones, you managed the situation competently. The Met Office can be proud of you, and I'll tell the Director how I feel. However, can I ask for your private opinion? Do you feel this is a naturally occurring phenomenon that will reoccur?'

'Prime Minister, I could, at a stretch, assume the airflow to be a natural phenomenon, although there is nothing like it in the history of meteorology; with no explanation, I must accept we don't know everything. However, I've no idea how a low-level air mass, travelling slowly, could pick up thousands of plastic bags or decide to dump them over Rugby, which is no hillier than the land it had passed over. Combining the two, I conclude this was completely unnatural. I feel that recurrence may depend on other factors.'

'Right, has anyone an inkling of who or what did it?'

After a minute's silence and a shaking of heads, Charlotte spoke again.

'Prime Minister, meteorologists watch for weather changes worldwide, and we all saw the whirlwind in the Middle East desert. We have concluded that it was impossible, and none of us agrees it was an act of God under the usual definition, which is a natural phenomenon occurring at an unexpected time, place, or strength. Instead, we accept that Divine Intervention occurred to send a message. What happened last night is in that category.'

'Does anyone agree or disagree?'

The Minister of the Environment claimed a lack of expertise, but the others said no. The Minister of Industry said, 'If Ms Jones thinks it is a message, can she tell us what it is?'

'Minister, I don't know; it would also be pure conjecture. The world attributed the desert whirlwind to an intervention by the Storyteller of Allah, as is the recent change to the statue of *Christ the Redeemer* in Rio, and the spectacular departure of the dictator in the far east. All we know about the Storyteller is the story he told and its message, which was to stop destroying the planet. We all know we have polluted the seas for decades and have discarded tons of plastic and plastic bags into the sea. The message is straightforward, yet twofold. *"Stop using plastic and discarding it in the ocean,"* but the method used to send the message is the other half. *"If you don't clean up the ocean, I can take all your pollution and drop it on your heads."'*

The Minister of Industry said, 'Prime Minister, our GDP would suffer an enormous hit if we banned plastic.'

'Is there an alternative?'

'Not that I know of.'

'Then you and Science had better collaborate and find one. We have five months until the general election, and if Ms Jones is right, we must take precautions now.'

'Has anyone anything else to say?'

Charlotte did. 'Prime Minister, we don't know anything about those plastic bags. Can someone collect a selection and give them to a lab to discover if there is anything about them that might indicate their age, where they have been, and anything else significant?'

'Science, that's a damn good suggestion; please do it.'

'Ms Jones, any other thoughts?'

'That the plastic collected in Rugby should not return to the sea.'

'Environment, make sure that happens.'

'Thank you all, especially you, Ms Jones. It has been a pleasure to meet you.'

25

Charlotte took the train to Cardiff and then went to her parents' home for the weekend. She bought four newspapers to read on the journey, all of which featured Rugby pictures.

One of them had a letter to the editor. Mrs Grundy complained that a savage creature had attacked her on her garden path. A passing student had saved her. He photographed the wild beast and posted it on his Facebook page. When Charlotte looked for it, she found a brown crab, missing its smaller claw, waving the other in the air with what looked like nylon tights wrapped around it and trailing behind.

A second paper had an interview with a retired gentleman. He had told the reporter, 'I was going home, walking along minding my own business, with my umbrella up 'cos it was raining, when this enormous fish fell out of the sky, hit my umbrella and broke it. Damned near knocked me flat; it did. What I want to know is who will pay for my umbrella.' Charlotte thought it fortunate that the reporter didn't ask why a retired gentleman was walking home at four in the morning. Instead, he had asked about the fish, a dead cod.

It was daytime in Washington, and Meghali arrived in Patrick's cubicle.

'Okay, Patrick, I'm a believer.'

'Oh, why?'

'Rugby, the town in England, has had light rain with plastic bags floating down. The BBC is running the story in a continuous loop.'

'Have you other reports, Meg?'

'Not yet. The Prime Minister has called for a Cabinet Meeting; I should have a list of attendees by ten am and a copy of the minutes by one pm. They don't report chit-chat but will tell us what happened as the Prime Minister must inform the ministers.'

'I'll watch and record the BBC announcement.'

'Okay, I'll send you anything I receive. Believing makes my job easier; I'll reference and investigate every name I note to spot anyone trying to wreck the Storyteller's task.'

That night, Meghali told Patrick. 'There's an odd actress in the English movie.'

'What does odd mean?'

'She's a meteorologist based in Exeter, far from London, but she was at the Prime Minister's meeting.'

'What's her name?'

'Charlotte Jones.'

'Was she mentioned in the BBC broadcast?'

'I don't think so. We can rerun it and listen.'

...

'Meg, she's not mentioned, but look at the caption at the bottom. The BBC quotes her as a consultant. I'll bet the Prime Minister included her in his meeting because if she was not there thousands of voters would want to know why he didn't ask the expert.'

'Okay, I missed that. Will the Prime Minister invite her again?'

'Yes, if there's a rain incident somewhere else. If there is, it'll be a new scene. I call it *The Gathering of the Force.*'

'What's that, Patrick?'

'It's when two or three people, farmers usually, set out to seek justice, and as they ride towards the town, others join them. The editor cuts in all sorts of people, some with wooden legs, others with eyepatches, old and young. The scene demonstrates determination: the baddies had better surrender or go elsewhere. The next rain will have gathered much more than plastic bags in this context. Right now, how about some determination to achieve a successful result?'

'After dinner, Patrick. I brought sushi with me.'

'Who's she? And is she beautiful?'

Meghali threw herself at him. The sushi had to wait.

On Monday morning, when Charlotte returned to her office, she found an email from the CIA in her inbox. It contained links to two Facebook pages and the sender's name, Meghali Azzaro. Charlotte looked her up on Google and then reviewed her Facebook posts. She thought of phoning Meghali, but checked the time difference. Meghali would be sleeping.

Rob Butler was sitting with his colleagues in the Edible Bags rumble room. Morry announced, 'Guys, we must decide if we are making bags to save the planet, or food to eat. I vote for saving the planet.'

Moments later, Simone, the sole employee who functioned as secretary and performed many other tasks, came and said they had a visitor.

They went to the reception area to meet a young man in a suit. Rob recognised him immediately; he had met him as a student at activist meetings. 'Henry, what a surprise. Have you come to see me?'

Rob introduced him to his colleagues. 'Henry Johnson, a fellow activist.'

After handshakes all around, Henry said, 'Actually, Rob, I'm now doing my best for ecology from the Department of the Environment, and I didn't know you were here.'

'So, how can we help you, Henry?'

'The foundation that gave you a grant for development suggested I see you; I'm trying to discover how to replace plastic bags.'

They told him, handed over samples, let him eat one, demonstrated its uses, and then took him to the rumble room. The secretary had done a quick clean and tidy, so they sat around the table while the secretary made tea and coffee.

'Henry, what do you think of what we've shown you?'

'First, my congratulations. Second, apply for your patent immediately; do not wait; if you want to add variations to the patent, do so; if you can think of different uses, do so. The patent is worth a lot, and you must do it now.'

'I'm not sure we can afford it.'

Henry dug into his jacket pocket, produced a small book, flipped the pages, and said, 'Write this down.' When the secretary had her notepad in front of her, he provided them with the name of a legal firm, Fitzgerald, Smithers, and Bellingham, along with its address and telephone number. Then he took his phone from another pocket and tapped in the number. They heard him say, 'Henry Johnson, Ministry of the Environment, Mr Bellingham, please.'

After a short pause, he said, 'Good morning, Mr Bellingham. I have the Director and owner of Edible Bags with me. The Ministry will support an immediate provisional patent application; we request that you file it tomorrow or the day after. Can you meet Rob Butler, the owner, tomorrow morning?'

After a pause, he said, 'Thank you, Mr Bellingham. Nine am then. We shall be there.'

Turning to Rob, he said, 'That's it. Now, collect some samples and write up a description of how you make them. You can say how and from what. There are no secrets between you and your lawyer. Then, draw up a list of things, such as cups, containers, wrapping, and things that use plastic, that a manufacturer could replace with your material. Think carefully about it. Bring that with you and meet me at that address in London before nine am tomorrow. Bring a suitcase, be ready to stay in London until the weekend.'

'Then what will happen?'

'Bellingham will draft and apply for a provisional patent to give you worldwide cover for a year and file for permanent ones as soon as possible. He'll offer you a contract for patent management and protection of commercial rights. Additionally, demand that they register the trademark and copyright the names 'Edible Bag' and 'Bags'. You have stamped the bags you showed me with a blue dolphin logo. Request that the trademark be registered and copyright-protected as well. Please remember the plural; they should do so anyway. You can license manufacturing to existing bag manufacturers with the protection the lawyer supplies. There will be complicated legal agreements; leave that to the lawyers. You won't manufacture any bags. Your job will be researching and policing the quality of the material and bags produced according to your patents.'

'Whew, we must take this one thing at a time.'

'Yes, but at some point, you must employ someone to manage reporters unless one of you does it, but ask a farmer to keep a cow, pig, and chickens in a yard nearby. Nothing will work better than showing a reporter and camera the animals eating your product, especially fish.' He grinned at them. 'Offer them a bag salad too!'

'Right. Simone, have you recorded all that?'

'All noted, Rob.'

Rob asked, 'What's the market, Henry?'

'For shoppers' carry-bags, very little; they can and do use cloth bags. I expect a few million tons monthly for supermarket and food packaging.'

Rob was on time the following day – after a sleepless night, he slept on the train.

Five days after it rained bags in Rugby, Travis Grantham dropped his girlfriend off at her flat in Knightsbridge after their evening at the theatre during his night off. They had continued with dinner, then a nightclub, so much later, after one am, he drove away from her door in Myddelton Square Gardens. Travis was a careful driver, so even though the streets were empty on his way to his Hammersmith apartment, Travis obeyed the speed limit and stopped at every red light. He wasn't concentrating on driving; the few rain spots hitting the windscreen reminded him that the weather forecast was light rain.

However, Travis didn't lose focus on the question in his mind. Did he want to move out of the flat he shared with Mike and move in with Anne? He had asked Mike for his opinion, and the reply had been sharp and short, 'If you must ask, don't.' He felt he should be contemplating marriage at thirty-two, although he didn't want to change.

He switched on his windscreen wipers as the rain increased. The first scrapes of the wipers made the visibility much worse, so he slowed and switched on the windscreen washer. It improved things, but a dirty collection of grey sludge had collected at the bottom of the windscreen. He touched his brakes and felt the ABS vibrate under his foot, just as it would on an icy road. He allowed the car to drift to a stop at the side of

Rosebery Avenue. It wasn't cold; the temperature reading on the screen was twelve degrees, so why had the ABS kicked in?

Travis forgot Anne as he had a problem to solve. Why had the ABS triggered? Opening the door, then reaching out to the windscreen, he collected a handful of the greyish sludge.

It wasn't ice. It seemed to be a greasy sludge holding hundreds of minute flakes. As Travis rubbed his fingers together, he could feel the slipperiness.

The airport meteorological office was open twenty-four hours a day. Travis called the duty officer and explained what he had found, then ended the call saying, 'I've no idea how widespread it is; call some fire departments and the Police, ask them to go outside and check. It's a definite hazard on the road and will be on the runway; cars may slide all over the place in less than an hour if it continues.'

Travis wiped his fingers on a tissue, reached for the door handle to close the door, and stopped halfway, amazed when the street lighting and headlights lit up several thong sandals swooping down from the sky. A woman's nylon panties landed on the bonnet.

Travis drove the rest of the way carefully.

26

Simultaneously, a truck carrying ten tons of refrigerated meat drove down the A40 into London; its destination was Smithfield Market. The driver followed the route he took at least twice a week; it should have been easy to spot the turnoff into Snow Hill Road, but the muck on the windscreen made it difficult, for his washers had run out of water after continued use since reaching London. As he passed over Farringdon Street, easily visible from the overpass out the side window, he slowed down to a walking pace. He opened the side window, which gave him a better view of the roadside and allowed him to follow the wall peeling off to the left as Snow Hill came into view. He turned slowly into the downhill off-ramp, then stamped on the brake pedal when he saw a large black mass blocking the road. The truck skidded and swung slowly left until the rear hit the central island.

The driver now couldn't see what was blocking the road, so he opened the door and climbed down from the cab; then, at the front of the truck, in the light given by the headlights and the truck's flashing hazard warning lights, he stood bemusedly looking at a whale lying across the road.

He did what any sensible Londoner would do. He dialled 999 on his phone.

'Emergency service, what service do you want?'

'I don't know, the one that removes dead whales from the street.'

'Sir, this is not a joke line. Do you want an emergency service?'

'Yes, the police.'

'You're being connected.'

'Metropolitan police, can I help you?'

'I drive a truck, and I deliver meat to Smithfield. My lorry is jammed across the road on Snow Hill, blocked by a dead whale, and the road is slippery.'

Fortunately, the police officer was well-trained.

'What is the number plate, sir?'

'The whale doesn't have one.'

'The number plate of your truck, sir.'

'BD51 SMR'

He typed it in as he heard it, and the computer showed him a ten-ton delivery truck.

'Thank you, sir; a squad car is on its way now.'

'Tell him to be bloody careful; oil or something covers the road.'

'Thank you, sir. I shall do. You say there is a dead whale across the road?'

'Bloody well is, must be several tons, dunno where it came from, maybe fell off a truck.'

'Can you see a police car yet, sir?'

'No, I can hear a siren, though. Yes, there it comes. Tell the driver he's going too bloody fast.'

The police car slowed, then managed to stop metres before hitting the back of the truck. One police officer opened the boot and started placing warning cones with flashing yellow lights across the road, far away from the police car and truck. The other officer approached the truck driver.

'Good morning, sir. Where's this whale?'

The driver pointed. The silence lasted several seconds, then the constable exclaimed, '*Holy shit!*'

'Yeah, that's what I thought.'

'I must call this in.' He returned to the police car and began talking on the radio. His colleague donned a yellow jacket and took several more cones up the road to warn on-coming vehicles.

Within a few minutes, the public works people were leaving their beds, as was the veterinary service, and several more police and fire department vehicles were on site. The trucker said to the officer beside him, 'I'm not going to stand anymore in this mucky rain; tell me when you want me to move,' then climbed back in his cab, removed his sticky wet jacket, pulled on his spare, and opened a thermos of coffee.

The warnings went out over the radio following a red alert from the meteorological office. It repeated every ten minutes from three am, warning all drivers of London's slippery road conditions. The police had phoned every borough around London; they had a list of affected areas; the warning applied to a part of Central London. Heathrow, oddly, was unaffected, nor was London City Airport.

There were some interesting phenomena. A hundred and twenty-two thong sandals decorated Trafalgar Square: one teetered on a lion statue. The person who phoned in the report said they had fallen gently from the sky, behaving like gliders, doing loops and rolls as they descended. He didn't mention the two figures sheltering under the National Gallery entrance; the young girl had clapped her hands when the sandal landed on the lion.

The early papers had nothing; the newspapers must print them the evening before. The late editions published at dawn were full of stories. By nine o'clock, the BBC news and special newspaper editions included much more information.

Uniformed men had collected buckets of the slime and flakes off the streets as the rain had stopped. Fish glue can be tenacious when it dries. The buckets went to several university laboratories for analysis.

An email arrived on the London Mayor's desk; he read that chaos would happen within minutes if it rained. The solution was to wash the roads, so the mayor called in the fire department. The city had few tanker trucks; Harry Drummer had to work twelve-hour shifts.

That afternoon, the Prime Minister answered questions in the House of Commons in Parliament. Several members representing London boroughs placed urgent applications on the Speaker's desk. However, the Leader of the Opposition was the first to stand and speak.

'Would the Prime Minister enlighten the members by telling us what he intends to do with the whale found this morning in London?' He then sat; sitting down is the accepted signal that there is nothing more to say.

The Prime Minister stood and replied most unusually, 'I intend to do nothing, as I have yet to decide. However, I'm sure the Right Honourable Leader of the Opposition can help by telling me what he thinks needs doing,' then sat.

The Leader of the Opposition, somewhat taken aback, made a weak reply. 'I would think the Prime Minister would at least be able to report on what investigations the government is undertaking.'

'I can assure the Right Honourable Leader of the Opposition

that investigations are ongoing and will continue until I know more; I regret I cannot satisfy his curiosity.'

The first university reports arrived at the Prime Minister's office later. He called a cabinet meeting at nine pm. This time, he requested Charlotte and instructed the Chief of Staff to arrange for a flat in Kensington until after the crisis. He asked the Lord Mayor of London to attend.

The Lord Mayor had no choice, named as he was by title.

Charlotte had a second helicopter ride. The pilot was a squadron leader; she thought him handsome.

PM: 'Ladies and Gentlemen, the analysis of what fell on us last night is precise and identical for all samples from different London boroughs. The report states that it is ninety-five per cent seawater and plastic waste, ranging from minute particles to a few new bags. Ninety per cent, they say, by volume, is the remains of plastic bags of all types.

'The report suggests filtering polluted seawater would produce the same gunk, and the dead fish, the whale, the plastic and rubber sandals, and pieces of fishing line and fishnet are collateral items.

'The whale was a young Orca, which the veterinarian says died due to a ball of plastic bags and a fishnet in its intestines.

'Charlotte, good to have you back again; is this another Rugby?'

'I don't think there is any doubt about it, Prime Minister. A similar message, but with a different emphasis.'

'What?'

'The last time I said the message was *"If you don't clean up the ocean, I have the power to take all your pollution and drop it on your heads."* This time, as there has been no visible reaction, it's to emphasise that it's not plastic bags alone that will fall on our heads, but a lot more. We must consider everything we have dumped in the sea over centuries.'

'Why centuries?'

'Whereas most pollution might have degraded in a hundred years, sunken wrecks that have lain in the sea for centuries are still found. Some pollution lasts much longer, like concrete-encased poisonous or radioactive chemical waste drums. Some, such as thousands of containers lost from ships for varying reasons, may not release their contents until they have corroded away.'

'Does anyone have a suggestion?'

After a minute's silence, Charlotte said, 'Make an announcement, Prime Minister, anything that makes it clear Britain intends to stop polluting the ocean and will do it immediately. Like a total ban on plastic shopping bags, people can use cloth ones. You may need to compensate some manufacturers in the interim, but it might stop a further deluge.'

A typical politician, the Minister of Home Affairs, said, 'Prime Minister, I agree with Charlotte. Think of this speech line: "Everyone feels immense pleasure when the Orca at Sea World entertains us; we are British and not a cruel people; the Orca found yesterday in London died in terrible agony with a stomach full of plastic bags. I ask people to use reusable bags for shopping out of compassion and kindness. I shall place an immediate ban on the use of plastic ones."'

The prime minister thought. 'Needs some work, but it's acceptable. I agree; I'll go ahead.

'Lord Mayor, are you cleaning up the mess?'

'Yes, Prime Minister, we have a problem washing down the streets; the fire department must do their best, but if you want the plastic content kept from the sea, we must re-route or pump the rainwater drains to a settling dam, not the Thames.'

'Charlotte, is that necessary?'

'I'm sure it is, Prime Minister; it would be better to do so than risk its return in the next rain.'

After the meeting, Charlotte put on her coat, and the Chief of Staff approached her. 'Charlotte, is the apartment satisfactory?'

'Oh yes, it's comfortable and well placed. I must do some shopping and settle in.'

'Excellent. The Prime Minister asks if you'll agree to a secondment to the Prime Minister's office as an advisor and consultant. I'm afraid there will be many reporters and ongoing publicity, so you should have an official position and status.'

'And I must not talk to the press, I suppose?'

'Yes, sorry, that too. But it will mean less hassle.'

'Okay, I agree.'

It was daytime in Washington, and Meghali was in Patrick's cubicle. 'Patrick, have you watched the BBC news?'

'The whale?'

'Yes, that and the other stuff. I expect to receive a meeting report later this evening. You were right again.'

'It has happened in a thousand movies, Meg; it was an easy forecast. Have you found a second odd actor?'

'Yes, a man called Travis Grantham called in the Meteorology warning broadcasts to London.'

'What's odd about him?'

'He works at Heathrow. The Meteorology system records all phone and radio calls that warn them about weather incidents. Charlotte called him early before the first plastic rainfall, and he called her back shortly before it fell. Is it an accident that he's involved in the second incident?'

'You're trying to find a human link, Meg, when a possible one is staring at you. I'll load the first meeting report again.'

....

'There, Charlotte said, *"or decide to dump them over Rugby."* What time did Travis call her, and when did the rain begin?'

Meghali checked her file. '03:12 in the morning, and the rain fell at 03:45.'

'At what time did he initiate the London broadcasts?'

Meghali checked, '01:28 from his car, on Rosebery Avenue, not far from the whale.'

'Okay, Meg, I need something about Travis. Have you checked him out? Has he done anything associated with the sea?'

'I've got his history. He has a master's degree in meteorology awarded by Sussex University. That's in Brighton, by the sea.'

'Can you find his master's thesis?'

'I have the title, *"The effect of inshore currents on local weather"*. How does that help.'

'I'll give you my analysis of facts that would justify the scenario they experienced. The Editor decided to try rain with plastic bags. There's no point without publicity, and Heathrow, a mega airport, has a Met department open 24/7. He sent the rain and then monitored the Heathrow personnel. Charlotte called Travis. It was unexpected, but he focused his attention on Travis. When Travis called Charlotte, he decided to route the rain around Heathrow and drop the bags. That's why it fell on Rugby. He had drawn the attention of two people who could publicise it. For the second rain, after learning that Travis has studied ocean currents, he decided to drop a whale next to him. The whale missed, but Travis got the rest. I'll bet both will be further involved.'

'Patrick, you have a gift for creating a plausible story. What happens next?'

'I'll bet He will activate the crabs and the octopus; what they will do, we will soon learn. Shall we visit a restaurant for dinner tonight?'

'If it's vegetarian. I couldn't eat seafood.'

'Then I'll meet you at your apartment.'

27

The small port of Bridlington is home to a fleet of small fishing boats. They catch lobsters and crabs using traditional lobster and crab traps, a type of trap developed centuries ago. It's not unique to Bridlington; boats go to sea every day around the coasts of Britain and Ireland. At least on the days when the weather is good enough to haul up a basket, remove the lobsters or crabs from the trap, insert a new bait, and lower the pot back to the seafloor. Bridlington, known as the lobster capital of East Yorkshire, depends on the catch.

Each evening, trucks, some from far away in Europe with water tanks on the back, some local vans and pickups, some just the chef from a nearby restaurant, gather on Gummers Wharf to receive the catch from the returning boats. The industry contributes a hundred and thirty million pounds to the GDP of Britain.

On Monday, after Charlotte returned from a weekend in Exeter, Grampa Hinton met the first boat home to tie up. He came when he needed to, about once every three days. Retiring after a lifetime as a fisherman, Grampa had traded on his reputation as a lucky fisher for years. He met the first boat home and received a free lobster or crab for dinner.

He was disappointed that day. 'How's the catch, Andy?' He asked the owner.

'Nothing, Grampa, nary a single crawler. The pots were crammed full of plastic bags.'

'I never *seed* that before.'

'Nor me, but it was a wasted day.' Turning to his crew, Andy said, 'Jimmy, go down the wharf and fetch some big rubbish bags; we'll pack the plastic and put it in the waste collection container.'

'Sorry, Grampa, maybe you'll be luckier with one of the other boats.'

He wasn't, apart from a dead crab or two; none of the boats had a live catch, but they all had plastic bags.

The fishers discussed the day in the pub that night. They agreed that it must have been due to an odd current in the bay that had brought the plastic bags to their pots. One of them said there must be tons of them in the sea.

None of them agreed with one old salt who said, 'I reckon the beasties have it in for us; they packed my pots real tight.' A much younger man said, 'Come on, Dad. Next, you'll tell us they will climb aboard and eat us alive.'

There was laughter when Dad replied, 'If they ate you, it would be no loss, but I expect the ones that do will fall ill.' It earned him an extra beer.

After catching nothing for four days, the fishermen were angry, the town was worried, and the mayor was frightened. Newspaper reporters were photographing the mountain of plastic bags at the dump and interviewing everyone, including those who knew nothing but were willing to talk. The mayor visited the Member of Parliament for Bridlington. Like most Yorkshiremen, he was blunt. 'If the government doesn't do something, we have a revolution coming.' The opposition party had already scheduled a political rally at the town hall.

The member promised to ask a question in the House of Commons next Wednesday during the Prime Minister's question time.

Two ports on either side of Bridlington had pots stuffed with plastic bags the next day, and as each day passed, the problem spread further.

The Prime Minister called another cabinet meeting. Knowing what it was about, Charlotte called the CIA and asked for Meghali. She did check the time difference; she called at two o'clock.

'Meghali Azzaro.'

'Good morning Meghali, Charlotte Jones in England.'

'Charlotte, I wondered when you would call; I've been following the English news.'

'Meghali, I need some advice. I looked at the Facebook links you sent, and now the Prime Minister wants my advice tomorrow, and I'm way out of my depth. Can you help?'

'Possibly; what do you want to know?'

'Well, do you know what is happening? Why have we had a downpour of plastic bags, and why are the lobster pots stuffed with them? I told the Prime Minister that the bag rain was a message to stop using plastic; he did ban plastic shopping bags, but what do I tell him now?'

'Charlotte, please take what I say as guesswork; I have a brilliant guy who works for me. He sometimes has what appears to be crackpot ideas, but we do agree that your rain was a message and that the Storyteller is behind it. We also believe the Storyteller doesn't want to annoy the population or injure them. The rain was to show that he was around. Patrick, my aide, thinks the Storyteller will attack the economy and, therefore, the government until the government acts. As nutty as it seems, he believes the Facebook pages show that sea life will bring pollution from the sea for people to collect and throw away. That's what the sea life is doing with the crab pots.

'He says the Prime Minister must publicly ban the *manufacture* of plastic and that he must declare a beach every few kilometres around Britain to be a waste collection site and clean it daily. I've no idea how you can persuade the government to do this without you and them appearing crazy.

'I don't think it will die away; the plastic and rubbish in lobster traps will now start spreading north and south from Bridlington until every crab and lobster trap in Britain fills daily with plastic bags. When Britain learns how to deal with it, it will go to Europe, America, and the rest of the world.

'It's the beginning. If I'm right, we still have plastic shoes and buckets, plastic boxes and wrappings, bottles and toys, and only the Storyteller knows what.

'I sympathise with your problem, but stand up and tell them. Here's an association that might help. Humanity has trained dogs to fetch a ball and return it to us. Can we train sea life to collect our pollution? Study the intelligence of sea life to understand octopus, mammals, lobsters and even crabs' behaviour.'

'Thanks, Meghali, I shall.'

'Call back and let me know how it goes.'

Charlotte took the evening train to London, where a chauffeured car took her to her apartment in Kensington. The chauffeur said he would call the following day at eleven.

She called Travis at Heathrow; she had never met him but knew he had studied ocean currents and didn't know who else to call.

'Travis Grantham, good evening.'

'Travis, Charlotte again.'

'Hi Charlotte, it was an interesting event you gave me last time. What do you have this time? Raining bicycles?'

'Nothing so ordinary; I need to know which beaches around England will likely have close onshore currents at depths less than fifteen or twenty metres.'

'Whew, you do ask some interesting questions. Why did you call me?'

'Because I know it's your hobby.'

'How do you know that?'

'As long as you don't assume I have a crush on you, I looked you up in the employee files. It's all there, including your master's thesis.'

'Oh, I forgot it was there. I might be able to help you.'

'Then tell me how I can discover if crabs bring plastic bags and stuff onto the beaches.'

'Oh, whew again. You can't, Charlotte, but the Air Force can help if someone tells them to fly low-level photographic passes along the beaches just before sunrise, after sunset, and on clear nights with a full moon. That's when the crabs will be active.'

'Thanks, Travis. Are you still working nights?'

'This is my last night; I have tomorrow off, then I go on days for a month.'

'Give me your cell number, please; I might have something that interests you.'

At eleven-thirty, she entered Number Ten.

The meeting now included the Minister of Defence, who introduced himself. Charlotte took her notepad from her bag and laid it on the desk.

'Charlotte, you know everyone, so let's start the day's business. Have you followed the events in Bridlington?'

'Yes, Prime Minister, with great interest.'

'You said it was a message when we had a plastic bag manifestation. How is it happening now, and what do you say is the message?'

'Prime Minister, I don't know how it is happening, although I can guess. I have two Facebook posts I would like you to see.' She opened the notepad and passed it to him.

After reading the posts, he passed them to the Minister next to him, and they circulated the table; once everyone had seen them, he asked, 'Charlotte, I don't know if you can use the meteorology computer system to search for data other than mete-orological data. I doubt you have the personal computer capacity to track Facebook posts. How did you find these?'

'Prime Minister, the CIA Director of Analysis is a friend. She knows everything that has happened in England, and as these are English posts, they are not a CIA secret. She sent me the links.'

The Prime Minister had to think this over; for Charlotte to have a connection in the top echelons of the CIA was a shock. 'So, what do you think of the posts?'

'I don't think they are false; I suggest you ask someone to check. If crabs and an octopus can deliver bags to a five-year-old to throw in a dustbin, they can stuff plastic bags into crab and lobster traps.'

'That's certainly a logical conclusion, whether true or not. How would we prove it?'

'The Air Force can help. Low-level photographic passes along the beaches just before sunrise, after sunset, and on clear nights with a full moon. That's when the crabs will be active.'

'You at least provide sensible and practical suggestions, Charlotte. Defence, please do so immediately.'

'And the other half of my question, Charlotte, what is the message now?'

'My CIA friend says her analysts believe the Storyteller does not intend to inflict harm on ordinary people. So, my original thought that the message was *"ban plastic or I'll drop it on your heads"* was, I'll admit, wrong. But that doesn't apply to governments. The message is for the government, specifically for you. *"If you don't stop polluting the ocean and clean up the mess, the ocean will ruin your economy.'*

Silence reigned until the Prime Minister said, 'First, you suggest a crazy idea that lobsters are stuffing traps with plastic bags, then you say they are out to ruin the economy. The members would roll laughing in the aisles if I said that in Parliament, but let me give you a chance to suggest something sensible. What do you suggest is the solution?'

'Prime Minister, I said what I did, anticipating your reaction, but it is what I believe. Do you have a dog? If not, does anyone here have a dog?'

'This becomes odder by the minute. I have a dog, not here, a Collie at my country house.'

'And does it fetch a ball when you throw it?'

'Yes, but what has this to do with plastic bags?'

'Have you been to the circus and a Marine Park?'

'Yes, to both. I have a clue of what you're trying to say.'

'You know that marine life, dogs, donkeys, and horses are trainable, as are many other animals and birds. Have you noticed that when the person who feeds the fish approaches their tank or aquarium, all the fish gather at the side? What is so surprising to think that something that can turn a man into a pig or create a whirlwind that rises to the stratosphere can teach a lobster a simple task like stuffing plastic bags into a trap?'

'You have a point. That explains why you think that. But how do you suggest we stop it?'

'Don't try. Ban plastic totally, except for exceptional cases. And then train the sea life to bring the pollution onto specific beaches for collection and treatment.'

'How do you propose we do that?'

'If you ban plastic, the Storyteller will know it. Then, designate a beach every few kilometres along the coast, starting with one on each side of Bridlington, and arrange for a daily clean-up. You'll find a heap of things to collect each day, and the heap will grow; simultaneously, the other beaches will remain at a low pollution level, and lobsters will stop stuffing traps.'

'So, you think a pristine beach will be an attraction, like food in a fish tank?'

'If you want to think of it like that, yes.'

'Maybe you aren't as crazy as I first thought. Have we found a replacement for plastic, gentlemen?'

The Minister of Science and Technology answered, 'Environment has told me of a startup company that makes bags from some plant materials; they are edible. Users don't need to throw them away; they can feed them to pets, chickens, and the farmyard. Fish become frenzied when fed fragments. Anything leftover doesn't need composting; it is dug directly into a flower bed.'

PM: 'Can humans eat them?'

Environment: 'They eat them, cut in strips instead of lettuce in their canteen.'

'Science, have you checked on the report?'

'We are going tomorrow, Prime Minister.'

'Industry, you go with them. I want a report tomorrow evening.'

'Certainly, Prime Minister.'

Charlotte asked, 'Prime Minister, can I go with them? It might give me ideas.'

'Of course, Charlotte. Industry, take Charlotte with you.'

'Environment and Home Affairs: Find beaches and organise cleaning. Then, science and Industry will find a way to treat and dispose of it. It's urgent; an election is coming. I would like to know how much of this we might need to manage.

'Charlotte, can you ask the CIA if they have any idea?'

'Yes, Prime Minister, I also have a colleague at the Heathrow Met office who specialises in coastal currents. He might be of help to the Ministry in choosing beaches. I'll give his number to the Minister.'

'People, we have made progress. We are meeting tomorrow at nine pm.'

28

When Charlotte returned to her flat in Kensington, she called Meghali and told her about the meeting.

'Fantastic, Charlotte, well done. Regarding the figures, I have a meeting next Friday at the Scripps Institute in San Diego. I would like to know the numbers for the United States. I can ask for the UK numbers, but if you want to attend the meeting, you're welcome; I would like to meet you.'

Charlotte said she would consider it.

The next evening, after the visit to Edible Bags, the meeting was short. Charlotte met the Minister of Fisheries.

PM: 'Science, what did you discover?'

Minister of Science: 'We are fortunate; the non-plastic material does everything they say. So far, they have made bags. However, they have made food containers to replace supermarket packaging and disposable cups. They are strengthening the liner for hot drinks; I learnt it resembles the glue made from fish bones. They said they would make a hot drink cup that lasted an hour; we drank our coffee in the mugs, and they told us to eat them after drinking. The mugs weren't bad tasting. I expect they will go to the farmers. They are researching a replacement for the PET bottle, but can't estimate when they will succeed. Perhaps a different strategy, at least temporarily, is required.'

The PM laughed, 'That must have been interesting.' In a cheerful tone, he asked the Minister of Industry, 'How long before we can bring this into service?'

'I'm sure we must convert existing manufacturers. The first one will take perhaps three months. If you shut down all plastics overnight, we will have chaos. Declare a total ban on plastic or plasticised carry bags; people can use regular cloth bags or buy them in the shops. Rubbish bags will be a problem, but waste collection services must find a solution to this issue. Politically, we can sell it to help the fishers and put lobster back on the dining table. The supermarket packaging must follow once we have sufficient raw material produced daily. I doubt we can achieve that in less than six months.'

Charlotte interjected, 'Prime Minister, the alternative is a ban on carry-bags of all types, give a tighter schedule for supermarket packaging, and leave people using cloth bags forever.'

PM: 'That's good thinking. Industry, how much money do you need?'

Industry: 'I can obtain figures for you in a few days; we can loan the capital needed for the conversion. It means we need not restrict the amount, but we must support the labour force at the factories until they are in operation, which will be a straightforward cost to the fiscus.'

'Finance, have you a comment?'

'No, Prime Minister, we will lose much more if the lobster industry crashes. I can suggest that PET bottles become returnable. Tax all new bottles produced or imported at one pound a bottle; recyclers can reimburse the deposit to those who return their bottles.'

'Then meet with Home Affairs and propose. I'll announce the carry-bag ban and say we intend to replace plastic packaging. It's full steam ahead. Now, how is the beach research doing?'

Environment: 'The man Ms Jones gave me is excellent; I'll arrange to second him to Environment from the Met office until further notice. We will clear two beaches for daily cleaning with existing machinery; he suggests asking manufacturers to propose special equipment. Home affairs must organise transport to a collection zone in collaboration with the mayors. Once we know what we are collecting and how much, Science will propose a treatment plant. I'm afraid it will take a few weeks to complete a list of beaches around the country because Travis must visit them, and we may need some help from the Minister of Fisheries to check on currents.'

Fisheries: 'Tell me what you want to do; I have a thousand boats and fishers who will do it immediately.'

PM: 'I'll not announce the beaches project; let's keep that close for the moment, for when we need to, but tell the people on-site it's an experiment in beach cleaning methods. Thank you, everyone. I'll notify you of the next meeting.'

Travis called the following evening at six.

'Hi Fruitcake, I owe you at least a dinner. Are you free tonight?'

'That's a very flattering way to say hello.'

'Well, at the Ministry today, I learnt what you told the Prime Minister; it's the only description that fits.'

'I must think up one for you after we meet. Where and when – it will solve my food problem.'

'Do you like Italian?'

'Yes, almost anything.'

'Olives, 140 Gloucester Road. I have a car; I can pick you up, or you can take a taxi.'

'My apartment is on Stanhope Gardens; wait a moment while I look on Google.' After a minute, she said, 'It's close by; I'll walk.'

'Okay then, seven-thirty or eight?'

'I'm hungry. Seven-thirty.'

'It's a date; how do I recognise you?'

'Oh, that's easy; I look like a meteorologist, one metre sixty-seven and eighty kilos, brown hair, knock knees and flat feet, with a bent nose and thick-lensed spectacles on eyes of different colours, brown and green.'

'*Whee!* A film star. I'll see you there.'

Charlotte recognised him from his Facebook photo as soon as she stepped through the door. He had blonde hair, was one-eighty-five tall, and weighed about eighty kg, but he had a more rugged look than the photo. She smiled at him. It might have been the smile, but he immediately knew her and stepped forward. 'Your description was perfect; you look just like a fruitcake. I'm pleased to meet you, Charlotte.'

'Likewise, Travis, the web says the food is good here, and I'm starving.'

A waiter showed them to a table, and they didn't waste any time before choosing from the menu. It took a moment to agree on a Chianti.

'Why do you owe me a dinner, Travis?'

'I'm now on secondment to the Ministry, with a big jump up in my salary.'

'I heard from the Minister that he had taken you on, not about the salary. You know that I'm now an advisor and consultant to the Prime Minister?'

'Not officially, but I read the papers and watch the news. No one has sworn me to silence, but I imagine you have been because I haven't seen or heard any direct quotes from you.'

'It's all new to me, but I'm trying to toe the line because it's interesting. I've already changed my opinion of the Prime Minister.'

'In what way?'

'I thought he was a typical politician, making vague speeches, waffling on, changing his mind daily. I find he's a politician, very much so, and I don't expect him to change ambiguous speeches because that's what politicians do. Still, he's unexpectedly open-minded, listens well, and when he needs to be, he is decisive.'

'He sounds much better than the Minister of Environment; he won't decide unless three different people have checked every detail.'

During the pauses between the courses of a typical Italian dinner, interspersed with sighs of pleasure from Charlotte, they discussed what Travis had done. Charlotte listened; talking to someone she felt was an expert, especially a handsome one with a pleasant voice, was a pleasure.

When she learnt he had a problem with beach currents, she asked, 'How will you obtain that data, Travis? There are hundreds of beaches.'

'I had a call from Fisheries; they offered me a thousand boats and crews, so I've asked for a fishing float with an aerial on top, a second with a fifteen-metre weighted line, a drogue chute at the bottom, and a recording system. The crews can release one of each into offshore water; then, the recorder will record the current at both the surface and at depth. The boat's GPS position will be part of the data.'

'I may visit the Scripps Institute in San Diego next week to learn about ocean pollution. Do they measure currents?'

'They are the world leaders on an ocean scale. What I'm doing is Mickey Mouse in comparison. Visiting them is a chance in a lifetime.'

'Would you like to come?'

'Would I like to go to the Moon? Can you swing it?'

'I don't know. I'll go on Thursday to visit Scripps on Friday and would like to stay over for the weekend, leaving on Sunday night or Monday. Can you make it?'

'To visit Scripps with a Fruitcake? I would paddle the whole way.'

'Then I'll see what I can do. Do you like Asian food?'

'My father was a keen cook; after he retired, he spent his time cooking and regularly replaced a chef at restaurants in our town. Although my mother repeatedly said he was light on the chilli powder, he was especially fond of Asian dishes. He taught me, and I cook up a spicy meal regularly.'

'Warm up the girlfriend, I guess.'

'English girls don't like spicy food, so it doesn't do much good. They don't return after one visit, so I chose Italian tonight.'

'Well, this Welsh girl loves it.'

Charlotte spent the rest of the evening listening to Travis talk about Asian food. She hoped he was a lot better cook than Greg; he was a lot more rugged; at least a hormone made her feel it was likely.

As they left, she said, 'Travis, I'm a poor cook, but if you can teach me to cook a decent curry, tell me what to buy and come Saturday to my apartment.'

'I'll accept, but I'll bring the ingredients.'

'Where do you buy them?'

'At Southall Market, I'll go on Saturday afternoon.'

'Pick me up, and I'll go with you. I know nothing about London or about buying Asian food.'

The next day, she spoke to the Chief of Staff at Number Ten.

'I've spoken to the CIA, and they have arranged a meeting with the Scripps Institute next Friday to study pollution quantities. The man I recommended to the Minister of the Environment, who employed him, took me to dinner last night as a thank you, and I learnt he has a problem with measuring ocean currents for the beach project. Scripps is the world leader in ocean currents, so it might be a clever idea to tell the Minister I'm going to Scripps and Travis should come too.'

'I don't know him. Have you known him long?'

'No, I spoke to him on the phone once or twice at Heathrow, but I met him for the first time last night. His name is Travis Grantham.'

It happened as she hoped it would.

Travis fetched her on Saturday; Charlotte enjoyed the Southall Market and learnt about spices, common Indian fruits and vegetables, and much about rice. She found, unexpectedly, that cooking with Travis was amusing and exciting. The dinner was superb.

'Travis, it was the most exotic and tasty curry I've ever had; every bite was a delight.'

'Thanks, but you did half of it yourself; now answer your question: did it warm up the girlfriend?'

'I don't know, but the fruitcake feels like it has just come out of the oven.'

The car stayed outside that night; they went boating on the Thames on Sunday.

Travis started a blog titled '*The Planet Fights Back.*' The beach photographs and the plea to visit beaches and see what was happening generated millions of replies. Travis had to call the Minister of Finance and request a budget to launch an entire internet operation; he soon had over a hundred people recording data.

Travis drafted a report that the environment minister presented at the next meeting. He reported that people worldwide had seen every known sea creature cleaning up pollution from the sea. A man reported seeing dolphins and whales towing fishing nets toward the shore, while others claimed to have seen shoals of fish dragging pieces of plastic bags. Beach observers reported crabs of every type and size carrying plastic up the beach, from minute flakes to buckets. A King Crab can weigh many kilograms and haul a large object.

The following week, Fitzgerald, Smithers, and Bellingham added forty or more employees daily. They did so by taking on many more partners, not in London but spreading throughout Britain's industrial areas. The contract signed between Bellingham and Edible Bags was their charter. Within days, Bellingham signed many licenses on behalf of Edible Bags, and three weeks later, the first mass production of Edible Bags began. Within four months, raw plastic production dropped by seventy per cent. The other thirty per cent would be more difficult; the speciality engineering plastics used for gears, cogs, bearings, motor vehicle dashboards, bumpers, fenders, and doors needed research. But this was not plastic discarded into the sea. Recycling plants took it.

29

Meghali and Patrick boarded a flight from Washington Dulles to San Diego. Meghali had told Charlotte which hotel to book and would meet her and Patrick at the airport for a limo ride to the Valencia Hotel in La Jolla. Their appointment with the Scripps Institute of Oceanography director was the following day. They dined together in the hotel restaurant; neither couple remarked that they were sharing rooms, although they were unmarried; the close relationship between the couples made it unnecessary.

Patrick thought Meghali and Charlotte were similar in their outlook. Meghali thought Travis was quite different from Patrick, but when she heard Travis call her Fruitcake with affection and tenderness, she decided he was an excellent match for Charlotte.

Meghali had told the Scripps Director they wanted to know about pollution in the ocean. Specifically, she mentioned the USA contribution, past and present, and the estimates for the UK; she also said Travis was interested in coastal ocean currents.

A delegation met them in the reception hall. When Meghali said after the introductions that she had never expected such a welcome, the Director replied, 'Ms. Azzaro, when the CIA is interested in ocean pollution, our people, who are passionate about the seas, want to know what's going on, especially when you bring the consultant to the Prime Minister of Britain and a representative from their Ministry of the Environment.'

They went to a meeting room, and the four visitors sat through presentations on ocean pollution for three hours. They remained wide awake the whole time; their minds loved it. Patrick built movies in his head that pictured what might happen, and Meghali associated one fact with another, even a point in the first presentation with one in the last. After tea and cookies, Meghali summed up.

'I know we came to the right place; your presentations were clear, competent, and relevant, and the information you have at your fingertips is superb. Charlotte, have you learnt what you wanted?'

'Much more than I expected, thank you.'

Meghali continued, 'However, let me give you a CIA analyst's viewpoint. Over the years, the United States has released millions of tons of pollution into the ocean. If the planet is about to throw it back at us, a considerable proportion is an economic threat, nothing more. Although an economic threat can be detrimental to our standard of living, it does not directly cause death, and every country in the world has a similar problem. To face this, we must treat everything thrown at us without it returning to the sea. That alone is a significant task, but one that science, industry, and organisations can solve. I don't know what role you can play, but I'm sure you'll have one.

'However, your presentations included estimates of the heavy metals and chemicals, such as pesticides, discarded over the years. The first question I need answered is: Will the planet return these to us? If so, in what form, and perhaps the most important, will it be a direct threat to life?'

In the silence that followed, a researcher said, 'That's a hell of a question.'

The Director asked, 'Does anyone have an idea? And don't suggest pumping the ocean through a giant filter.'

A researcher who had worked for years on red tides, a toxic plankton bloom in the sea, said, 'I think I might have an inkling.'

'Go ahead, Ken.'

'Red tides may be phytoplankton, but the toxicity is due to Ciguatoxin produced by the dinoflagellates and bacteria. I've read multiple papers on soil bacteria; two genes in their DNA frequently feature in the documents: the AR and MR genes. The AR resists the absorption of complex chemicals, such as antibiotics, and the MR resists the uptake of metals. Metals are necessary for bacterial reproduction, so bacteria take them up; however, excessive absorption can be fatal, which is why the MR gene exists. If a mutation allowed the absorption of enough metal to kill them, and this is something I'm studying for red tides, then whatever material hosts the bacteria becomes toxic to life.'

Meghali asked, 'So you suggest the equivalent of massive red tides could clean the oceans of these poisons?'

'Yes, the massive ones are related to fertiliser runoff, but it might not be the kind of red tide I study. The host material could be of a low density or frothed by aeration, creating scum on the beaches if blown ashore. In the extreme, it could be an oyster or any filter-feeding organism, and rain might carry a low enough density material, a toxic rain that could fall anywhere.'

'And the consequences?'

'If people ate the oysters or other filter feeders, or the fish that eat them, they could suffer from severe illness and even death. Toxic rain would poison the land, livestock, and food production, much like red tides poison fish. Then, the poisons follow the food chain into humans, gaining toxicity at each stage. If cows eat toxic grass, we eat a toxic concentrate in milk and meat.'

The Director broke in at this point. 'I think we should go for lunch, and then I've organised a tour of the labs; I think Travis will find the ocean current recording equipment interesting. Then we can meet back here at four to hear any suggestions and discuss other matters.

'I know Travis is interested in ocean currents close to beaches, but I don't know what data we have for him. The thought of poisonous material washed onto beaches suddenly makes knowing more about inshore currents a major priority. So, add this to the afternoon's agenda.'

All four went on the tour after a simple lunch in the canteen. Travis was thrilled in the ocean current lab to find something suited to his needs: a bright orange ball that floated with a weighted keel tube underneath and a Man Overboard Beacon on top. It could bob in the sea, providing a direction and distance signal to a receiver or recorder. The software displayed a map with the ball's wanderings as a dotted line. A second, more sophisticated one had a buoyancy chamber, a small reservoir of compressed air, and floated at a fixed distance from the sea surface; it maintained its depth by making minute adjustments to the air in the buoyancy chamber, just as a scuba diver's buoyancy jacket does. The beacon used a different frequency to indicate the underwater ball moving in various directions relative to the surface ball.

When the director learnt that Travis had a thousand fishing boats to take measurements, he immediately suggested that Travis contact Plymouth University, as they might be able to help. Travis received two balls as a gift, along with a set of design specifications and an agreement to share data and conclusions.

The afternoon session was disappointing, as Scripps had done little research into ocean bacteria, despite ocean samples worldwide showing varying levels of metals and dissolved pollutants. The estimates of the total amount shocked the visitors, as did the amount attributable to Britain and the USA. They decided that if Travis could persuade a University in England to work on it, Scripps would try to obtain funding for similar research in cooperation. It was then that Meghali remembered the jellyfish, her mind locked in a logical association. *Brighton Beach-jellyfish-filter feeders.*

'Ken, could jellyfish collect heavy metals and chemicals?'

Silence reigned for a minute, and Patrick smiled at Meghali; he remembered, too.

Ken replied, 'They are filter feeders, so theoretically they could; there are so many of them they account for a considerable mass of sea life. They are active feeders, pumping water with their umbrella-like structures, making them efficient. There are thousands of species, so if each species developed one gene to collect a chemical or metal, they could manage everything we've discharged into the sea. However, if they died, fish would eat them before the sea could wash them onto a beach.

'However, I don't think they're in the red tides class, seaweeds that absorb bacteria, and it's the bacteria that absorb the metals. But they might absorb pesticides. We know little about the *Nomura*; it's a Japanese jellyfish pest that weighs up to two hundred kilograms. I guess something that big could absorb massive quantities.'

The Director said, 'We can collect twenty or more species and analyse them for pollutants.'

Charlotte replied, 'I think you should; I'll ask Cambridge to do analyses and repeat them monthly.'

Meghali and Charlotte huddled over one set of data with two Scripps researchers. Past data were sparse, but they had done their best to correlate the data to determine the rate at which the metal load pumped into the seas had increased. The curves reminded Charlotte of the world's population curve, so she asked a researcher to impose one on the screen. Fifteen minutes later, it showed a near-perfect correlation. Charlotte asked for an email with the link to the graph. She had an idea she might need it. When Meghali showed Patrick, he said, 'You have all you need there to calculate how much we've thrown into the sea. Director, if you can obtain a reasonable estimate for any year in, say, the last ten, an integration using the population curve will give the total.'

Then Patrick asked, 'Director, we've discussed solid pollution, metals and chemicals; I'm not proud to say the US may have poured more oils and tars into the ocean than any other country. What happens to them? I know the crude and the bitumens have dangerous levels of heavy metals.'

'They do. If the product is light, such as motor fuels and kerosene, it floats and evaporates. The heavy oils float. If the spill is close to a coastline, you've seen the newsreels where hundreds of people do their best to clean the beaches and any wildlife. In the open ocean, wave action breaks down the oil slick into balls that eventually absorb sufficient solids, lose their volatiles, and sink or arrive on beaches as tar balls filled with sand.'

'Does Scripps have data on the quantities that countries have discharged?'

'No, we can try to gather some numbers, but this pollution must be worldwide, and I can't imagine any possible collection means. We should try to stop it, but as many ships discharge ballast at sea in international waters, I don't know how we could do so.'

Charlotte replied, 'That's easy, Director. Use Satellite surveillance to spot an oil slick, followed by an interdiction for the ship to enter a country's territorial waters, and, supposing it does, seize and dismantle it. With cooperation between countries, such actions would halt those practices.'

Patrick asked, 'Charlotte, when the UK collects the beach rubbish, can you sort and weigh the percentage of tar balls? Like measuring heavy metals and pesticides. That will give us a baseline from which to work. We mustn't overlook the possibility that sea life can bring tar balls onto the beaches.'

'I'll ask for that when we return.'

Meghali and Patrick went directly to the airport. Charlotte and Travis stayed for the weekend, went to the beach, and ran with the Californians. Charlotte wore a bikini, and Travis a Speedo. After returning to England, Travis spent more nights and weekends with Charlotte than in his apartment. The physical pleasure was a bonus because they both enjoyed each other's company.

That night in bed, lying enlaced, Meghali asked. 'Patrick, tell me your thoughts about Charlotte and Travis. I feel they have an unusual connection. Almost atomic, she's the proton, and he's the electron, as if they were bound together.'

'I agree, Meg, and I couldn't help wondering about us. Perhaps it's the Scripps atmosphere. I thought we were a molecule of two tightly bound atoms joined forever.'

'Not the Scripps atmosphere. We are joined right now. I'll prove it.

'There, can you feel what I feel...'

'Meg, has the molecule disintegrated?'

'Not yet. Maybe later. If the Storyteller wants a female Prime Minister, what about Charlotte?'

'Too young, no political experience or skills, no party position, and no parliamentary seat or constituency to vote for her. She might make an excellent Prime Minister with Travis's and our help, but for the storyteller to overturn hundreds of years of British tradition is a massive task. In the USA, all you need is fame.'

'I suppose you're right, although I would like to see you fail, but not for an hour yet...'

30

Armed with the Scripps figures, Charlotte approached the Prime Minister with a proposal and received her first rebuff. 'Prime Minister, we must place a pollution trap at the end of every river discharging into the sea.'

'What would that look like, which rivers, and what would it catch?'

'I've no idea, but every bit of waste we can stop going into the sea is waste we won't need to collect.'

'I won't authorise or legislate for anything where we don't know what we will do, who it will affect, or how much it will cost. If you want to investigate, go ahead; I'll authorise a research budget for a university to find a solution to a barrier and cost it, but nothing else at this stage.'

'So, there's no point in me mentioning a worry I have?'
'What?'
'The sea is full of heavy metals, chemicals, and pesticides we have discharged for years and continue to do so. Scripps is trying to estimate the amounts. If the ocean throws that stuff back at us, it's poison.'

'That's a big *if*, Charlotte; keep your eye on it; let me know if there's any proof, but I won't do anything unless there is.'

Travis helped her draft a research proposal, and the nightly sessions further deepened their relationship. Charlotte insisted that the proposal carry both their signatures. She sent it to five universities, asking if they could do it and provide a cost estimate. The Prime Minister honoured his promise and called the Minister of the Environment, asking him to support the proposal. Loughborough was the best offer, and the minister approved the budget. Loughborough completed the final barrier design to collect floating and underwater rubbish within four months. The Public Works Department built the first one across a local river as a final test. If you asked the workers what they were making, they replied, '*A Charlotte.*' Interested reporters followed the development; five newspapers and the BBC serialised the news of the '*Charlotte*' development, and although she never said a word, her name became synonymous with the efforts to combat pollution.

Years later, the name was as commonplace as a weir when a *Charlotte* stretched across a river mouth.

Travis handed the Scripps transmitter balls to the Ministry of Science and asked them to find a manufacturer, for he wanted two hundred pairs. Then he scrolled through the thousands of photographs taken by the RAF. He started with the beaches on either side of Bridlington and identified the two with the highest visible crab activity. The cleaning teams swung into action, and shortly after, Public Works modified the beaches, eliminating dunes, dips, and buried trees to allow cleaning machinery to operate in a straight line.

The daily tonnage collected rose steadily, and the Bridlington fishing boats caught Lobsters and Crabs. Still, it had become common knowledge that the beasties were busy bringing rubbish to the beaches. Until the quantity of collected rubbish dropped, catches would not return to pre-crisis levels, as the beasties were busy. The fishers became very protective of their catch; they had to release every undersized lobster or crab, as well as all breeding females. Whereas before, they had hurled them overboard, where the seabird flock that followed every boat preyed on them, now they lowered them carefully into the sea.

When Travis visited the fishing boats to organise the current tracking floats, he noticed it and ordered a long tube from a local supplier with a Teflon lining. The supplier, sensing a new market, didn't charge. The first fisher to try it, hooked on the gunwale at an angle, slid the crabs and lobsters down it, where they exited two metres under the surface, out of sight of the birds and beyond harm from the propeller. When asked about it, the fisher said, 'That's a *Travis Tube*, that is, keeps our under-sized catch alive for the next time.' They became standard equipment on the boats. The birds still flock to the boats because they throw anything dead overboard.

Scripps formed a partnership with Cambridge to research bacteria that absorbed metals. They collected a daily sample from the beach waste collection teams for analysis and then gave routine reports to Charlotte on the toxicity of the waste. When the toxicity numbers began to climb, Charlotte spoke at the next pollution progress meeting.

After the Prime Minister congratulated everyone on the progress and increasing catch of Lobster and Crab, the environment minister replied. 'Prime Minister, my team, led by Travis Grantham, has made excellent progress in ocean current research, for which the Scripps Institute thanked us in writing. We have identified the remaining beaches we should clean, and I hope our lobster and crab catch will approach normal levels in a few months.'

'Please convey my thanks to Mr Grantham, Minister.'

'I shall do, Prime Minister; I understand that Plymouth University intends to award him a Doctorate in recognition of his work.'

'Excellent news.'

The Minister of Industry, not to be left out, said, 'Our production of edible plastic material in Britain is now at levels where all plastics, except the critical and licensed items, are replaceable. It is not the raw material holding us up, but the conversion of machinery that makes the plastic items.'

'That's also excellent news.'

The Minister of Finance added, 'You'll have seen, Prime Minister, that the lobster and crab fishers in Europe are now beginning to suffer from the trap-packing phenomenon we have successfully overcome. Patents fully cover the Edible Bag material, and I foresee strong inflows of royalty fees from outside the country beginning soon.

'A consequential problem may arise because the price of lobster will soar. I'm concerned about the illegal sale of undersized catch. If prices soar, our people will complain that the French are buying our food.'

'Can we limit exports?'

'I've no idea; Industry must look at it.'

'This has been a successful operation, and I thank everyone for their contributions; with the elections five weeks ahead, I think we will win a majority again.'

'Prime Minister.'

'Yes, Charlotte.'

'I did warn you some time ago about the metal and pesticide content in the oceans.'

'Yes, but nothing has transpired yet, so I think I was justified in my decision.'

'Well, I must add a further warning. Cambridge University sent me a report yesterday in which they remark on a slight increase in the toxicity of the collected waste materials. They have run projections based on the current low levels. Depending on the formula used, they might measure dangerous toxic levels in one, three or five years. They state there could be significant errors.'

The Prime Minister was optimistic, 'Then I don't think we need to worry about it until after the election.'

Ten days before the election, Charlotte spoke again at another meeting.

'Prime Minister, I received a report from Cambridge University last night. It says toxicity levels are climbing far faster than expected, and it ends with a recommendation that all waste collection and management staff don full HAZMAT suits until the situation clears.'

'We must keep this quiet and investigate it fully.'

'I'm afraid that's impossible; Cambridge has sent a warning to the Ministry of Environment, and all the waste collection depots, coupled with the Cambridge sample collection staff donning full HAZMAT suits to make their collections. Once the crews see them, they will strike until they receive suitable protection.'

PM: 'Environment, what if we temporarily lay off the collection crews?'

'We can do so; it might keep the toxic information quiet for a day or two, but not much longer, and certainly, the media will be on us like a ton of bricks.'

Charlotte added, 'Stop cleaning the beaches, Prime Minister, and first, the lobsters will stuff the pots with plastic all around the country within twenty-four hours, and second, it will set the collection program back six months.'

'So, what can we do?'

'The toxic waste must be collected and treated for a long time. But if, and I only say if, you announce a ban today on the use of all pesticides and chemicals containing heavy metals, including their manufacture, the toxic levels of waste may remain steady or even drop slightly.'

There was silence while the Prime Minister thought about it. Then he said, 'Go ahead with the HAZMAT suits. I'll call a press conference at three pm. I'll announce a rise in the toxic level of the waste and that we are ordering everyone involved to wear HAZMAT suits until the toxic wave is over. We must delay until after the election. Then I can ban pesticides.'

'Thank you.' He left the room.

Of course, the media did their investigation. You cannot keep many secrets, and there are always leaks. Charlotte said nothing but did so with a stern face, pressing her lips together without her usual smile. That alone was enough for them to pressure other sources.

Then, six days before election day, a Commons member of the ruling party with a marginal seat had a mild heart attack. Told by his doctor to withdraw from the election, the party organisers had a problem. They solved it when one of the election committee members, whose constituency adjoined the vacant one, suggested that Charlotte might be popular enough to keep the seat; he guaranteed the fishing industry would vote for her, so they entered her as the replacement. She had no time to campaign with three campaigning days left; the party marked the parliamentary seat as lost.

However, the BBC owed Charlotte several favours and arranged an immediate interview with the surprise candidate. After questions about the deployment of the *Charlottes*, she made a novice politician's mistake, saying she would vote in favour of any anti-pollution bill proposed by her party or the opposition. On election day, the politicians didn't miss the strong signal that pollution was far more important than voting for a party.

Charlotte won with a 68 per cent majority from an unheard-of 78 per cent turnout. The election committee member who had proposed her as a candidate said he had told the fishing community to persuade everyone to turn out and vote.

The party won a narrow majority, but the Prime Minister lost his seat. The surprise was still to come. Due to the Westminster political system, the parliamentary party, without an elected leader, had to organise a leadership election. The party's members, fully aware of Charlotte's voting score and popularity, proposed one candidate and elected Charlotte as Prime Minister without a leadership contest.

That night, Meghali called Charlotte's private phone.

'Hello, Charlotte, congratulations. I imagine you're exhausted and wondering what to do next.'

'Right on both counts, Meghali.'

'I assume you walk into Number Ten tomorrow and then must choose a cabinet?'

'As I understand it, yes, after my appointment at Buckingham Palace.'

'Patrick has a suggestion.'

'Go ahead.'

'If you can believe him, He says that when there's a shootout in a cowboy film, the winner is the guy who looks in the other's eyes and doesn't waver. In practical terms, appoint the entire existing cabinet and warn them that their appointment will depend on performance. But appoint Travis as the new Minister of Pollution Collection and Control. Let him take whoever he needs from the Department of Environment.

'Ban pesticide use unless it's fully biodegradable in less than two months, and ban all metal used in everything that can end up in the oceans. That includes all the fancy and unnecessary vitamins, cosmetics, and paint. Announce that, unless it's necessary for health, with a certificate issued by a doctor, the government will immediately shut down any business that transgresses without compensation. Not fines and continued operations.'

'What about metal additions in fertilisers?'

'Ban them except on an application proving the soil is deficient in a metal. Approval is for one application, and the amount purchased must match the application.'

'Thanks, Meghali. I'll think about it. I want to return to the beach in San Diego right now.'

'I know how you feel. If you need money to research the disposal of ocean toxins, let me know. We have rich philanthropists in this country. We are just beginning to feel the problems you have experienced. Bye.'

Travis walked in. She put the phone down and told him what Meghali had said.

'I think she's right; aim straight at the target and don't flinch. You must make a speech tomorrow at Number Ten. It should be easy; let's do the first draft. I intended to celebrate with a Moghul Emperor's curry, but I'll order a pizza, then we'll sleep, and tomorrow morning, we'll polish up the speech before your driver collects you.'

'Okay, but tomorrow, you're coming with me to Number Ten; I want to introduce you to the media.'

In Britain, the new Prime Minister reached dizzy heights of popularity, for as a Welsh girl, she could do no wrong in Wales. The reaction was surprising in Scotland, possibly best illustrated by her first speech to the Scottish Parliament.

After the introductions, she started with a story.

'I am, the historians tell me, the first Welsh Prime Minister of England since Lloyd George over a hundred years ago, the second Welsh Prime Minister and the first Welsh woman to hold the position. I dreaded coming to make this speech, but this morning at the hotel, my fears disappeared.

'An elderly gentleman came up to my breakfast table. It usually takes me a minute to decide someone's nationality, so I wasn't sure until I realised that, being in Scotland, he was probably a Scotsman. Then I felt sure,' she paused for five seconds, 'because he was wearing a kilt.'

She paused until the laughter died. 'Then I learnt that the Scots are not shy about giving credit where credit is due, for the old highlander said, "You're okay, you are, lass." I haven't been called a lassie in England since I was ten.'

After another round of laughter, she said, 'I asked why I was okay, thinking maybe he agreed with my policies. He replied, *"Because ye're nae a Sassenach."*'

Delivered with a perfected Scots accent, the standing ovation that followed put Scotland into her hands.

'Patrick, I've won the Gold Medal at last. You were wrong.'

'I wasn't thinking clearly, occupied with something else.'

'Not when you said that Charlotte would not be Prime Minister; something else came afterwards.'

'Then I thought of it, but I can offer an excuse. I'm mortal.

'Meg, that's three countries and three towns where women have replaced the male leaders.'

'Which three countries?'

'Middle East, East Asia, and Britain. The Americas, Africa and Australia remain. I wonder which will be next?'

31

It was a routine CIA meeting to review the recent intelligence. There was nothing new, except for the events in Britain. The rest of the world held its breath as it observed the struggle unfolding there.

Meghali had asked weeks earlier for observers at the ports of the Maine lobster belt to check on the lobster catch, primarily to report on the presence of plastic bags in lobster pots. She had a graph with the reports.

'Director, as most of us have, I've been following the events in Britain, and we have waited now for months, in vain, for a similar polluted rainfall to occur. My analysts agree that it will not happen as it was a warning, and the signs, although heard and acted upon by the British Prime Minister, were noted by every country in the world. So, it doesn't need to happen globally.'

'That's a relief, Meghali, so we have no threats on the board?'

'Quite the reverse, Director. It may be early, but the number of reports about lobster pots packed with plastic bags is growing, and I now have sufficient data to show that the lobster industry will cease to exist in four months if the United States takes no action. If not a physical threat, this is of significant economic and social impact, identical to the event in Britain.'

'So now we are going to be attacked by lobsters. Don't you have a more credible threat to report?'

'Director, that's not what I said.'

'That's what I heard, and it's what the President and every person in the USA would hear.'

'Director, the whirlwind in the desert that buried thousands of terrorist soldiers is now accepted as being Divine Intervention. The Pope has declared the change to the *Christ the Redeemer* statue to be a divine intervention. The Prime Minister of Britain has classified the actions of lobsters, crabs, and other sea creatures as a Form of Divine Intervention. I'm afraid no alternative definition is available when our lobster industry crashes. It is not a case of lobsters attacking the USA; it's an intervention by a force we cannot understand; humanity has not understood it for millennia, which is why the churches are full of people praying to it.'

The Director was scornful. 'So, I should tell the President that lobsters are attacking us, or God, is that what you are saying?'

'No, Director, I suggest you tell him the facts: that the CIA forecasts that the lobster industry will disappear within four months, that it appears identical to the events in Britain, and the sole solution we can propose is that followed by Britain. You may add that if we don't act, Washington, DC might experience a severe plastic bag storm.'

'Although I don't think the President will take seriously an increasing number of lobster pots stuffed with plastic bags, I can do that.'

He did, but the way he said it implied he didn't consider it seriously, so apart from laughter, the meeting in the White House forgot it. The prospect of the Washington Football Team losing against the Kansas Chiefs in the upcoming game was a more significant threat.

'Meg, my AI has flagged a news item from Japan.'

'Why, Patrick?'

'I told it to note all unusual marine events. This news report is not much more than a one-liner on page six of the Mainichi Shimbun, a national paper, but the AI found the original article in a local journal, printed for the residents of a small fishing port town.'

'So, what does it say?'

'That the number of *Nemopilema Nomurai*, usually called *Nomuras*, has soared, and they may become a fishing problem this year.'

'Is that the giant jellyfish Scripps mentioned some time ago?'

'Yes, they grow to two metres in diameter and two hundred kilograms.'

'Are they the biggest jellyfish?'

'No, the *Lion's Mane* jellyfish can grow bigger but are solitary, unlike the *Nomura*. The stings of both don't kill directly, but can make a person extremely ill. The *Nomura* are densest in the Yellow Sea and the Sea of Japan. The *Lion's Mane* is found everywhere in cold water.'

'What's significant about that report?'

'Nothing startling, but once before, in the 2003 to 2004 fishing season, a bloom of *Nomuras* impacted the fishing, as nets had tons of jellyfish. A boat capsized under the load.'

'I'll call Scripps and ask if they know about it.'

'Good morning, Meghali Azzaro from the CIA speaking. Is that Shu Fen?'

'It is, Ms Azzaro. It's a pleasure to hear from you. How can I help?'

'I would like to speak to the Director. Can you arrange a time for me, please?'

'He's in his office, Ms Azzaro, and has ten minutes before a meeting; if that will do, I can connect you now.'

'Thank you, Shu Fen, please do.'

'Meghali, this is a surprise. Do you want to visit again?'

'I do, Director, but not now. I have a question about jellyfish. The species *Nemopilema Nomurai*.'

'Are you in Japan? They asked about that jellyfish two days ago. They are experiencing a bloom.'

'I'm in Washington, Director. Patrick picked up a news article and is listening. Can you tell me anything about them? What do the Japanese want to know?'

'Essentially, when will they disappear so they can begin fishing. The boats are reluctant to leave port. Unfortunately, I don't think we can help. *Nomuras* are common there. One of our guys looked at the satellite weather pictures. They don't show *Nomuras*, but they give sea temperatures. They are slightly above average, and I guess that's the reason so many have collected there. The *Oyashio* cold offshore current has moved away from the shore, and the warmer *Kurashio* is now between it and the land. We can't forecast when it will return. The *Tsushima* current carries the *Nomuras* from the Yellow Sea, where they are endemic, and they travel through the strait between Honshu and Hokkaido. The *Tsushima* current may be stronger than usual, pushing the *Oyashio* to move away.

'I will offer a Scripps research team and a ship to measure the currents.'

Patrick tapped Meghali's arm. 'Thank you, Director. Patrick has a question.'

'Hello, Director, how are you?'

'We're all well, Patrick, but worried about the toxic waste. Everyone is working hard on a solution. What is your question?'

'I could find out from other sources, but as you are online, I thought I might ask. Japan fishes for Bluefin tuna. In which current do they catch them?'

'Tuna don't restrict themselves to specific waters and conditions, but they do prefer colder water; however, their prey is often in neighbouring warm water where other species breed faster, so I would suggest that in Japan, they are cold water dwellers that feed in warmer water. Then return.'

'So, if the *Oyashio* current has moved offshore, the tuna will be farther from the land?'

'That would be a reasonable assumption.'

'Thanks, Director. I'll take it from there. Goodbye, and good luck with the toxic waste. The world needs that solution.'

'Goodbye, Meghali. Goodbye, Patrick. Thanks for the call.'

'Now something makes sense.'

'Patrick, you're being enigmatic again.'

'Sorry, Meg. When I read the *Nomura* article, I couldn't help but ask if it wasn't a lobster case, but one factor makes similarity impossible. Crabs and lobsters have brains; they hunt or collect, deciding what to eat. Jellyfish don't; they drift aimlessly, catching whatever collides with their tentacles. It's impossible to train a brainless creature; therefore, a bloom of *Nomuras* in a port must be due to currents. Given a week or two, the port authorities can organise the collection and composting of the *Nomuras*, so there's no threat to the Japanese economy. However, if the Tuna are going far offshore, and the Tuna catch is dropping and continues to drop, Japan's favourite food will disappear, and the government will be in trouble.'

'I could ask why, but I'll guess it's whales.'

'I agree, Meg. I once said the editor likes elephants and rhinos and hates poachers. The International Whaling Commission bans whaling, and Japan flaunts the ban. I'm sure the editor also likes whales and is proposing a choice. Whales or tuna.'

'Norway also hunts whales, and the Faroes have an annual whale hunting festival.'

'I know, Meg; once Japan folds, the threat will move there, although it will be different. We need to know if the Bluefin catch in Japan is dropping.'

'Japan and the US share intel, and I know an analyst in Tokyo, or we could ask Charlotte to call their Prime Minister.'

'Call your analyst; we need proof before going to that level.'

'I've received the weekly count for the last three weeks, Patrick. Both the weight and numbers are dropping, and the rate is increasing. If it continues, they'll catch very few Bluefin tuna in four months.'

'Thanks, Meg. I'll call Travis. He might know their Minister for the Environment.'

Patrick called and explained. Then, Travis followed diplomatic protocols to arrange a call with his Japanese counterpart.

Travis received the call at eight am. 'Good afternoon, Minister.'

'Good morning. First, congratulations on your doctorate and your promotion. Can we dispense with the titles and return to where we were when we last met in London?'

'Of course, Kaito, I'm still learning to live with the title, so it's a pleasure.'

'Then, Travis, I hope you won't say our lobsters will pack our traps with plastic bags.'

'I won't because your success in recycling plastic is well known, so I feel that won't happen.'

'That's a relief, so why did you call?'

'I'm sure you know my doctorate is the result of ocean current studies that I did with the help of Plymouth and Scripps. Scripps called me and asked for my opinion on a question they received from Japan. Do you know of the problem with *Nomuras* near the Pacific end of the *Tsugaru Strait?*'

'I do. Scripps hasn't replied yet.'

'They will do; they will say it's essentially due to an increased flow through the strait from the Sea of Japan, which has caused the *Oyashio* to move away from the shore, and at least a part of the warmer *Kurashio* is now between it and the land. They asked if I could forecast when the phenomenon will reverse.'

'And can you?'

'Yes, but you won't believe it. However, Bluefin tuna are cold-water fish that feed in warm water, so the tuna in the Oyashio area have moved far from the usual fishing areas. I have requested the catch history because, although Japan receives priority for catch sales and has not experienced a change, the export clients have. Within four months, Japan will experience a drastic shortage of tuna. Please don't accept what I say. Check it yourself.'

'And when will it reverse?'

'I said you won't believe me. Suppose you announce a ban on whaling, with drastic punishment; announcing any transgression is classified as pirating and will carry similar penalties. If you do, the situation will immediately stabilise and begin a recovery.'

'Travis, even if I believed you, I couldn't sell that to the Prime Minister.'

'Kaito, I've told you, ask your scientists to study the currents, keep a daily tally of Bluefin catches, and when you're ready, ask your Prime Minister to call Britain's Prime Minister. She will tell him it has nothing to do with science, but that the Ocean is fighting back. Call me any time if you have questions.'

'Thanks, Travis, I shall study it immediately.'

'Patrick, Travis talked to the Minister and told him. He says we'll have to wait a month before he's convinced.'

'Okay, now I wonder what the editor has planned to convince the Norwegians.'

'What resource could he threaten?'

'There may be several, including the fjord fish farms. I'll bet the editor can train a Giant Pacific Octopus to tear apart an open sea net and let the fish out. We'll have to wait and see.'

'And the Faroes?'

'During their traditional *Grindadráp* festival, the men are usually in the water up to their waists. The editor might influence the currents around the Faroes and surround the islands with *Lion's Mane* jellyfish collected from all over the Atlantic. The jellyfish are extremely poisonous, and their tentacles can be thirty metres long. Several of them near a beach make the water unapproachable.'

32

Two months later, the European Union banned the use of plastic. Fitzgerald, Smithers, and Bellingham opened four hundred more branches.

'Patrick, in one of Charlotte's early meetings with the last Prime Minister, she said.

"Whereas most pollution might have degraded in a hundred years, sunken wrecks that have lain in the sea for centuries are still found. Some pollution lasts much longer, like concrete-encased poisonous or radioactive chemical waste drums. Some, such as thousands of containers lost from ships for varying reasons, may not release their contents until they have corroded away."

I don't know how we could find those items; they could be anywhere in the world, at any depth. That may be why we haven't had any warning to collect them. Do you think the Storyteller will let it pass, or do you know what he will do once the world has solved the current pollution collection problems?'

'Meg, I don't have a scenario that provides a possible solution, so it's up to logical thinking. The storyteller is far too powerful to ignore the undersea pollution. What is the first problem?'

'There's just one. I asked Scripps, and they replied that sonar scans of the ocean seabed would take decades and cost a fortune, but if I could accurately pinpoint an object, they could arrange for removal. They gave me a maximum depth of three thousand metres.'

'Then I shall guess that whales or squid that can descend to those depths will provide us with a marker. The storyteller could move anything deeper into shallower water. Unseen, we would never know he did it. What the marker will be, I don't know. Let's ask Travis. Maybe he has an idea.'

'Good evening, Travis. Meghali's with me.'

'Hi Patrick, hi Meghali, how can I help?'

'We want to know how the Storyteller can inform us of all the sunken containers in the sea.'

'I have no idea, Patrick. It would be easy in shallow water, such as a massive seaweed growth, but currents would take untethered markers a long way once the depth exceeded thirty metres. A similar problem applies to oil spills from sunken ships; we must start at the spill on the surface and scan the seabed up current until we find it. Generally, this is extremely expensive as the search area grows in proportion to the distance from the surface spill. I'll think about it and call you if I have an idea.'

Before he had spent enough time thinking, he had the solution thrust on him.

In a second underground room at Fort Belvoir, an analyst sat in front of his terminal, reviewing a sequence of satellite photos taken as a satellite passed from west to east over the Caribbean. Due to drug smuggling across the Caribbean, the satellite density gave constant coverage. Most of the images scanned by the computer software produced no significant results. Many small blobs were ships. Although they moved between one satellite pass and another, the computer identified them from memory. Investigated and named when they first appeared, the AI software updated the last known position if they kept their course and speed. For any change in direction or speed, the software printed a message on the adjacent screen. Anything new appeared on the monitor with a red dot and the label '*Unidentified Object*' and its coordinates.

The eleventh image showed a red dot. The analyst zoomed in to see a black patch on the sea. Its shape was a familiar oil spill shape, starting at a point and expanding as the spill swept away with the current until it faded. He had seen many. The long oval ones were the most common, where a dump of oil or chemicals spread in all directions, dragged by the current. This one was like a leak from the seabed, continuously feeding at one point.

He checked the instruction book, notified the Department of Ecology and the Scripps Oceanic Institute, and set a computer watch for a future satellite pass.

The image two hours later showed the dot, and it had neither moved nor grown.

Three days later, it disappeared overnight. By then, the Scripps exploration ship had left port.

Arriving at the coordinates, it found nothing, so the scientist on board launched a sonar search of the seabed.

It didn't take long to discover an object directly below the coordinates of the inkspot. The object's sonar image, boat-shaped, showed it was approximately twenty metres long. The water depth was forty-two metres.

The scientists on board packed up; since nothing was scientifically unusual, the captain notified the Department of Ecology that a sunken vessel required recovery to prevent further fuel leaks.

A sailor shouted as the crew lifted the sonar probe from the water, 'Oil bubble surfacing.'

A second sailor threw a bucket into the water, attached to a rope and collected a few litres of black seawater. One of the scientists came down from the bridge to look at it. After dipping his hand in the bucket, he said, 'It's not oil, but a black dye. We must analyse it.'

Two hours later, as the ship returned to Galveston, the onboard lab identified the substance as a complex organic dye, primarily composed of the compound melanin, and the closest match in the Scripps database was squid ink. The captain remarked, 'If the surface slick was squid ink, the number of squid must be enormous.'

It was enough for the ship to collect a diving crew and gear and return to the site.

The divers found the boat; it was recent, and they estimated it to be less than a year old. It was a high-speed fishing boat with gasoline engines. The divers reported a curious dolphin but no squid at all. A crane barge lifted the wreck onto the barge, where they found a little gasoline in one tank, the others packed with cocaine, and the boat's bow crushed as if it had collided at high speed with a half-sunken container.

The Scripps scientists held a meeting to discuss where the squid ink came from, but they hadn't concluded when a new report of an identical spill a hundred nautical miles from the first site arrived.

The ship headed straight for the new site. One of the scientists, who had answered questions from the British Minister of the Environment several times, called him.

'Travis Grantham, good morning.'

'Travis, this is Ben from Scripps. I have a phenomenon here in the Caribbean, and I want your reaction.'

Ben explained what had happened.

'Ben, I don't know for sure, but if you want a guess, I'll say if you analysed squid ink, it was squid ink.'

'Okay, Travis, but where did it come from?'

'The squid went to the site, rose vertically, ejected ink below the surface, and waited a while. When you came, the squid left.'

'Travis, you're nuts; why would they do that?'

'Ben, you said it yourself. To show you where the boat was so you could remove it from the seabed.'

'Will you tell me next that the Dolphins or Whales organise it?'

'No, Ben, you said a dolphin nosed around your divers. They might find the wrecks. I don't think they carry plastic buckets up the beach, but something does. Go to the next ink spot; if there's a sunken boat or container, it will confirm it. And if there's a dolphin, please let me know and then ask Scripps to take action to help me. I'm starting a blog to protect the Dolphins because they play a crucial role in helping humanity. I want sonar buoys deployed in any area where active fishing is occurring. Throw your institute behind the proposal and persuade the universities to back it.'

A week later, it rained on the White House and the surrounding twenty hectares. The composition was identical to the rain that fell in London, except the smell of dead fish was overwhelming. It was impossible to miss the whale on the White House lawn. The President left for Camp David to avoid the stink of rotten fish while the White House was cleaned and deodorised.

It didn't do much good. A lingering aroma remained in the area for several weeks, depending on the wind direction, for although the buildings were spotless, deodorising twenty hectares was impossible.

Then it rained at Camp David.

'Patrick, don't you think your scriptwriter is going too far?'

'No, but I must admire him; I would never have imagined his script.'

'Which one? The ink spots?'

'No, that's a detail; I imagine the dolphins thought it up themselves.'

'So now the dolphins are managing the world?'

'Well, they are intelligent; give them a ball to play with, and they invent games to play; now they've been given humans to play with, and they have invented a game called *"Deliver the wrecks."*'

'I knew you were crazy the day I met you. Explain the script you're talking about?'

'Think about the facts, Meghali, and let your mind form a conclusion.

'Fact one: The sea creatures collect pollution and push it onto the beaches.

'Fact two: Human beings are collecting and disposing of it.

'Fact three: Bacteria in seaweeds absorb the dissolved pollutants, die, and the waves wash the seaweed onto beaches.

'Fact four: There has not been a single case of wanton destruction of human life except for three vicious nut cases.'

'What can you conclude?'

Meghali responded immediately, 'Looked at like that, I would say it is a case of co-operation between species.'

'Yes, and it took a genius to think of it; humanity has useful tame dogs and horses, so extending to dolphins and other sea creatures only requires an open mind. I think the mechanism to clean the oceans is in place, and the Storyteller is training the humans to cooperate.'

Travis changed his blog, recommending cooperation with sea creatures as a better solution to cleaning up the detritus that rained down daily. To many, it was a ridiculous suggestion. They ignored it, but the UN kept a tally, and soon published figures proved him right; the mass collected on the cleaned beaches grew while the others dropped.

Pushed by citizens tired of living in towns and cities with a dead fish smell, reluctant governments soon followed suit. They could now collect the pollution without fish falling from the sky, but they still had to process it.

33

The CIA Director's meeting had every head of a department in the room once again. The attendees were having quiet discussions with their neighbours. The door opened, and the Director did as he had done the last time, placing one hand on each side of the file he had put on the desk.

'Has anyone a fresh idea of what's going on? We are the CIA, dammit, the intelligence organisation of the United States. I now have the same list as before, but it has more items.

'There were fourteen, and I still have no explanation for them; now there are three more.

'Fifteen: The entire population of sea creatures and a mass of bacteria collect the last hundred years of solid and liquid pollution from the sea, and someone is dumping it in Washington, on the White House and Camp David. The President is pissed off, guys; his house smells like a fish market.

'Sixteen: A nut case British scientist heads up an ecology movement. They believe the planet is fighting back, and we should cooperate with the sea creatures. That's bad enough, but now he claims squid are marking the spots in the ocean where containers or shipwrecks of poisonous material lie on the seabed, and the organisers are the Dolphins.

'Seventeen: Lobster fishers are going wild, and the lobster business is in trouble because they are stuffing the pots with plastic bags instead of going in themselves.

'I repeat, gentlemen. Has anyone got a fresh idea? I must report to the President. What do I tell him? The CIA is asleep?'

The Head of Analytics, the sole speaker at the last meeting, replied, 'The weight of the evidence is overwhelming; the mystery man is a messenger of God. No one at the CIA has the least idea of what God will do next. But I can tell you what he wants.'

'What?'

'What has happened in Britain. Britain is a small island, a first-world country, and nowhere in Britain is far from the sea. I believe it's the reason Britain suffered first. But they have been pragmatic about it. They collect pollution from the beaches; they report that specific beaches receive pollution for collection while others don't. I asked the Prime Minister. It might seem ridiculous, but she said that if they clean suitable beaches daily, they are the beaches that receive pollution. They are working hard to find ways to treat it. They have banned insecticides and plastics and placed barriers or nets across all rivers where they discharge into the sea to collect any other rubbish. They no longer have polluting rain or lobster pots stuffed with trash. With drastic punishment, they have banned all goods containing metals that might end up in the sea. The manufacturers cease to operate if they break the law. The government doesn't collect wrecks or sunken containers; they publish a satellite map of inkspots, and the treasure hunters fetch whatever is in the sea under them. Their biggest problem is keeping historical treasures from the illegal market. It's a cooperation between humans and sea creatures, no different from the collaboration of horses, donkeys, and dogs that we have known for centuries.

'Britain also bans any ship leaving an oil slick identified by satellite from entering their territorial waters, whether identified inside or outside their territorial waters. If the ship enters their waters, it's intercepted by their navy and confiscated. They are dismantling the third such ship in the Clyde and have five more in the queue; other countries with navies have announced a corresponding law, and those without navies are negotiating joint ventures.'

'So, what do we do?'

'I said last time, Director, what the British are doing. Like Kennedy, who dedicated America to putting a man on the moon, the President must dedicate America to saving the planet and decree that we must take the first step, as Britain is doing. God will likely do something to upset our apple cart if he doesn't. What, I cannot foresee. We are the most significant source of pollution in the world. Unless we take radical action, I believe an event will force an election, and a female ecologist will win the Presidency, as has recently happened in Britain.

'I'll add, if we don't, we shall all die through our inaction.'

'Shit, you want me to tell that to the President?'

'I formally request you do. If you don't, I shall resign and say it on television. Like all of us here, I'm primarily a citizen of this planet, and for us, as the French President once told Congress, there is no Planet B.'

The Director didn't tell the President, but gave him the meeting minutes and the recording.

Meghali received what she asked for, which was a surprise. The President did what she said, but like all politicians, the President had informers and learnt who had made the recommendation the Director of the CIA brought to him. He also read all the previous minutes. The President replaced the Director, promoted him to Chairperson of the CRAP bunch and promoted Meghali to US Ambassador to the United Nations. The president had read her warning that a woman might win the presidency, so he moved her out of Washington.

Meghali would have to move to New York. Patrick resigned;

his mind wouldn't allow anything else. He bought a large house in the Hamptons on Long Island for the two of them and moved his computers into the basement. He did an upgrade simultaneously, becoming the first private owner of two supercomputers.

He didn't believe it was over.

From doing nothing, the President became an advocate of massive anti-pollution programs. Patrick said he was terrified of receiving more whales on the White House lawn. He passed a Scripps proposal into law.

Squid and octopuses worldwide produced inkspots; cranes lifted hundreds of wrecks and sunken containers from the seabed, many of which contained fuel oils, chemicals, or other toxic substances. Sonar buoys protected the Dolphins.

For the next two years, the world's stock exchanges experienced a boom-and-bust cycle they found impossible to manage. The oscillations ultimately died out, and significantly few brilliant economists believed they knew what had happened.

Patrick had watched the activity; his conclusion was radically different. The editor was back at work. It didn't stop Patrick from making another fortune or three, but he thought the editor was studying a new screenplay. After the first crash, he noted the effect on the emerging markets and told Meghali.

'Meg, the editor is back at work. He's painting a new backdrop, building a fresh movie set, but I haven't figured out what the screenplay will be.'

'What are the factors?'

'The money flows on the world exchanges are odd; an unusual amount of capital flows to the emerging markets, and it's doing so in bursts. The IT companies are doing well in upgrading the IT structures of third-world countries to first-world levels. However, they have a long way to go, and there has been a rise in the computer game market in those countries, probably due to the IT infrastructure.'

'So, the odd thing is the money flows?'

'Yes, I can accept the rest as a result.'

'Do you see any purpose?'

'No, unless there is a consequence from an increase in playing computer games.'

'Look for one. If people overcome the urge to slaughter others by killing avatars in a computer game, does it affect anything, like making them more peace-loving?'

'I never thought of that. I'll collect data on computer game sales and wars.'

The results showed a strong correlation.

'Patrick, there's your answer.'

'But why, Meg?'

'You wrote a paper once about global warming; in it, you said that humanity would need to learn how to live without many of the things we take for granted. If you take something from a group of people, what do they do?'

'Go to war. But computer games are too incidental to fit a screenplay. They must be a diversion; there must be something else.'

'War requires a national identity; migration destroys that cohesion. Does IT infrastructure encourage migration?'

Then Meghali added, 'Not necessarily migration of people, but migration of capital. Would country A go to war with country B if A had major investments in country B?'

'I doubt it. Can you obtain figures from the UN?'

'I can try, Patrick, but many countries don't keep those statistics.'

'It's worth a try; if true, global warming comes next on his agenda.'

'If, as you believe, the editor is still here.'

34

The young woman, tall and athletic, with long blonde hair, dressed fashionably in a high-necked white blouse, a long skirt, and low-heeled open-toe sandals, stepped out of the taxi in front of the United Nations building in New York at nine am for an interview appointment at nine thirty in the language section offices. Soraya carried a large handbag with a shoulder strap.

There was nothing strange about her appointment. Soraya Badawi had completed an online application form a week earlier, which included the medical certificate, providing her with a full UN health clearance and the application number. She received the number a week before the session, during which she completed an online IQ test and had her photo taken. The section on languages listed the UN's six official languages: Arabic, Chinese, English, French, Russian and Spanish, with checkboxes for *Speak, Read, Write, Fluent* and a recently added one, *Native*. She had checked every box. Then, in the line below labelled Extra Languages, she wrote 'Hindi, Zulu and all others.'

A computer processed the application. It checked with the FBI for any known records, confirmed her birth in Luxor, her English father and Egyptian mother's deaths, and her visa into the USA. Then it determined a rating. It added a point for each of the checked boxes labelled Speak, Read, Write, three for the Fluent box, and four for Native. The programmer had never considered that someone could have more than one native language; at most, two. The highest scores were forty-four.

The computer accepted sixty, which had never occurred before, as it had never learnt forty-four was the maximum, so her application was at the top of the list for the next interview session. The computer made the appointment, so the first time a human viewed the application was three minutes before she walked into the first interview office. There were six interview rooms, sometimes more, and the computer also generated a schedule for each room, assigning one of the six languages to each interviewer. The first step was an interview with a different person for each of the six languages marked as fluent in the application. The young woman sailed through all of them in under two minutes each, for after a few questions, the checkbox on the application for each language, labelled 'verified', received a checkmark. The computer rescheduled the next appointment, so she didn't wait more than a few minutes. After the six interviews, her smartphone received a message notifying her of an appointment with the department's head at 9:30 am in two days. That was two days ago.

The department head was a woman, and when she reviewed the day's applications, the first candidate she saw was impossible to ignore. Good-looking, with a clean medical record, an IQ test above the maximum, and verified in six languages. After twenty years with the UN, she knew that if the impossible were to happen anywhere, it would happen at the UN. So, she checked the Director of the Language Department's schedule and booked an appointment for 10:45; she could cancel if it proved unnecessary.

Her secretary ushered in the first candidate, and she was as good-looking as her photo. As she displayed no signs of candidate nervousness or tension, the first question was immediate, rather than the usual small talk used to calm a candidate. 'Ms

Badawi, thank you for coming; you have written the extra languages on your application: Hindi, Zulu, and all others. How many do you speak?'

The reply was a question, 'Principal languages or dialects?'

'Principal.'

The answer bemused her, 'All of them.'

After considering this momentarily, she repeated the answer as a question, 'All of them?'

There was no hesitation, 'Yes.'

'And dialects?'

'I don't know, I've never counted; they are just a question of usage. Spend some time speaking one, and it comes naturally, for most of the difference is in pronunciation or accent, plus some local words. Do you have someone here who speaks a dialect with whom I can talk?'

The Head of Recruitment turned to her computer, set up a search for a Nepalese speaker, and found a suitable candidate. She called the translator and asked if she could spare five minutes. The petite woman who came into the office looked curiously at Soraya and asked, 'Mrs Johnson, how can I help?'

'Good morning, Bhavaroopa. I want to introduce Soraya Badawi; she says she can speak your home language.'

Soraya spoke to her in Nepalese, 'Hello, Bhavaroopa; where were you born in Nepal?'

When Bhavaroopa answered and named a small village in the mountains, Soraya replied in the local dialect, 'It's a beautiful part of the world. I spent some time in the peaceful area, and the air was so clean. You must be homesick sometimes.'

Bhavaroopa's attitude switched suddenly to that of a sister in the same household. The two, oblivious of the watching Head, began discussing the sights and places in the town until the Head said, 'Excuse me butting in. I wanted to know if Soraya spoke Nepalese. It seems she does.'

'Oh yes, ma'am, but we were talking about the village where I was born; not Official Nepalese, it's our local dialect, and she speaks it just as I do.'

'I expect you will tell me no one speaks Official Nepalese. Am I right?'

Soraya replied relaxedly, 'That's about right, ma'am. The official language is written and possibly spoken by translators but not by the Nepalese people.'

'Not even in government offices?'

'No, ma'am, it's like India; they might try to speak a generic form of Hindi but never succeed. Each person colours their language with an accent and different words, but they understand each other if it's not too different.'

'Bhavaroopa, do you agree?'

'I think that's a very accurate description, ma'am.'

'Well, thank you for coming, Bhavaroopa; we have an appointment with the Director.'

While the pair bid each other goodbye and exchanged phone numbers, she mailed the Director a brief note: *Read this. Coming to your office.* She included a link to Soraya's file.

She turned to Soraya and said, 'Please come with me,' then led the way to a staircase, went up a floor, and along a corridor to the Director's office, where she knocked on the door and entered his secretary's anteroom.

As they came in, the secretary said, 'Good morning, Martha; take a seat; he has someone with him; he'll be out in a minute or two.'

Two minutes later, the door opened, and the director ushered his visitor out. Then, he turned to Martha and Soraya. 'Good morning. Please come in. Would you like something to drink?'

Martha said, 'I need a coffee; Soraya, how about you?'

'Tea, please, mint if possible.'

The director turned to the secretary, 'Jennifer, can you organise it, please?' He followed the two women into his office and sat in a large leather armchair behind his desk, while the two women sat in more upright chairs, also in matching red leather. Soraya looked around with interest; the office had a few official documents in frames on the wall, a picture she recognised as the Taj Mahal, and a large window looking over the East River.

'Well, Martha, what is the problem?'

'Have you looked at the application I sent you?'

'No, I haven't had a second to spare.'

'Then I think you should read it; the link is in my mail. We'll wait.'

He busied himself with his computer for five minutes while the secretary brought in their drinks, and Martha and Soraya sipped quietly. Twice, he looked up and studied Soraya; on one occasion, he caught her eyes, and she smiled at him. Then he pushed the keyboard away and, turning to Soraya, spoke to her in Hindi, 'This is an outstanding CV; how have you learnt all these languages?'

She replied in perfect Tamil, 'Travelling with my grandfather.'

He was about to ask a second question when he realised that though he spoke Hindi, she had replied in his home language. 'How did you know I speak Tamil?'

'When you speak English, your accent is that of Sri Lanka; your Hindi has the accent of a Tamil.'

'Amazing. Martha, you still haven't said why you came to me.'

'Soraya is so gifted in language abilities that our department would be a frustrating place to work. I've assessed her; she claims to speak all the world's principal languages and many associated dialects. I believe her. There must be something in the UN where her abilities would be of much greater value.'

The director decided to discover more about Soraya, pulled his keyboard back, and prepared to take notes as Soraya finished her tea. He then began the question-and-answer session, which lasted half an hour. He had to instruct his secretary to reschedule his day, as her history fascinated him. When he asked why she had applied for a job at the UN, she replied, 'Just before my grandfather passed on, he said the UN was where I should be.'

He had almost run out of questions when his secretary buzzed, and before he could press his communicator button, the door pushed open. A senior UN diplomat from the Secretary General's office strode in. 'Rihaan, ladies, sorry to butt in, but I have an urgent problem. I'm meeting with the Yemen ambassadors and their government leaders at one-thirty pm. I expect they will speak Arabic; I know the Ambassadors will, but each pair can speak their respective dialects. The translator I had lined up has called in sick. I'll not follow the Arabic translator's conversations if they talk to each other in their dialects. I need someone urgently who can translate for me.'

Rihaan turned to his computer, but before he could start a personnel search, Soraya spoke, 'One will be a Houthi following the Shia branch of Islam, the other from the government, a Sunni. The Sunni will speak good Arabic with little dialectical difference; the Houthi's language will be quite different. It is still Arabic but a more basic form with Iranian phrasing. His UN Ambassador will translate it into standard Arabic, but with little nuance, and the Ambassador's opinions will influence the translation.'

The diplomat looked at her in amazement. 'And you can speak their languages?'

'I can.'

'Then my prayers have been answered. Will you help me out of my predicament?'

She smiled at him. 'Of course, it's what I came to do.'

'Rihaan, Martha, I'll borrow this young lady and return her tomorrow. Thank you.' Turning to Soraya, he added. 'Tell me your name.'

They left the office, and Rihaan told Martha, 'It seems your problem has been solved, at least for a day.'

'The diplomatic branch is the place for her. I can't work out what she meant when she said helping Charles was what she came to do.'

The meeting took place on time, and unusually, Soraya, although officially a translator, sat beside Charles; she said translating speech from headphones didn't supply the nuances and body language necessary to translate dialects. She had also changed; she was now wearing a pure white Kaftan decorated with gold embroidery and a pair of sandals with jewelled straps. Charles asked where it came from; she said she had brought it for evening wear in her bag.

The visitors arrived in two groups: The Houthi, an unofficial Ambassador, and his leader, with an assistant carrying a briefcase. The Yemen ambassador was with the president of the southern half of Yemen and an Imam. Charles met both delegations at the door to the meeting room, welcoming them on behalf of the Secretary-General and confirming that they were to meet her the next day. They sat at tables separated by a metre and angled to face the table where Charles, Soraya and a diplomatic assistant sat. The Imam and the assistant with the briefcase sat behind their respective leaders.

The Yemen Ambassador was the first to speak; he had met Charles as the two men had crossed paths several times in the UN building and at receptions. He leant forward and said into the microphone in diplomatic Arabic, 'Before we begin, please inform us of the reason the young woman beside you is here.'

Before Charles could reply, Soraya said, in the Arabic accent of Yemen, 'Ambassador, I am here as an assistant of the United Nations, as I am familiar with Yemen's languages.'

Surprised, he spoke directly to her, 'Certainly with mine, but also of the Houthi?'

She replied by speaking to the Houthi leader in his dialect, 'Eminence, I am here as an assistant of the United Nations, as I am familiar with Yemen's languages.'

He had understood both, so he smiled as he thought she had scored a point off the Yemen ambassador and replied, 'I've no objection.'

The Imam, who had seemed quiet and retiring behind the two in front, sat up straight and looked carefully at Soraya and her dress. The gold embroidery appeared to be Arabic letters set within loops and whorls. He couldn't make out the words, but one almost certainly was Allah. For the next thirty minutes, he discreetly watched her every move, trying to read the embroidered lettering.

Charles started the proceedings, speaking into the microphone, 'I would like to welcome you for coming to discuss the problems in your country; I must report to the Secretary-General before tomorrow's meeting if we have progressed towards a permanent ceasefire between the north and the south. Can I ask the Yemen ambassador to explain the current position of the Republic of Yemen?'

35

The Yemen ambassador reached into the pocket of his *thawb* and drew out several sheets of paper. It took him ten minutes to read a lengthy list of complaints about Houthi activities. During the speech, the Houthi ambassador whispered several things to his leader.

Soraya wrote notes on a sheet of paper.

Although not officially recognised by the UN, the Houthi ambassador took a similar folder of papers his assistant handed him and repeated the same complaints. Soraya noted the comments made between the Yemen ambassador and his president.

After both sides had finished reading their lists of grievances, the Imam was confident he knew the words written in gold on her dress, and Charles felt depressed. It would be another pointless meeting.

Then, when Soraya spoke, the room fell silent. She used the Arabic vocabulary and pronunciation of Yemen's people, which is common to both sides in their daily activities.

'You are behaving like two three-year-old boys fighting over a ball. They will receive a smack from their mother, but no more, because she knows they will learn to work together for their mutual benefit when they grow up. You have people dying in both North Yemen and the Republic of Yemen; you have poor schooling for children. Men, women, and children are suffering from malnutrition, sickness, and inadequate medical treatment. And yet you squabble like little boys when you could make Yemen into a rich and peaceful country by working together. How you can pray to Allah, I do not know.'

In the silence, the Imam stood and walked between the two desks. He placed a hand on the leaders' shoulders on each side of him, then said in a muffled voice.

'Beware of what you say. A young woman spoke in a mother's voice, but the words are those of Allah.'

He bowed to Soraya, then returned to his seat.

Charles, now wholly out of his depth, said nothing.

The Houthi leader, who had studied her during her speech, said, 'Please tell us what you think we should do.' He had a sense of humour, so he grinned and added, 'Mother.'

Soraya looked at him and smiled, then stood. 'Confuse the world and take advantage of how it can work in your favour. You will both announce to your backers that you have concluded a peace agreement between you. To Saudi Arabia, Iran, and their allies, tell them you need aid. Still, in your arrangement, whichever side receives help will share equally with the other according to your respective populations. Your contract allows the North and South to govern the areas for which they have fought.

'Here in this building, you will ask the UN to recognise Yemen as two self-governing territories. You may not have two votes in the General Assembly, but you will insist on two ambassadors.

'Then you will both ask your backers for a new hospital, but the Houthi will insist their backers build the hospital in South Yemen, and the South's backers will construct and equip the one in the North.'

She sat down. The Houthi leader then spoke, 'It sounds crazy; why should the backers build the hospitals on the other side of the border?'

'Because national governments do not think. If you ask Iran for your hospital, you will receive a small one, and the world will say you are unimportant and cannot negotiate a big one. Saudi would also give a small one to the south. If the hospitals are on opposite sides, the Saudis will build a big one; the world will see a gift; the Saudis are not a country to give cheap gifts. Give the hospital the name of the Saudi King. They will make it even more significant. Iran will not allow the Saudis to outdo them, so it will also build a big one. Say it will carry the name of the Ayatollah.

'Men value pride and status above all things. Although Shia and Sunni Islam worship Allah, the Shia Ayatollahs will not allow a small hospital to carry the name of an Ayatollah in a Sunni country. It is true for the other.

'I suggest we leave you here. We shall send refreshments, and you can compile a list of what you need to make your country rich and powerful again, as well as identify who to ask for help. Your country is positioned strategically on the shipping routes. Offer to open the port to the world's navies without favour in return for building port infrastructure, allow them free use of the port buildings they construct and use, but tell them you have no army or arms to protect them. They must defend themselves, and you as well. Play one against the other without becoming a vassal to one. Arabs have been traders for thousands of years. Without wasting your energy and time on fruitless fighting, join and show how good you are at trading for your country.'

The Yemen President asked, 'How shall we draw up this agreement?'

Soraya walked around the desk to stand before them, then asked the Imam to join her. Then, before them, she said, 'I ask your Imam to judge the truth of these words. I spoke of traders, of thousands of years when men sealed contracts without paper or pencil. The world knew that shaking hands with an Arab trader and swearing this oath: *"I call on Allah to witness this contract"*, was better between honourable men than any paper. I suggest you do the same in this Imam's and Allah's presence.'

The Imam said, 'I've waited all my life for someone to say those words. My Lady, in the name of Allah, I shall always be your servant.'

The Houthi leader of North Yemen and the President of the Republic of Yemen looked at each other and laughed. The president said as he put out his hand, 'As you said, it sounds crazy, but it might be a lot of fun.'

As did the President, the Houthi leader shook his hand firmly and repeated the oath.

Soraya turned to Charles and said, 'We must leave them now, organise for refreshments; strong mint tea, your canteen must know, every thirty minutes, with some Arab sweetmeats to eat.'

As they approached the door, the Imam bowed to Soraya.

'My Lady, your dress has embroidered words; if I've read it correctly, you believe in the Storyteller of Allah.'

'Indeed, I do. Perhaps it is why my behaviour today was strange to you.'

'The Force of Allah is mysterious; we can only obey. It will be a pleasure to meet you tomorrow.'

Once out of the room, Charles told his assistant to organise the refreshments, then returned to his office with Soraya, where he slumped into his chair and said, 'Neither the translator speaking in my ear nor I could follow your conversation fully. But I understood the gist of it; somehow, you persuaded the two sides to kiss and make up; it was the handshaking bit. Now, they are compiling a list of demands for the UN and its backers for us to consider tomorrow. Am I right?'

'Yes.'

'It's incredible, but I suppose we have weeks of writing and rewriting a peace agreement.'

'Not at all; the agreement is signed and sealed.'

Thirty seconds later, Charles shut his mouth and squeaked, 'Explain.'

'They shook hands and swore an oath before the Imam and Allah that peace would prevail, and they would work together. However, I've committed the UN to one thing. It will recognise Yemen's governance separately as two separate territories and allow two different ambassadors, although it may be one country with one vote in the General Assembly. There will be things to work out, and I think the UN can help, for example, by ensuring that trading rights granted to Yemen apply to both parties, establishing a single passport system, and ensuring that the police cooperate effectively. You might need a UN office in both territories, including one here. It is administrative and minor diplomacy; I'm sure the UN can do it, but don't wait until someone asks; suggest it as soon as you find something you can do for them. It might mean a revolution in the UN if the UN logo were on every Yemen passport issued by the UN, and if the UN stated that they don't need consulates, as the UN would take on this role. Over time, the territories will naturally rejoin. Oh yes, they have agreed to share all aid and assistance received by either side. You can be sure they will honour their agreement and share fairly.'

'I still can't understand how, after years, you achieved all this in less than two hours. But I'll see the Secretary-General.'

'Oh, I can tell you. I told the two leaders they behaved like three-year-old boys fighting over a ball, and a mother would give them a spanking. I said it was time to grow up.'

'You didn't!'

'I did; check with the translator; he must have understood most of it.'

Now completely bemused, he said, 'Soraya, please be here tomorrow at nine. I've much to digest, and I must see the Secretary-General.'

He saw the Secretary-General. The United Nations is a living organism; its food is rumour, suggestions, and innuendo. Without expressing it, the workers know that informing others is a way of gaining brownie points; it is impossible to keep anything secret. As Charles entered the Secretary-General's office, she looked up and said, 'Good afternoon, Charles. I hear you have been a naughty boy and rude to the Yemen delegation.'

'Madam Secretary, that's not quite true; the young woman I had as a translator is the one who was rude.'

'What, exactly, did she say?'

'I didn't receive an accurate translation; she spoke a Yemen dialect, but I learnt from her afterwards that she told the President and Houthi leader they were behaving like three-year-old boys fighting over a ball, they deserved a spanking, and their country would do a lot better if they grew up.'

'My God, I've frequently wanted to say something similar over the last thirty years. Good for her!'

'My feelings are akin to yours, but it's not exactly how diplomacy works.'

'No, what was the outcome? Have the delegations left the UN in anger?'

'You'll not believe this, ma'am; they have agreed on peace. So far, there is one condition: the UN recognises north and south Yemen as two self-governing territories with two ambassadors.'

'And it was your young woman who did this? What's her name?'

'Soraya.'

'I've never heard of her; it will be interesting to meet her. Is she coming to the meeting tomorrow?'

'Yes, she's critical to a successful conclusion.'

'Well, you had better assemble a legal team to write an agreement quickly; we must have their signatures before they leave.'

'Soraya says they don't need to sign anything; they have shaken hands and sworn a witnessed oath in front of the cleric who was there; he was part of the South's delegation.'

'This becomes stranger and stranger. What do you want me to do?'

'I think you might ask them to announce their agreement in the General Assembly together.'

The Secretary turned to her computer, tapped a few keys, then said, 'There is a slot Thursday evening and one on Friday afternoon due to cancellations.'

'Not Friday; it's their day for prayers.'

'Okay, I've booked Thursday provisionally. See you tomorrow, Charles.'

The following day, Soraya was on time at Charles' office. His secretary showed her in with deference she had not shown before. Charles was busy with his computer and making phone calls. Between calls, he said, 'Please be patient; the Yemenis have asked if they can meet the Iranian and Saudi Ambassadors; I'm trying to arrange a meeting.'

The secretary brought mint tea for Soraya without her asking while she listened to his conversations and heard him say at least twice, 'Yes, she'll be there.'

After forty minutes, he finally breathed a sigh of relief. 'Done. One-thirty this afternoon, and the Secretary-General will try to find a moment to join the meeting.'

'I heard you reassuring them the Secretary-General would be there.'

Charles was puzzled for a moment, and then his frown cleared. 'No, I reassured them you would be there. It's a nice dress you're wearing.'

'Thank you, Charles. It's the same style as yesterday, but embroidered in red.'

'If you wear them often, you'll start a new fashion in the UN. Now, we have three hours. Unless you have any other suggestions, I'll ask Ines to show you around the Diplomatic section of the UN.'

His secretary was delighted, hoping to learn a titbit or two to share with her friends. As they walked around, the secretary became progressively more impressed as Soraya happily conversed with all the Diplomats in their native languages. As a result, they finished the tour in time for a quick lunch and returned to the office at one p m.

36

Charles was ready. As they took the elevator to the meeting room, he told Soraya he thought he had enough support for at least a temporary recognition of two Ambassadors.

The Yemen delegations were already in the room, shortly joined by the Saudi and Iranian Ambassadors, each accompanied by assistants.

Charles, Soraya and his assistant took the facing table; there was an extra seat for the Secretary when she arrived.

The Saudi Ambassador was the first to speak, 'We are here at the invitation of the Diplomatic Corps of the UN. I have an official notification that the North and the Republic of Yemen have agreed to a ceasefire. We would appreciate learning the terms of this ceasefire agreement.'

The Houthi leader nodded at South Yemen's president and said, 'You explain; your Arabic is more like theirs.'

The explanation followed: when the President said they had agreed to disarm entirely and to split aid and help into fair shares between the two sides, the Saudi Ambassador was visibly agitated. The Iranian Ambassador, the more astute of the two, then asked, 'That is an announcement for the General Assembly; why are we here today?'

The Houthi Ambassador answered, 'My colleague and I, with the guidance of our leaders, have drawn up a list of items necessary to overcome the current poverty and sickness in the country, both north and south. It includes humanitarian aid, hospitals, schools, suitable equipment, and the necessary support to run them, allowing us to train Yemeni staff. We intend to request assistance from UN agencies on specific issues and have compiled a list for the UN's consideration. We are here today to discover what your two countries can do to help and on what terms.'

It was a straightforward request, and the Ambassador passed over the list. The expected haggling then began.

Charles intervened on one occasion when asked how the UN could help with medical personnel.

After an hour, Soraya caught the eye of the Imam, who had looked her way repeatedly. The gesture she made was invisible to the others.

Then the Secretary-General entered; they all stood while she took her chair and said, 'Please continue.'

There was a brief discussion among the members, then the Imam stood, walked to the front, and the conversation ceased. He said, 'I've listened for an hour to the discussion; perhaps a short pause will help. I would like to hear my Lady Soraya's opinion.' He bowed and returned to his seat.

The Yemen delegation nodded and said yes; the others, astounded, said nothing. Soraya stood, paused, and then smiled. 'I've been listening with interest and conclude you are arguing about the unimportant. As a woman, I know some priorities far outweigh the measures of exchange. If a neighbour needs rice because she has none to eat, I give her half of what I have, trusting Allah will ensure she returns it when I have a similar need. You are playing in the mud like children when you could be building a castle with bricks.'

The silence was total when she continued, 'Saudi and Iran are great countries with large populations and enormous wealth, so great it does not matter if they give a small fraction to Yemen, but you, the Ambassadors, know that to keep your position in power, the populations must also agree. When Allah gives a gift, you do not question its value; you do not ask what motive is behind it; you accept it with thanks to Allah. Today, Allah has offered you a gift with bountiful returns, and you cannot see it.'

She was about to sit down when the Imam said, 'My Lady, we are but mortal men without a gift to understand the wishes of Allah. Can you please explain?'

'This planet received a message from Allah, told by the Storyteller. The words I shall remind you of are: *"You are destroying your planet, and one day, it will be a dead world like your neighbour, Mars."*

'You know most of the world's people believe this to be true and would like to save the planet; you understand further that if you impose restrictions on your people for this purpose, they may rebel. Therefore, progress is slow, and our Earth dies.

'Today, you have an opportunity to announce to the world that if you cannot fix the entire world, you can fix Yemen; your people will not rebel; they have little to lose. Announce that you intend to aid Yemen to become a zero-carbon emissions country, a zero pesticide use country, and a zero plastic and toxic waste economy. Every assisting state can concentrate on one type of pollution. It will shame countries that do not assist; they will come forward with expertise or additional help. Let Yemen become a shining example of achievement when great powers unite. If Allah so wills, the knowledge from Yemen will spread to other countries. It does not mean free handouts; it will not be easy; it means negotiating goals and plans between those with the means and Yemen's leaders. Not the giving of gifts wasted in the pockets of evil men. Let the world of Islam declare Jihad to save the planet. Your people and the world will applaud.'

As she sat down, the Imam bowed to her and said, 'The words of Allah are truly marvellous.'

The Saudi Ambassador stood. He said, 'I must consult with Riyadh. Can this meeting be adjourned until tomorrow morning?'

The Secretary-General said, 'If the members agree, I can arrange it.'

The Iranian Ambassador said, 'I agree, for I have the same necessity as the Saudi Ambassador.'

The Yemenis agreed, and the Secretary said, 'Tomorrow morning then. I shall let you know tonight. Will ten o'clock be suitable?'

No one objected, so they all left the room. The Secretary said, 'Charles, Soraya, my office, please.' She left, and Soraya waited while Charles ordered his assistant to arrange the next meeting. Then, they joined the Secretary.

The Secretary stood as they entered, and Charles said, 'Madam Secretary, you have not met Soraya, although you heard her speak at the meeting.'

The two women shook hands, the Secretary looking keenly at her.

'Soraya, I heard you speak; I've never heard anyone in this building talk as you did nor be so forthright in condemning diplomatic behaviour. Why did you do it?'

'Ma'am, they are all men of God; perhaps you do not appreciate the depth of their belief, a belief which sometimes becomes fanatical. I do, for I spent years in the East. I spoke today in the Arabic that their religious leaders use; my words were the words of God, and they cannot deny them. You heard the Imam confirm this when he said, "The words of Allah are truly marvellous." But they are men and must see a reward from any decision; I gave them the vision.'

'And what will happen now?'

'You are occupied full-time with international political affairs; perhaps you're unaware of how the different branches of Islam have moved closer together since the Storyteller visited a remote village in the Middle East. Led by the Aga Khan, the Ismailis are attracting followers from both the Sunni and Shia communities. These two are shifting their religions closer to the Ismailis to avoid the loss. The Sunni Imam at the meeting has become my ally; he knows a powerful Ayatollah leads the Shia and, unlike the fragmented Sunni, can rapidly move to support a Jihad. He'll call a Saudi Imam in Riyadh. The Ambassador's instructions will include approval of Jihad. Still, most importantly, it will say Iran should not have an opportunity for publicity and political gain that Saudi Arabia does not have. And the Iranians will do the same, except for a positive instruction to call for Jihad. The Saudis will have to agree.'

'My God, things have changed. Please tell me what you would do now?'

'Very little, they will do it themselves; when it is a matter of Jihad, it is better to leave it to the believers. However, I did explain to Charles. I suppose the UN wants to maximise its gains. It should supply support via the agencies. Don't take a leadership role, discover where they need help, and offer it with an excuse, like 'We have excess capacity in agency X; if you can use it, please do not hesitate.' They are proud men; pride is a fundamental aspect of Arab culture. Make it easy for them to accept.'

'After thirty years at the UN, I never expected to receive a worthwhile lesson in diplomacy from a young woman. In which department do you work?'

They were both left speechless when Soraya smiled and said, 'Oh, I don't work for the UN.'

Charles broke the silence with a stutter. 'But...but...but. You were in Rihaan's office with Martha when I searched for a translator; I thought you were part of the language department.'

'No, it was my first time in the building; I thought my language skills would earn me a job. But I haven't been offered one.'

The Secretary picked up her phone and called Martha, and a minute later, she was reading the application form. She noted but didn't question the IQ; she already knew Soraya's intelligence. Martha's scribbled note: *All principal languages and many dialects* raised an eyebrow.

'Soraya, we have a job for you in the Diplomatic Corps. I'll send your application to the recruitment department with a recommendation. They will contact you shortly. For the moment, consider yourself hired as a diplomat.'

Soraya's radiant smile was enough, but she said, 'Thank you, ma'am.'

'Now, I assume you and Charles will be at the meeting tomorrow, and there is a time slot booked in the evening for an address to the Assembly. Do you think you'll make it?'

Soraya replied, 'Yes, ma'am, but I would make one request. To make the announcement physically believable, could you please rearrange the seating in the Assembly so that all the agreement participants are together? It will increase the statement's impact when shown on the news media.'

'It's a headache, but I'll ask protocol to work on it immediately. You continue to surprise me, Soraya.'

The next day's meeting was much shorter; Soraya's dress had blue embroidery, and everyone was cheerful and encouraged even more when the Saudi Ambassador said he had arranged a celebratory dinner at the Langham Hotel.

They settled down to work on the list of items the Yemen team had made, and there were many suggestions from the Saudi and Iranian Ambassadors, so the list grew longer, with many list items carrying the letters S or I. An S or I with a question mark, meaning the Saudis or Iranians agreed to investigate them, and some with a question mark for examination by both sides for proposals. They adopted Soraya's hospital proposal without demur. When Soraya suggested adding two orphanages attached to schools for each territory, and the Imam gave his approval, it became an item on the list. The Secretary-General arrived an hour later, just in time for them to agree on the last line of the list. Amazed by the room's atmosphere, she later told Soraya it was like seeing boys playing Age of Empires, where the players build empires. Soraya noted this for later consideration.

The Secretary-General inquired about the meeting's progress. The Saudi Ambassador said it was complete; only a document remained to sign. With everyone focused on the Secretary, Soraya caught the Imam's eye, so only he saw her gesture, clasping her two hands together in a simulated handshake. He nodded, then stepped forward.

'Madame Secretary, two days ago, at a meeting in this building, the North and South Yemen leaders sealed an agreement between them. There was nothing written. Many employees must discuss many details and record and sign the results. Today, it is unnecessary; I shall repeat the words spoken by my Lady Soraya so the Ambassadors of Saudi Arabia and Iran can hear them.

'"I spoke of traders, of thousands of years when men sealed contracts without paper or pencil. The world knew that shaking hands with an Arab trader and swearing this oath, *I call on Allah to witness this contract*, was better between honourable men than any paper."

'We are honourable men; I suggest we do the same.'

They did.

They then agreed to meet for the celebration; the Secretary said she would have come if she had known, but she had appointments that were impossible to change.

When the delegations had left, ready to prepare for the Assembly announcement later, the Secretary looked admiringly at Soraya. 'I still don't know how you did it, but I've arranged the Assembly as you suggested, warned the media, and made an enigmatic announcement to all the UN delegations. I think the Ambassadors will pack the hall.

'Soraya, I don't know where to place you in the UN, so I've decided to appoint you as an assistant in the Secretary General's office; one of your first tasks will be to help Charles and anyone he names to run with this project.'

'Thank you, ma'am; I'll try not to disappoint you.'

'I doubt it will be the case, but I must warn you. You'll shortly find yourself extremely busy; although few people know you, you already have a reputation. It will result in numerous requests for help. I must remember to introduce you to the Chinese ambassador, Han Ah Soo; he's a valuable ally in matters concerning Asia.'

The unexpected reply stunned her. 'If the Ambassador is the nice man who was a professor at Shenzhen University, I know him; I met him when I studied at the Confucius Institute in Beijing.'

The building manager allocated an office to Soraya. Assistants had to share offices, but for unexplained reasons, she never did. Her office changed several times until it was next door to the Secretary-General's office. Every time she moved, although there were no framed photos, a small statue of the *Redeemer* found a discreet place to stand.

Fade Out

Travis and his team at Cambridge, boosted by scientists from Scripps and others from the USA, developed a treatment system for bacterial toxic waste. The funds came from Britain and the USA, whose investors insisted on a one-dollar technology license; the metals refining paid for the collection costs, as it is a patented technology. Other countries have had to pay.

Now a freelancer, Patrick increased his earnings with royalties from ad campaigns. The first one he did for free for Charlotte, the little boy was not Louis, but it won *Best Ad of the Year* three years running, and fifty-four countries paid him royalties.

A year after Soraya joined the UN, she met Meghali. It was a polite meeting, nothing more. Still, Meghali told Patrick about their meeting that night. Then she added, 'Patrick, I had an uncanny feeling that she knew everything about me as if we had met years ago, although I've never seen her before.'

'I sometimes feel like that when I meet someone; it's usually an actor who lived long ago, whom I remember from a movie. But often, Meg, what you feel turns out to be true.'

'How can it?'

'We may learn one day.'

Five years later, Yemen was the shining example Soraya promoted, and many of the world's smaller countries followed the Yemen example. When the Secretary-General's contract ended, the General Assembly appointed Soraya unanimously, influenced by the Chinese Ambassador, the Arab bloc, and the United States Ambassador, Meghali Azzaro.

Patrick's computer algorithms added Soraya's appointment to his oddly designed database.

Charlotte's party won an overwhelming majority at the next general election. With the legislative power available, she and Travis began to nibble and bite into fossil fuel use through legislation that made petroleum products more expensive and other taxes less onerous. Patrick advised.

Meghali, as the US Ambassador, made an official visit to view the mosque built by the Emir, met the Imam, whose name was Jamal, and asked if she could meet Fatima. She did, in a small villa that her husband, the Emir, had built for them near the mosque. They met in a lush, scented garden with a tinkling fountain, surrounded by palm trees and green grass. Meghali congratulated the Emir as they sipped mint tea, and then managed to ask a question: 'Who was the young girl with the Storyteller, and what happened to her?'

Fatima the Blessed replied, 'Soraya was an orphan I looked after. She left with the Storyteller. We heard of her three times after they left, but I've heard nothing since. Sometimes, I wonder what happened to her. Do you know anything?'

'A suggestion. Surveillance film at the statue of *Christ the Redeemer* shows a visit before the statue changed, of an aged man with a staff and a young girl; they behaved as any tourists would. I cannot tell you anything else.'

A week later, Fatima returned to where she first saw the

Storyteller; the street was quite different. The mosque builders had dismantled the buildings for materials and replaced them with modern structures. She walked on the paved road made of fused sand bricks. It was then that she thought of Meghali's reply.

'I cannot tell you anything else.' It was ambiguous.

Two years later, the Kings of Saudi Arabia and Jordan visited the United Nations simultaneously, ostensibly for distinct reasons. A news entry stated that they had met with the Secretary-General for a courtesy meeting. Patrick's AI program promptly searched the UN database for the Secretary-General's meeting schedules. It noted the courtesy meeting was a private meeting of all three, with no record of the discussion or the Secretary-General's favourite Imam's presence. A recording of it would have created waves after translation from Arabic. Many years later, the King of Saudi Arabia's autobiography included the details.

'Your Highnesses, the Arab countries have spent eighty years in an expensive and unsuccessful quarrel with Israel. I wish to propose an idea.'

The Saudi King courteously said, 'Please go ahead, Secretary-General. We will always consider your suggestions with respect.'

'Build a band of industrial production and wealth with a high standard and quality of life along Israel's borders. Do so with Arab money; do not allow investment by external interests. Ensure the industry does not pollute or use fossil fuels. The world is working to eliminate pollution, and you can achieve a leadership position without relying on fossil fuels.

'Do not engage the government of Israel, but slowly encourage the Imams to tell the people who live and work in this band that Jews who wish to cross the border to work in these industries are welcome, as Allah demands tolerance. Preach that Jews are Semitic people who worship Allah with different rituals and know the value of money, as do Arabs. Governments change; we cannot trust them, but individuals will shake hands and respect personal agreements.

'Their skills will be of value. Allow them free entry, whether they come to work daily or for extended periods. Peace will come to the area, and after many years, the Government of Israel will change because the Jews no longer fear. Fear no attack from Israel, as their people will live there. Not the economic benefit, but Allah's praise will be your reward. The land will remain part of your kingdoms, but allow Palestinians of all religions to live under your laws.'

Patrick looked at the data the AI reported and felt satisfied. He didn't know, but he thought the editor was an expert; she had beautifully crafted the fade-in to a new scene. The future would be fun.

A year later, Patrick's financial programs detected unusual money flows, and the AI routines made connections. He thought an opportunity for profit might soon be visible.

After Meghali had blended an eclectic mixture of ingredients at breakfast, he said, 'You asked some time back if the Storyteller had gone. He has; that movie has ended. But although the world has done a surprisingly respectable job of cleaning up the oceans, and marine life has rebounded, the big problem is yet to come.'

'What's that?'

'Global warming, but it might be a few years yet; there's a new scriptwriter on the job, crafting the sequel.'

'Who?'

'The Secretary-General of the United Nations.'

'But that's her job.'

'Exactly, where better for a scriptwriter to work?'

'So, what is your forecast?'

'There are many alternatives; the first might be replacing natural gas in fertilisers, although I fancy geothermal electricity.

'Meg, the next presidential election is in two years. I think you should stand.'

'No woman has ever won the Presidency; what makes you think I can?'

'I think the editor will be on your side; combating global warming requires a resolute leader.'

Patrick's ego was too big. He never imagined that an infinite power would know his thoughts. Or that it might be using Meghali and him for something.

The President met a Senator from Alaska three months later. The White House refused to give the reasons for the meeting, but Patrick's AI noted the visit and reviewed all the recent data about Alaska. A company that had announced two years earlier that it was drilling for oil with a newly granted exploration licence had terminated the employment of its on-site personnel.

Three days after the meeting, the White House press attaché announced a significant magnesium find in Alaska. 'We will keep it as a strategic reserve,' the spokesperson said.

It took three more days for one of the dismissed employees to post on social media, 'We were drilling for oil and found enough Milk of Magnesia to give the entire world the screaming sh..ts.'

(The media site AI changed his final three words to 'runny tummies').

Patrick remarked that night to Meghali. 'You'll win the Presidency. This President has just taken the same road as the

British Prime Minister before Charlotte.'

'Explain, please.'

'You once told me you had thought the unexplored oil fields might have vanished. The editor has a sense of humour; one in Alaska has changed into a liquid laxative, and the President is in denial mode; he hasn't mentioned the oil is no longer there.'

'Patrick, I would have to win my party's primary; that may be possible, but the president will stand for a second term, and beating the incumbent is rare. Standing for Senator would be safer. For a four-year term.'

'I don't think so, Meg; if the editor needs you, I'm sure she'll provide the means, and I'll run your campaign on the media and television. It'll be fun.'

'Okay, I must resign, but for courtesy, I'll tell the Secretary-General first.'

'Good morning. Madam Secretary.'

'Good morning, Ambassador. We've worked together many times, and you requested a courtesy meeting. Can we use first names?'

'Of course, it's a pleasure.'

'Then, Meghali, what's it about?'

'I'm about to resign from my post and stand as a presidential candidate.'

'Why? I can't imagine a better candidate, but your reputation is international.'

'Patrick and I have discussed it for hours, Soraya. I believe this country will fall apart from internal battles if pressure builds to stop the consumption of carbon fuels. All the current possible candidates will vacillate between policies instead of taking a clear stand.'

'I know your objectives, Meghali; you've made it abundantly clear over the years, so I hope you succeed. I'll follow the primaries and then the election daily. So I wish you good luck. Come to see me at any time if you need advice.'

'Thanks, Soraya.'

'If I'm going to stand for President, I want you beside me. How about a quiet ceremony somewhere?'

'I was about to ask tonight, Meg.'

'In bed?'

'Yes.'

'Then please do.'

...

'Patrick, ask now. I've never imagined wanting to hear the magic words that drive girls hysterical, but I do.'

'Why, Meg?'

'Because of your expression, it gives me a fluttery tummy.'

'Then will you marry me?'

'Yes, and now show me how much you love me.'

...

'Meg, it can be a simple ceremony, but a big party. At the end of it, you can announce your candidature.'

'Why?'

'It's an opportunity we should not miss. You have many friends at the UN; we'll invite them all to a wedding in New York, and include Charlotte, Travis, and Scripps. If the Secretary-General attends, it will guarantee nationwide publicity in the journals, legitimising your candidature amongst politicians and putting your face and name on every TV screen.'

When Charlotte announced the date for the next UK election, Meghali called.

'Hi, Charlotte. If you win this election, you'll become British history's longest-serving woman Prime Minister.'

'Thanks, Meghali, but once the pollution problems have ceased to be important, the next term will be the last.'

'Patrick thinks there's an even bigger problem coming, Global Warming, and he has a few suggestions. He says you must build a war chest and will post his suggestions in a secure file.'

'Thanks, Meghali; Travis proposed, I accepted, and we'll marry in Wales, then make an official trip to India for our honeymoon.'

'Then our congratulations. I called to tell you that Patrick proposed, and I'm about to resign and stand for president. I'll send you a wedding invitation.'

'That's marvellous, I hope you win.'

Intermission.

Author's Note on the Sequel

Act II begins with Meghali and Patrick planning an election campaign, but soon they are diverted by a sinking oil tanker that threatens the East Coast of America with a massive oil spill. Meghali resigns from her post as Ambassador and takes charge of the cleanup operation. At her wedding to Patrick in New York, she announces her candidacy for President.

When the President doesn't assist with the oil spill, she risks an accusation of piracy he launches. With help from her ambassador friends at the UN, she foils the attempt to convict her.

Then begins the hectic race to persuade the American voters they need to *"Make a New America."* From one state to another and back again, facing hostile crowds, antagonistic media, fake news, and entrenched interests, until Meghali wins the primary, debates the sitting President, and wins the election.

But she doesn't stop there. She has made public promises and is determined to keep them. Will she manage to do so? The opposition is wealth and personal interests; she and Patrick, with many supporters, need every trick in the book, and some new ones.